"Ismailov tells a haunting tale of an Afro-Russian boy's search for love. Generous in spirit yet unsparing in its honesty, *The Underground* illuminates a loneliness that is as devastating as it is universal. In breathtaking prose, Ismailov reminds us again and again that even the slimmest thread of light can pierce through the darkest of days."

—Maaza Mengiste, author of *Beneath the Lion's Gaze*

"In reading Hamid Ismailov's *The Underground*, I found the hard-won wisdom of Ralph Ellison's *Invisible Man* in conversation with the boyhood lyricism of Anne Carson's *Autobiography Of Red*. But most crucially, simmering just under the skin of every word, I heard Ismailov's own heartbeat: haunted, beautiful even when strained, and insistent. The world has conspired to keep this necessary and timely novel a secret for too long."

—Saeed Jones, author of *Prelude to a Bruise*

"Hamid Ismailov has the capacity of Salman Rushdie at his best to show the grotesque realization of history on the ground."

—*Literary Review*

"A writer of immense poetic power."

—*The Guardian*

"*The Underground*, Ismailov's latest novel published in English, depicts the brutal separation between the hopes and realities of social integration on the threshold of the collapse of the Soviet Union. The dark and picaresque tale follows the life and death of the young Mbobo (also the book's title in Russian) in a series of vignettes marked by the grand stations of the city's metropolitan transportation system."

—*F Newsmagazine*

"Wonderful.... Intimate details from a specific era and location enrich Ismailov's novel. Kirill's memories of seasons and stations become a nostalgic elegy for the bittersweet cityscape of late-Soviet Moscow.... The imagery is visceral.... Ismailov's work, like Pushkin's and like Platonov's, is a profound and haunting exploration of place and time. Just as *The Railway* conjures up a multifaceted Uzbek town and *The Dead Lake* is rooted in the tortured vastness of the Steppe, so *The Underground* creates a spiritual and cultural map of Moscow."

—*The Kompass*

"Ismailov's works blend a keen awareness of the cosmopolitanism of the Soviet project, with its feverish drive for modernization.... It also pays homage to the rich tapestry of Russian—and Soviet—literature, and the interplay between the two. *The Underground*'s structure is reminiscent of Yerofeyev's *Moscow to the End of the Line*; and Ismailov delights in pan-Soviet literary references, from Abkhazia's Fazil Iskander and Chuvashia's Gennady Aygi to Odessa's 'Ilf and Petrov' and Nobel laureate Ivan Bunin. Ismailov sees himself as part of the Russian literary tradition (his prose has been compared to Bulgakov, Gogol, and Platonov).... Ismailov's novel is a deep examination of the confusions of Soviet and post-Soviet 'Russianness.'... An intricate portrait of an all too foreign loss: the disappearance of one's country."

—openDemocracy

THE UNDERGROUND

ALSO BY HAMID ISMAILOV

The Dead Lake
A Poet and Bin-Laden
Googling for Soul
Hostage to Celestial Turks
The Railway
Two Lost to Life

THE UNDERGROUND

A NOVEL

HAMID ISMAILOV

Translated from the Russian by Carol Ermakova

RESTLESS BOOKS
Brooklyn, New York

Library of Congress Cataloging-in-Publication Data: Available upon
request.

ISBN: 978-1-63206-044-0

Ellison, Stavans, and Hochstein LP
232 3rd Street, Suite A111
Brooklyn, NY 11215

www.restlessbooks.com
publisher@restlessbooks.com

The publication was effected under the auspices of the Mikhail
Prokhorov Foundation TRANSCRIPT Programme to Support
Translations of Russian Literature.

 transcript

He felt that they saw him as some kind of rare beast,
a peculiar, alien creature accidentally transported into their world,
a world he had nothing in common with.

—Pushkin

1984 Chiasma

*The meaning of words that have gone before
is lost, although something still remains to be said...*

I am Moscow's underground son, the result of one too many nights on the town. My mother Moscow (though everyone called her Mara, or Marusia) was born in some little Siberian town or other, maybe Abakan, maybe Tayshet and, with that town's strange name in her passport, she picked me up in the year of the Moscow Olympics—or maybe earlier, during the preparations—from an African sportsman from a "friendly country." She was one of the *limitchitsa*, come to Moscow on a temporary permit, in the Olympic village. "We were sent to them, but they came in us, all right!" she explained later, drunk. And so that is how I came about, a cross between a bulldog and a rhinoceros: Kirill, by the name of Mbobo. My mother died when I was eight, and I died four years later. And that is all there is to my Moscow life. The rest is just decaying, late-blown blooms of memories.

When you are condemned to spend your largely unlived Kha-kass-nigger life underground, your closest friend is not the maggot chewing on your slit-lilac eyes, nor the roots of the disheveled fir tree sucking the dark paint out of you in the night, nor even the other dead, each rotting alone; no, it is the metro that becomes your best friend. And not because, when you reached the age of five, out of lack of money, your sobered-up mother gave you a many-hued metro map and said: "This is a portrait of you, Mbobo, my prickly little sunshine!" And not because I always fled from the terrors and delusions of life on the surface to the kingdom where even I was a pale shadow, indistinguishable by color or fate; and not even because my days ended there and my nights began in that neighborhood. No! The metro became my best friend simply because when the ground hums, when a passing train shivers not far away, then bones knock together, teeth chatter in rhythm, and little ants, building their abodes, scatter and creep through the darkness where there once was skin.

"Ladies and gentlemen, this train terminates here. Please exit the cars..."

Komsomolskaya Station
Sokolnicheskaya Line

The first book Mommy bought me was about a scary plant named Periwinkle. I was afraid to be alone with that book, especially the rough sketches of a prickly burdock that teemed over the pages from all sides. One day I decided to get rid of that book, so I took some matches to the garbage chute at the top of the staircase in our hostel and torched that book. But then that Periwinkle, with its dry bract, flared up in such a way that the flames jumped over onto my wide *sharovari* pants, and I yelled as loud as I could. The neighbors came running out, rolled me around on the floor, put out the flames but not the fear that was still afire in me, screaming, "Don't tell Mommy! Don't tell Mommy!" But they told Mommy as soon as she came home, and then she whipped me over and over in our tiny room with her thick ladies' belt.

I remember how my black skin burned under each stripe being laid out on my back and butt. I yelped in pain, but what I feared most was that Mommy would stop and tell me the most terrible thing, the thing I was more afraid of than pain: "Now get your things and go to your father!" Where in all of black, hot Africa—which sounded like hell to me—was I supposed to go? But having flogged me with her rhetorical: "Gonna do that again? Are you?" she left me pressed into the hot bunk as she crumbled dry corn onto the floor, then made me kneel on it with bare knees. That's how that stinking burdock got its revenge on me, laughing from the walls, masquerading as the metro map...

Later, when my first stepfather—Mommy finally told me not to call him "Uncle Gleb," but "Daddy"—gave me a book with drawings of an underground fairytale city called *Metro*, and an ABC book with pictures of that same system, I would spend the long winter hours when they had left my three- or four-year-old self by the window (double-glazed and with cotton wool stuffed between the two sets of frames to keep the draft out) either staring warily at these two books, with pictures that looked like they had been drawn with a wet crayon, or peering into Moscow's indigo darkness, which had something in common with those unearthly drawings, as well as with my warring, frightened innards. Maybe those books would bring some kind of misfortune down on me.

It was in that same third or fourth year of my life that I first dreamed about that underground town full of multicolored lights. And maybe because it was underground, or under floor, it shone much brighter than anything I'd ever seen in my waking life and, for some reason, it was this town I wanted to name after the word dearest to my heart: "Moscow."

Lightbulbs shone like stars, the noble polish of granite and marble glittered and gleamed, and that special warm and ethereal darkness made no distinction between the colors of faces—everything glittered and gleamed with the reflection of those same underground stars and underground moon, underground marble and underground granite, and I recognized that kingdom as my own. I dreamed that dream several nights in a row.

Then one day, not-Uncle-Gleb-but-Daddy took me to Moscow from Khimkion-the-Left-Bank, where Mommy and I were living with him. Everyone in the wintry *elektrichka* trolley gawked at me, the way you would stare at an exotic insect at the zoo. We got off and I thought I saw the Kremlin, but Daddy said it was just Leningradsky Station.

Then we crossed the square and found ourselves at some massive temple doors.

Remember the entrance to the metro from the Kazansky railway station? Regal doors flung wide open under eleven lamps, spanned by an enormous arch with the enormous letters METRO, and above the arch, like the turreted symbol of Moscow, synonymous with the Kremlin, a zigzag, the wide open legs of the letter *M*, luminous with ruby light...

I felt in my black guts that I was entering a new world. The air coming from those wide-open doors was stale with the smell of muscly sweat. People with suitcases and bundles were making their way, like ants, to the turnstiles. I knew two fairy tales that could help me here: one was about a little orphan boy whose mother disappeared into a gaping cliff, and you had to say: "Rock, crack open!" and then the monolith would open its great muzzle. And the second story was about Ali Baba, who could slip into his cave at will with the magic password: "Open sesame!" The first story terrified me; the second tickled my curiosity.

Uncle Gleb—Daddy—led me to the iron box on the wall and put a small coin into it. Large five-kopek coins spilled out in reply. Ah, how generous was that world! He handed one to me and explained how to slip through the gate when the rubber-ended metal pincers parted, and how it opened up for only a brief moment. Heart racing, I took a long look back at the entrance into this world where, going into the unknown, downward, lamps shone as figures floated past. "Daddy, why are we leaning backward but the people coming toward us are leaning forward?" I babbled on the escalator, hiding my fear.

"No, son," he explained. "We're all standing up straight. It's just that our escalator's going down, and theirs is going up. It's what's called an optical illusion."

"And what's an optical illusion?"

"You'll find out when you're older."

"And when will I be older?"

"When you find out what an optical illusion is."

I was flying along at Uncle Gleb's side, holding his hand. He yanked me off the escalator—you can't look back—and into the underground snow palace, a kingdom of marble and white stone, with pillars instead of columns, with a never-ending dome stretching to infinity instead of a ceiling. Never in my life, my life on the other side, on the surface, had I seen such beauty, such splendor. My Daddy, an experienced guide, didn't rush me as I stared, wide-eyed. He led me slowly and ceremoniously from one mighty pillar to the next; they stretched along the painted arc into the dome and were decorated with tendrils of stone leaves. This world entered my pounding heart in tremors, and I felt that no one would be able to drag me back from this world or this world back out of me...

But all of a sudden, into the hustle and bustle of people danced a thin whistle. The train, with a blue-green stripe, suddenly ripped between the pillars, gnashing and screeching. Terrified, I shrunk into a ball as my stepfather said: "Let's go!"

It was a metro train. Its doors opened and, like blood from the throat of a slaughtered rooster, people spurted out. The passengers on the platform, including us, were sucked into the void.

"Watch the closing doors!" a disembodied, rasping voice boomed out, and I sensed that the only thing ahead of me was oblivion, made more bearable by that same rough voice: "The next station is Lermontovsky."

But I didn't make it to Lermontovsky. I stayed forever at my primordial station, mired in my tears. If ever I was mortally swindled, then it was in the metro that day. Nurtured by my dreams and the pictures in the ABC book, I had never expected that this marble palace-station would suddenly stop short and that nothing but a dark tunnel would open up, as though it were pouring out of me with the involuntary muddy tears of childhood's unforgiving disappointment.

I couldn't believe my eyes.

This cruel deceit was so obvious: miles and miles of maggoty darkness, the sudden flashes of those mendacious stations—now a different one, then another—illusory, deceptive, ephemeral, so contrary to my dreams of my underground city that never ends. It was like drawing a picture on the first page of the ABC book and then simply leaving empty leaves, only to interrupt that emptiness later, on page ten or page twelve, with another colorful picture drawn with a wet crayon. The uninterruptedness of my child's world was broken once and for all. As I now understand, then and there, I was thrown against my will into the cobbled and re-cobbled world of the grownups, into the optical illusion...

Dzerzhinskaya Station
Sokolnicheskaya Line

My black body remembers how it traveled that first time, through the brilliant lightning flashes of the stations, connected by long and noisy darkness. A thin beam of light stretched out across the frowning arc of the ceiling, transforming the station sign into an overhead cross as we made our way to the exit. I didn't have enough air, either because of my unrestrained tears or because of the closeness of the subway. Once when Mommy was playing with me on our bunk bed she suddenly threw the thick, fleecy blanket over my head and giggled: "Can you see Africa in there?" Laughing, I tried to scramble out from under the blanket, but my mother blocked me in with her hands and feet, and I suddenly felt afraid. I started choking and I lost all strength. When my mother, laughing, threw the black blanket off my head, she found me unconscious.

That same feeling engulfed me as I was dragged upward by my stepfather. It seemed that a second longer and the darkness of those never-ending flights, prevailing between the sparse slits of the stations, would close over my head, like the blanket...

But we went out the same way we came in, and again a vast Moscow square with a lone, unarmed old soldier in the middle was turning white in the snow. My stepfather led me around the edge of the square to Children's World. In all my four years, I had never seen such a shop.

As we entered the hall, with its huge New Year tree and huge clock, I was so stunned by the vastness of it that I forgot all about my metro. I felt so tiny and wretched in the midst of it, but I sensed the others' stares falling on me like the toy snow from the railings, and I was afraid someone was going to ask me to do a merry dance or recite a little ditty like the one drummed into me at nursery school, the one we all heard as:

Even if I had procured a Negro
From the clown of the years
A bus of glum laziness
I would still have learned the fierce metal bracket Tony.
And why?
Because Lenin gave him a talking to...

The only thing I understood from that whole poem was that on one side there was a Negro—a professional clown, probably my father—and on the other side there was Grandpa Lenin, along with Tony, gathering the children from our school under the New Year tree, and "giving them a talking to," as he stroked their little heads.

But my stepfather spun me around the New Year tree, as if he were Father Frost and I were his little Snow Elf, and then joined the queue for the toy stall by the exit, leaving me to stand there in the snow, in front of a huge window, watching three motionless children within. For the first time in my life, the children didn't run up to me, didn't ask about me or my parents, didn't ask: "Why is he black? He's a Negro, isn't he?" And for that reason I felt a rare kindness toward those boys and the girl who were standing alone, looking off into the distance. I called to them but they didn't move. I thought they couldn't hear me through the thick glass, so I knocked.

They just kept gazing into the middle of the snowy square where that lone soldier poked out in his overcoat; he was probably their grandpa. I waved, but only my own reflection replied.

I felt ashamed for monkeying around in front of those still and solemn children.

When my stepfather got back, carrying a colorful bag of presents, I asked him: "Are they October Cubs?" His reply seemed even stranger to me: "No. That's a window display, and they're just mannequins."

"Can I make friends with them?"

My stepfather smirked and nodded. He said I could open my present in front of them. So, in front of my new friends, I stuck my little muzzle into the twinkling bag, full of chocolates, cookies, mandarin oranges. Right at the bottom, I saw a cracker with a toy inside.

"OK, Pushkin, hold on with both hands" Uncle Gleb said, "And I'll pull!" Afraid to slip in front of my serious comrades, I held on tight. My stepfather counted to three and gave a quick tug. There was a loud bang and onto the white, unsullied snow fell a naked Negro girl in a tub...

Park Kultury Station

I cried the whole way, but this time I cried like my new friends in the window display, without showing my tears. I didn't look at anyone; my gaze was so far off that I didn't even notice how the stations alternated with the dark tunnels, or how everyone in the carriage looked me up and down. We were carried out into a station with a forest of thin Egyptian pillars that made you want to hide behind them. The lamps on the ceiling made you think of flowerbeds of upside-down cakes, and Uncle Gleb explained: "This is Park Kultury." We walked for a long time over a windswept bridge, hung from iron straps like Mommy's underwear, and, finally, we walked into The Park of Culture.

It was crowded, especially around the fair and the stage, but my stepfather knew where we were going, so we followed the white river into the park's depths. Passing the red-faced hawkers in their fur hats and aprons as they clapped their mitts together, breath steaming, we came at last to the small square where an immense New Year tree had been set up, with children and parents frozen in a circle dance around it. As we made our way closer, Uncle Gleb sat me up on his shoulders, and I could see Father Frost entertaining the crowd with his live monkey dressed up as the little Snow Girl. When we got up to the rope that held back the crowd, Uncle Gleb set me down and shouted: "Lolik!"

Father Frost looked up and slowly headed toward us, still teasing the monkey. "And now, children, little Snow Elf Antoshka and I are going to find out what's hiding at the bottom of this sack, which I brought from a deep, dark forest of thick vines. Antoshka, do you want to pick out the prize?" The little monkey nodded, and the children squealed in delight.

"And how about you, boys and girls, do you want to win the prize?" Father Frost was right beside us, and the boys and girls all cried together: "We want to! We want to!" And someone shouted out of time: "We wants! We wants!"

Father Frost, his back to us, looked over his shoulder at my stepfather and asked: "Which is yours?" My stepfather gave me a shove that almost sent me flying, but luckily I got snagged on the rope. "Ah, so we wants, do we?" Father Frost shouted back, and everyone burst out laughing. Then, under his breath, he asked: "The little black one?"

My stepfather gave me another shove. "OK, then. Whoever Antoshka chooses, they'll win the prize! ONE!" Holding the little monkey on his shoulders, Father Frost swung him around. Everyone joined in: "O-nnn-e!" "TWO!" "T-ww-ooo!" "THREE!" As the children called out "Th-rrr-eee!" Father Frost deftly jerked the little monkey off his shoulders and it jumped onto me, sinking into my shoulders with its claws and digging its feet into my belly. I was scared to death and, when I opened my eyes, a pair of bored, scared monkey eyes was looking at me from under the white cap, and the whole crowd whooped and yelled: "There's another monkey!"

"Where? Where?"

"There! Look!"

"Dressed up as a person!"

Father Frost bent down, blew his vodka breath in my face, and picked us both up. He carried us to the middle of the circle. My head was ringing. I couldn't hear what the crowd was shrieking; I didn't see what Father Frost pulled out of his sack...

All I remember is that the pitiful eyes of that little monkey were nothing like those of the toy animal I took home that day from Park Kultury...

Barrikadnaya Station
TAGANSKO-KRASNOPRESNENSKAYA LINE

My stepfather got drunk in the park with Father Frost-Uncle Lolik and one of the red-faced, blue-veined hawkers in a black fur hat and white apron, clapping his mitts after every glass, steam coming out of his nostrils. The little monkey and I each got a pie, and mine stuck in my throat like a lump of ice. And then my stepfather said goodbye to Uncle Lolik and his monkey, promising to see them again in the evening, and took me to his office.

My stepfather was a writer and worked for the journal *Friendship of the Nations*, which had its offices on Vorovsky in an elegant old home. After a brief appearance at his cubicle, he led me through the courtyard, then through a basement to the canteen, which was dark and reeked of stale smoke. "Is this another metro?" I asked, and my stepfather mumbled, "Yes, Pushkin, sort of..."

We sat next to a woman wearing too much makeup, who ruffled my hair and gave me an overly familiar flick on the nose: "My, my what a cute little monkey!" My stepfather bought us sausage-and-cheese sandwiches, along with some vodka for the two of them. They drank, and I chewed my sandwich, trying to swallow the ice cube stuck in my throat. My stepfather pulled a few pieces of paper from his pocket. They were folded twice. He turned them over and said: "The Cat."

I pricked up my ears and hung on every word that passed slowly through stepfather Gleb's wet lips.

The Cat

I.

In the twenty-first year following her death, her soul moved into a cat. No, not a pedigreed cat, just a simple stray. But that's clear...

The wife brought the cat home. She carried it in a plastic bag and spilled it out onto the floor like a sack of potatoes.

"Otherwise, it will scratch," she said, her back to the family.

The husband didn't waste the opportunity:

"What will? The potatoes?"

He was ready to make the most of it, trump card in hand. "So the potatoes scratch? And does the oven bite? And do you want to know how the laundry sucks?" But his wife's gentle voice and Mboshka's delighted, idiotic yelp swallowed up his unspoken words.

The cat immediately deciphered his dirty look and darted quickly into the very darkest corner, to squeeze itself into the niche above the record player.

The husband, dissatisfied for the sake of the domestic balance, quite instinctively got up from the table with a steaming potato which had shed its skin, and found himself in the living room, instantly lit up by the trajectory of the cat's own dirty look. He involuntarily called her by name, and even held out his hand, but then jerked it back and, half opening the window with the mosquito net, went back to the table.

Even when his voice came from the kitchen—"I guess we should feed her..."—the cat was still trembling, as though it were galloping along that trajectory that had flared up for a moment.

The cat spent the whole night sitting on the record player. Just as plastic is impermeable to either cold or heat, so all her warmth came back to her just as smoothly as the saucer of milk Mboshka set in front of her reflected the pale dawn of her eyes.

In the morning, Mboshka was the first to come, his bare feet slap-ping, and he hung around the record player until it was time to go to school, when, scolded in no uncertain terms by his mother, he left in tears. In his wake, the wife went up to the cat, and sensing the smell of cat pee at close quarters, let the dogs out on the newcomer and then, under her husband's growling, "I told you so..." set about rubbing the carpet with a wet cloth. The smell of cat pee went from room to room with the cat's steps. After sprinkling the carpet with deodorant, the wife, too, went to work.

And he was left alone with the cat.

2.

He sat down to his notes, but the presence of someone in the house distracted him. So he got up to lift the sin from his soul, to try to make peace with the offended animal. The cat, posed like a sphinx, proudly turned away. Even more insulted, he locked himself in his room, but he couldn't get the sketches into his head. He thought about his wife's scheme. He thought for a long time, in detail, clearly. With all the energy allocated to translating. Then he set to sharpening pencils. He sharpened all his own Art brand pencils, and Mboshka's too. Cursed, brittle Art.

And when he sat down, not knowing what to do with himself, the doors of his room suddenly burst open, and the cat looked in at him. Or rather, threw a self-satisfied glance at him. Waiting until the doors grew still, she set about taking some kind of inventory, starting by sniffing his discarded slipper, then the dusty drawing paper—at which she gave a short sneeze—and so on, methodically checking item by item, object by object, finishing with the pins stuck into a sheet of paper on the desk. Her examination completed, she lay down on the manuscript in front of his nose, directly under the lamp, her indif-ference to his point of view throwing him into disarray.

He didn't know how one behaved with cats in such circumstances. Did one tweak their ears, spank their bottoms, or something else? He shouted at her, but it seemed silly in that empty room. Yet it seemed even more ridiculous to explain to this unthinking beast, as you would to a little brother, the indecency of her behavior. But for some reason he couldn't make up his mind to simply push her off the desk.

She slept on the translation manuscripts until Mboshka's arrival. He grabbed her impulsively, though she was still sleepy, and began kissing her on the nose. He began to tell his son off for such barbarianism: who knows what microbes might be roaming around on her? But Mboshka carried her off into his room and didn't show his kisses.

He realized that the cat had to be fed, a corner had to be prepared for her, and a place in the bathroom. In short, she needed to be trained. And so when Mboshka came out with her for lunch and attempted to feed the animal from his own spoon, he was abruptly intercepted and made to throw the cat onto the floor where a doll's saucer had been filled with warmed bouillon.

In the evening the wife came back, loaded down with "user guides" and "manuals," and began an unsuccessful attempt to feed the cat with Hercules porridge oats. But who's to know? Maybe their family's opinion on that point had spread to the cat right from the start and, no matter how hard the wife tried to force "the healthiest porridge" onto either the cat or her son, neither would eat it.

It was then that the wife, too, began to sense the appearance of some third force in the house.

3.

Days went by. Mboshka was surprised that his charge didn't have to go to school, didn't need to do homework or practice the piano. His father, too, pondered the fact that the cat really had very little to do. Sometimes he tried to feel sorry for her and would think up some activity. One day, when a pigeon landed on the windowsill, he opened the window leading to the porch roof and let her out onto the whole flock. The cat waved her tail for a long time, some vague instinct lent her courage, but the intellectual environment of the last few months had planted seeds of caution in her mind, and she worried that the window might bang shut behind her forever. Or maybe it was something else.

Finally, he managed to push her out at the pigeons, but when, having finished his urgent work, he peeked out the window, he saw the pigeons strolling self-importantly along the roof and the poor cat was hiding motionless behind some broken glass leaning against the wall.

He called her and she scrambled onto the windowsill as fast as her four legs could carry her. Startled, the pigeons flew up and around in every direction.

She snorted, grumbling at him, haughtily and huffily showing her displeasure in every way possible. Nonetheless, the window became her favorite training ground. She would sit there, lurking, or twitch her tail compulsively in time with each little step of the pigeons, and when sparrows flew along, well, she sprang into warrior mode.

She took up waiting on the sill for the tomcats to pass in the evenings. Lucky enough to be able to take a stroll along the porch roof, especially in the evenings when everyone was at home, and the pigeons had flown away to sleep, she even struck up relations with two shamefully young admirers who, following some timetable of their own, would come visiting in turns and bawl from below, throwing her into confusion or embarrassment.

When that happened, husband would say to wife: "Just imagine, some girls come by and she understands and keeps quiet..." At that the wife said nothing and went out to finish cooking the Hercules porridge oats or to help the son with his music.

But she would stay by the window, thinking of something quite different; contrary to Mboshka's belief, she wanted to go out, like those tomcats she saw below the roof.

Only Mboshka didn't think anything to himself but lived with the cat as though she were his own little sister or—to be more precise—daughter, passing his parents' pedagogical tricks on to her. He made her wash her hands before lunch, not leave the table without asking, not make a mess in the cupboards, not go out in the cold without a scarf, not... the cat reciprocated, coming and folding herself up on the piano while he was practicing, twitching at the rustle of the pages of his books while he did his homework, or simply sleeping on top of the bedcover at his feet.

Once the cat tripped and fell off the porch roof. Mboshka, who at the time was coming to terms with how he might release his charge into the big, wide world, leaned right out of the window but didn't find anyone outside. He howled, convinced that the cat had left him forever, and confessed he had made her stand in the corner that morning.

The father ran outside, under the porch roof. She was nowhere to be seen. The children playing nearby said that the only place worth looking for a cat was the cellar. There was a whole colony of them there. He went down into the cellar through the door to the trash chute and started calling her by name. No one answered. As usual, the cellar was flooded with hot water, and in the clouds of steam, which brought with them a foul, rotting smell, he started to cough and shout in turns. Somewhere above him, from where he had just come, her voice reached him. He turned around and saw her, sitting in the corner, hopeless and forlorn.

At home, Mboshka smothered her with kisses, whispering: "What did you do that for? I was so worried! Never do that again, OK?"

4.

The husband assumed he was the one who fed her. After all, without fail he would come home from the House of Creativity with a kilo of beef stroganoff or goulash, which he would pour into cups covered with cardboard that could easily be pushed aside, and leave them in various corners. Then he would leave again without even one bite for himself.

The wife thought it enough to give the cat an occasional stroke...

Mboshka probably didn't think much about anything—though who's to say—but he loved the cat more than he loved his parents.

And they all now felt that some sort of mirror had appeared and started to reveal things.

Catching sight of the reflections wandering through the rooms, each tried them on, and all of them together—as they used to say in the wife's theater—played the lead cat.

He would roam through the rooms for days on end, hating his translations, which never afforded him any inspiration: hadn't he himself called them a form of psychotherapy and advised his wife to bend over some Khakass folk tale in the evenings?

But she didn't have the strength then and certainly didn't have it now—she was spent after the shows—to hear about her husband's dissipating existentialism, which was darkly floating by, and, asking him to leave her in peace for half an hour, she would sprawl out like the cat on the couch to doze, answering every noise, every clang of the washed dishes, with a grumble.

Just what Mboshka did, no one was privy to. Maybe the cat knew, but, after having put the boy to bed, he would finish his milk and go into the parents' bedroom, where he was trying to rouse his wife and make her feel guilty, his caresses unanswered or met with grumbles.

The wife would wake up at two o'clock while he was fast asleep, having turned over and tucked the blanket under him, and she would set about doing the laundry, rattling her tubs and stools.

That was the cat's starry hunting hour, her zenith.

Crouched behind the couch, she would suddenly hurl herself at his big toe that stuck out from under the blanket and start gnawing his blisters. In the end, he wrapped a bandage on his toe, but it turned out that unwinding the bandage was even more entertaining than chewing on a dried wound.

And the wife, on her way to work, would purr in his ear: "Why didn't you come to me?"—and was lost again until the nightly wash.

In those days, Mboshka was rereading his cat literature, from Kipling's "The Cat That Walked by Himself" to Baudelaire's "The Cat." "Did a black cat cross your path?" he smirked and, singing some vulgar romance about how glum you feel when a cat paws at your heart, he would go off to school.

Then one day the cat was no more.

He came home from work, as he was supposed to, in time for lunch, but the smell of meat didn't send a little ball snorting and rubbing around his legs to greet him. He rushed to the window. It was shut. A lone crow was sitting on the porch roof. He began groping around in the corners. The cat was nowhere. Then he called his wife at the theater. She said she was on her way, but asked him to be gentle with Mboshka. He went to the school and asked them to let the boy come home under some pretext. On the way home, he began the conversation from afar, telling the boy about his mother's death, long ago. But when he got to his memories of how they took him out of school, he suddenly fell silent and saw tears in Mboshka's eyes. So he hurriedly blurted out: "I called Mom right away. She's probably already at home." But the boy's tears didn't stop. "You're so grown up now," he said, and made an awkward attempt to tweak his nose. The boy fell into his arms and sobbed his heart out.

Quickly, quickly the wife came home and, flinging wide the doors, threw them a mistrustful glance. And in the next instant, when the doors had grown still, she went and set about examining all the corners, cupboards, and shelves.

He ran through the trash chute door into the cellar; Mboshka felt over every inch of the porch roof.

But the cat was nowhere.

Then, in the middle of a working day, the three of them sat in the living room. Translations, roles, and lessons were all forgotten; they were thinking: where had the cat disappeared to?

Maybe she'd left them?

Or run away with an admirer?

Or gone away to give birth and would come home with kittens?

Or maybe simply... she had stopped being a cat?

. . .

Right about then I fell asleep, as I always did during my stepfather's long stories. I dreamed that our cat was actually a tomcat.

. . .

On Friday morning, instead of making Hercules porridge, Mommy initiated an argument as simple as Hercules. Seeing as they had argued over and over every angle of family relations to its sickening conclusion, boiled it down to a bare skeleton, for the sake of diversity, that morning she got started on the tomcat.

"See what you've done! Go on, get up and take him to the vet!"

"What? Where? Why? Well, the cat was lying under the door all day yesterday, as it does every time there's a thunderstorm—"

"He hasn't been able to urinate all day. Look at the poor thing, he's suffering!"

My father got up, went unwillingly to the bathroom and while peeing looked into the cat tray where the cat was sitting. "Go on, go on! Get to work!" was what probably ran through his head, but when the cat didn't react to the water flushing—which usually made him dive after it—but instead it just crossed its little paw with difficulty over the empty cat tray, he realized that something was definitely wrong.

"What did you feed it yesterday?" he asked the still sleepy Mboshka.

"Grass..."

"And where did you pick it? Right on the roadside, I'm sure! You know it's full of lead... I've told you a thousand times—"

Mommy was calling all the vets and other cat-herding neighbors.

"It's twenty-five rubles for a home visit, plus the examination," she called from the kitchen.

"Forget that!" he muttered. "It'd be cheaper to buy a rope—"

"Then go yourself!" She slammed the phone down. "There. Take the address—"

"But I have to—" he began, but just at that moment the cat slowly and painfully came into the room and looked at them with tired eyes. Then he made his way to the nearest corner and lay down.

"Go on, get the box ready, then," he ordered mechanically.

"What do you mean, 'then'? Just take a bedspread and carry him in that!" she snarled.

"But he'll piss all over me, from top to toe—" he barked, but cut himself short.

Mboshka silently, deafeningly stroked the cat.

He wrapped the cat in the bedspread, and for the first time ever the cat didn't struggle. After waiting with his wife on the side of the road for half an hour, he finally flagged down a taxi.

"He's in a bad way, your cat," they said at the first vet. "His urinary tract's full of stones—"

"What can I do?"

"Well, injections, for now. I'll write you out a prescription; you can get it in an ordinary pharmacy. Yes, I'll give him one jab. Then it's up to you for the rest."

He went to the pharmacist with his wrapped-up cat. My, how the old women scolded him: "There's children dying, old folks, and here he comes along with a cat." He silently took the American medicine.

Back at the vet's when he unwrapped the bedspread and put the cat on the table, the cat, cowardly jumped off the table and, flattening his belly against the floor, crept into a corner. And then he suddenly felt unbearably bad for his poor, sick tomcat.

"Come here, sweetie, come to me, little one. They'll give you a nice little injection and then you'll get better, you'll see..."

It hurt the cat, but he kept quiet.

The day went by, but there was no respite for the cat.

The next morning he gave the cat an injection himself, and together, all three of them took him to a different vet. It was Saturday, so there were hordes of people waiting. When their turn finally came, the vet said: "We need to put the cat to sleep."

They begged her to insert a catheter to drain off the urine and even put a ten on the operating table for her. She agreed, but warned them that the cat's condition was "serious." The cat went limp and looked them all wanly in the eye.

They were asked to step outside, and each alone paced the length of the waiting room amid people, cats, dogs, and disease.

When the cat was returned to them, he left another ten. He was overjoyed, and completely forgot to ask whether or not they'd extracted much urine with the catheter.

"He's full of stones," said the vet. "You know, we could only insert the catheter half a centimeter."

He imagined the cat's bladder, full of stones, and it was only after the hour and a half bus ride back home with the totally exhausted cat *that he suddenly realized with horror that the vet had said something about half a centimeter in the urinary tract.*

He didn't want to remember this in front of his wife, let alone discuss it; it would just serve as yet another famous example of his "total indifference to what's going on around him." He was only waiting for—in secret—Sunday, when the vet who lived on the next block would come home. He'd give her whatever it took, just so long as she saved the cat.

"You'll feel better now," he promised the cat, and sensed that, indeed; bursting below the belly all that time, toward evening the cat wilted and sagged.

"They probably drained off the urine with a syringe," he reasoned to himself, remembering the tiny drop of a bloody-watery mass in a jar beside the catheter.

"Give that vet another ring?" he asked his wife. "Maybe she can call in first thing tomorrow morning."

That night he slept with the cat. The cat wasn't the slightest bit better. Instead, he grew hopelessly weak and kept trying to crawl to a cool place where he could lay his hanging belly. At midnight, his overgrown claws scraping the linoleum, the cat crawled out from under the bed and, swaying as if he were drunk, crawled by way of habit to the cat tray, hung there by his front paws but couldn't raise his belly.

He stroked and caressed the cat, poor and sick. He stroked his perineum and mentally pulverized those cursed stones, whispering: "You poor little thing, in so much pain." But the cat just kept quiet and suffered his pain by himself.

Toward morning the cat grew more peaceful under a pile of fluffy scarves and blankets, and even lay on his side.

"Hold on till this evening," Mboshka asked him.

"Hold on," asked the wife.

Together, they gave him an injection and the cat convulsed with pain. For the last time, as it turned out. In an hour, he was no more...

* * *

When I woke up on the couch in my stepfather's office and told him my dream—admittedly, a simpler version in those days (now, in the idleness of my eternal loneliness, I draw out every detail)—he gave me a drunken, slobbery kiss and said: "Another shitty writer, Pushkin, you son of a bitch!"

After a while he led me out of the courtly courtyard to another kremlin, which wasn't Leningradsky Station, but Uprising Square. We crossed over the Garden Ring, went down, past this kremlin of the Uprising and then, near a bunker-like building, I noticed with horror three enormous granite figures toppling out of an equally stony wall. One of them, squeezed between the two others, was looking straight at me, as though they were the drunken parents of my three new friends, already waiting for me at the entrance to the metro.

You see, often when I came back to our stairwell from the apple orchard across the road, three people just like that—two guys and an "auntie"—would call me over, hiccuping: "Hey you, *hic*! Little black imp! *Hic*! Come *hic*! Here!" And they would push some candy into my mouth, or maybe a little tomato, as much to say: "Well now, *hic*! Help it down!" And once, when my stepfather was at a reading, those three called me over again—but imagine my horror when I recognized the lady in between them as my mother. She was drunk, and thus tearfully kind; she kissed me wetly in front of those two men, clucking and saying: "He's *hic*! my-y little black imp! *Hic*! My *hic*...!"

We went into the bunker and, still afraid, I kept glancing back, hiding behind Uncle Gleb on the escalator—were those three drunken giants coming after us? At last we were in the hall with its blood-red columns and stalactite lamps that zigzagged along the length of the ceiling. At first I thought that the light was behind my eyes, like it always was when my head split with pain after a long cry or a too-short nap, but I realized that above, a lamp was stretching its brittle folds in the opposite direction, crawling out like a sci-fi maggot from the cellar-like gray stone from which I, too, had come.

That maggot'll eat them up! I thought, and relaxed...

Taganskaya Station
Tagansko-Krasnopresnenskaya Line

It was completely dark by the time we came out of Taganskaya Station onto a smallish square, and I saw another kremlin, which my stepfather blithely called the house on Ploshchad Kotelnicheskaya. The square lit up a small, two-story house, and we headed toward it. Despite the evening frost, a crowd was bustling around the building. As we drew closer, they asked my stepfather: "Do you have a spare ticket?" My stepfather, still not fully sober, yanked my arm so sharply that I hung briefly in the air, as he laughed coarsely: "Here's my ticket!" The crowd parted, confused, until someone else asked the same question, and got the same answer.

My stepfather pulled this stunt for the ushers: I swung for a brief moment, and then found myself inside the building, as my stepfather whispered something into the ear of a genteel old lady. The lobby was neat, like a clinic or a barbershop; further back, a crowd gathered at the entrance to the concert hall, where some photographs were hanging on the wall along with some loudspeakers. We skirted the masses and went to the bottom of a staircase where, one after the other, step after step, just like on the escalator earlier, five or six Pushkins were standing. Then we weaved our way through some corridors until Uncle Lolik came out to meet us and led us to an empty dressing room.

There my stepfather said, "So, Lolik, let it fly!" Uncle Lolik switched on the tape recorder and a loud, husky voice burst out:

I run, I stamp, sliding
On the cinder path
Not allowed to eat, not allowed to drink,
Not allowed to sleep—not a wink.
But maybe I'd like to go out
To Gurev Timoshka's
But no: I run, run, I stamp
On the cinder path.

My stepfather kept drinking, and he and Uncle Lolik each slammed down a glass in honor of someone named "Volodka." Then Uncle Lolik turned to me and said: "We had to send your little friend Antoshka to the vet. He stuffed himself with all kinds of crap that day by the New Year tree. But I've got something else for you to do. You can sit here and listen to a story about Ali Baba. Do you know about him? And the forty thieves?" I nodded, although in truth I was mortally afraid of those thieves. "We'll take your dad into the main hall, and I'll keep an eye on you. Deal?" I nodded again.

My stepfather went off with Uncle Lolik, leaving my toy monkey and two boiled sausage and cheese sandwiches. I was alone in the dressing room, and the same throaty voice sang about my real Daddy:

And Sam Brook from Guinea
Overtook me by a lap
And yesterday all around
Were saying: Sam's our friend
Sam's our Guinean friend!
Our Guinean friend is shoving ahead
The gap keeps growing
But I hope that there will come
My second wind...

I glanced around. In front of me, directly opposite the three-leaved mirror, was a chair with a leather jacket flung over the back. The jacket was obviously too small for Uncle Lolik and on the chair, leaning against the jacket, was a well-worn guitar. In the corner was a china vase with a dour portrait of a face. On the table was a collection of little jars, tubes, and boxes. Two bare lamps on long, spindly legs stood on either side of the table, and on the wall behind them was a photograph of the same grouchy, hairy person on the vase. Admittedly, in the big photo, with the guitar he looked kinder...

Uncle Lolik came back carrying a portable record player, which he set on the little table in front of me. He turned off the song about my runner-dad:

> *I'm hoping for my*
> *Third, my fourth wind*
> *But on the fifth I'll cut short*
> *The gap between the Guinean and me!*
> *Well he's some good friend—*
> *Overtook me by a whole lap!*
> *And yesterday all around*
> *Were saying: Sam's our friend*
> *Sam's our Guinean friend!*

In the silence, he fiddled with the socket and put a record on. The record hummed to life, and music came forth. At first I was wary that the deafening frightening, husky man's voice would boom out again, but instead, sweet voices struck up: "*Pep-per-si-a, Pep-persi-i...*"

I couldn't understand. Were they going to sing about peppers? Peppers and me, or something? Uncle Lolik waltzed off, and once again I was alone with the voices, a story I hardly understood, but which didn't scare me, despite its scary name.

At night, Mommy often told me the Khakassian tale "Yaril Tas." I remembered it this morning when I first went to the metro. In the story, mother and son are living in poverty, and one day a rich villain wants to force her to marry him, but she runs away to the mountains and hides in a rocky cliff. One day, the son goes to find her in the rock and chants a little verse: "Rock, crack open! Let me see my Mommy..."

Mommy would say: "If you're not a good boy, I'll go away to the mountains and hide in a rock, and I won't open it up for you! Now, go to sleep!" And I, afraid of not being a good boy, would screw my eyes up tightly.

I very soon fell asleep, and dreamed of a cave, like a palace inside, where cut glass and gold leaf glimmered, where people moved grandly and silently like fish in a tank; where thirty-three thieving little monkeys suddenly appeared on the escalator, wave after wave of them, step after step, traveling down into the underworld. And suddenly a commotion broke out all around and everything spun in the whirlwind of their dance; the cut glass shattered into shards, the gilt crumbled into dust, and darkness pierced the cave, and I realized that I was dreaming of my Moscow metro where, like fear, Mommy's voice resounded:

"Watch the closing doors..."

Avtozavodskaya Station
ZAMOSKVORETSKAYA LINE

Rotting in the frozen, viscous Moscow soil is not much worse than growing in your mother's warm, slippery womb; your skin is just as dark, blending with the darkness around it, though it is, obviously, no longer stretching and expanding. What is worse, however, is being tortured by immaterial, futile memories, belonging not to you alone, deposited with the yearly or ten-yearly layers of earth. Even the slightest movement of a train through the earth—like the surge of blood through the veins—stirs up the many-layered soil above you, and all its heaviness presses down on your still-existing rib cage and the emptied space in it where your heart once was.

My mother came to work at the Moscow Car Factory "in the name of the Komsomol of Lenin" as other limitchitsa were traveling in the opposite direction, to her Siberian-Komsomolsk regions. Railway workers went to complete the Baikal-Amur Mainline, others to launch the Sayano-Shushenskaya hydroelectric power station.

My Mommy was put up in a shared room in a five-story hostel, almost directly opposite the factory's main gates. She worked on the conveyor belt, in the assembly shop, until she was dog-tired, but dreamed all the while of getting a job teaching nights at some art school. But somehow it never worked out and everything was always put off until next year. Then the Olympic Games came—or the preparations, when sailcloth suits with beige jackets and dark-blue trousers were sewn for all the workers at the car factory—and they were signed up as volunteer civil patrols throughout the city.

I don't remember that time, but I'd memorized my mother's tale of my disreputable conception and the nine months following, when no one had any clue as to the nature of the strange creature she was carrying. I was offended, but she was my Mommy...

She tried to get rid of me, but apparently she was so young and inexperienced on one hand, and so young and healthy on the other, that her attempts to abort using old wives' methods didn't work. The ambulance was called, and she was admitted to the so-called "observation" ward, where they could keep an eye on her for a while.

In the early months of her pregnancy, she went back home to Siberia, to her mother, the old lady who came to Moscow twice: once to collect her daughter's body, and again to collect a pension. I was ashamed of her in front of my friends, in front of the neighbors. She was shaggy and unkempt, with evil, slit eyes—a ready-made Baba Yaga. But she was my Mommy's mommy...

Back there, in Abakan or maybe Tayshet, Mommy almost married a former classmate who still pined for her. One day in mid-August, in the hellfire of a heat wave, he invited her to go sunbathing. They got in an old Moskvich—just like the one that took Mommy away, in the end—and rattled along the road for three hours. They spent all day in the sun at the lake, where he read to her from a book called *The Stranger,* by someone named Camus, which he'd gotten through his connection at the local library.

Mommy told me that, besides the sunstroke and nearly fainting in that stuffy old car, the episode also killed any interest in literature for the rest of her life: the sense-memory of the sun and the book's futility were so unbearably nauseating. And though Mommy said it had crossed her mind to present the simple

Khakassian with a little Negro six or seven months later, as revenge for the sunstroke—*the baby got overcooked that day by the lake!*—she felt sorry for the poor guy. Otherwise he would have ended up like poor old Ivanov in the joke she liked to tell:

* * *

A son is born to Ivanov the Russian, a Negro son. Ivanov is sitting in the maternity ward and the midwives didn't know how to tell him. Finally they call over the watchman, Rif the Tatar, pour him a glass of spirit and ask him to speak with Ivanov, to say something along the lines of: well, a dark-skinned child, there's been some kind of mutation of the genes.
   "Got it?"
   "Sure, I got it! What's so complicated?!" asks Rif. So Rif the Tatar, taking a sniff at his sleeve to help the spirit go down, goes up to Ivanov and says: "Ivanov?"
   "Yes, I'm Ivanov."
   "Ah, you're a fool, Ivanov, y'son of a bitch! Gotta keep yer mutator clean, see—a Negro's been born to ya, they've called 'im Jean!"

* * *

So she left her Ivanov the Khakassian in peace and ran away back to Moscow.

She went back to her Avtozavodskaya Station, with its elegant marble pillars that looked like a woman's legs, bare to the hip, and with lamps like bitch udders (that is how I pictured the station from her irate account) and, right at the exit, just under the transformer-like shell of a stylized *M* with an extra flourish, she fainted in a heap over her suitcases...

1980 Arch

a voice from the darkness
silently sways, having returned from its wanderings,
that air in which we wander too...

Paveletskaya Station

ZAMOSKVORETSKAYA LINE

As the birth drew closer, it wasn't her mother who came, but her father, a retired army colonel, a man with the genteel and ancient surname of Rzhevsky. He was vacationing somewhere in Nazran. Seeing how he had to change his itinerary and come through Moscow, he arranged to be taken on board the Nazran-Moscow train as guard for the restaurant car in exchange for free passage, and in a couple of days they pulled into Paveletskaya Station. However, as the train was late, my grandfather decided not to search in the wintry darkness for his daughter's hostel, but to spend the night in the restaurant car, thereby guarding it at the same time.

In the depths of the night, he heard a woman scream. At first he thought he had been dreaming about his daughter's labor. Coming to, he realized the cry was coming from outside. Being a gentleman and military man, he grabbed a fireman's hook and flung the doors wide open. In the narrow space between trains, he saw two shadowy figures in the violet darkness and heard a woman making sounds like a skinned sheep.

With a commander's bark, Grandpa rushed toward them, but before he could position himself for attack, the tool was pulled from his hand and my grandpa felt a sharp burning in his chest. As he collapsed under the train, miraculously, he saw a crowbar, which the trackmen use to check the wheels, chained up there. Grabbing it instinctively, he brought it crashing down on the dark character.

The blow landed on his attacker's head, dropping him like a sack onto the snow. The woman, beaten and tear-stained, crawled over to my grandpa and, seeing the dark puddle around him, began shrieking at the top of her voice. After a while, the station guards came running, called the police and the ambulance, and Grandpa—instead of a getting a trip to Avtozavodskaya Station—was taken to Sklifosovsky Hospital.

When Mommy heard the news, there was a terrible movement in her belly, as if I had found out, too. She was bewildered: should she go give birth or rush to her father in Sklifosovsky? First, they told her to go to Paveletskaya and pick up her father's things and documents and present them at Sklifosovsky, so she went to the metro. Under the arches, like the caverns of her father's lungs, slashed by the hook, or the splayed legs of a woman giving birth, Mommy forced herself to stay conscious, sniffing turpentine, as she dragged Grandpa's huge suitcase, full of vacation supplies and presents for the whole of Siberia, and—most important—his colonel's papers, to the station's military office. There, almost in labor, she left the suitcase and rushed to Novokuznetskaya Station, where, it turned out, lived the lady her father had saved. Her name was Irina Rodionovna Oblonskaya and she had phoned my Mommy after all the commotion and promised to help any way she could. She worked as the deputy head doctor at one of the maternity hospitals.

And why didn't Mommy go to her father? Because down there, in Paveletskaya Radial Station, under those bowed legs, her water broke...

Novokuznetskaya Station

ZAMOSKVORETSKAYA LINE

Do you remember Novokuznetskaya Station? The one modeled on the empty Yeliseevsky dining hall, or, really, on the hall of the dead from some Egyptian pyramid. My mother threw up at each of the throne-like benches and felt sick at the sight of the lamps that look like dentist's spittoons—and especially due to the innumerable fathers crowding around and racing off with fireman's hooks. The horde made her gag incessantly.

Her father's retirement papers were in a bag that was now overflowing with vomit, and the benches were now wet. A policeman came over, assuming she was a drunk, and tried to drag her by the armpit to the surface. Once she had spilled the whole bag of puke over him, the sergeant realized what he was dealing with. He left her on a cold (dry) bench, and he went off, whistling—either to call an ambulance or wipe the humiliation off his uniform.

I must have been uncomfortable in that sticky place with the seeping water and everything tightening like stretched skin. I began to stamp my feet, like a grasshopper or like a tiny blacksmith with a hammer; was I calling out for help? Later, after Mommy's death, I would often sit alone, in the fetal position, hunching myself up and crossing my legs as I tried to recall, reclaim, resurrect those pre-birth sensations that dissolved like a viscous mass into the subconscious. I relived that sensation only once when, at the age of seven, I fell into a vat of tar next to a building site, from which—luckily—an old man in white pulled me out. I think I saw him once more, but I didn't recognize him. But more of that later. I felt the momentary bliss of powerlessness as I shrank into a ball, about to dissolve into the mass, which neither rejected me nor quarreled with me in any way. But nobody let me die then...

They took my mother upstairs on a stretcher, and she felt a little better. She asked the good people to call Irina Rodionovna, who lived nearby on Great Tatar Street. They called, and Irina hurried to the station. The black ice was so dangerous that she quickly decided to take her patient by metro to the maternity clinic at Oktybrskaya Station, only two stops away.

On the same stretcher, now escorted by Irina Rodionovna, Mommy was carried onto the orange line, clean, severe, and sterile like a hospital ward. Startled passengers scrambled out of the car as the stretcher was carried aboard. As the metallic voice announced its usual "Watch the doors..." to the emptiness, Mommy and I felt together that my birth had begun...

Oktyabrskaya Station
KALUZHSKO-RIZHSKAYA LINE

The metro must be Moscow's womb, the belly from which everything springs forth. Moscow—my mother—remembers that day like a nightmare. "Oktyabrskaya Station," she would say, "it's even more sterile than Novokuznetskaya. More like an obstetrics ward than a station. Pity the Ministry of Internal Affairs is just next door; makes it like a friggin' funny farm. I nearly gave birth to you at that station. The cramps began. Just imagine—your birth certificate would say, 'Place of birth: October Natal [that's what she'd say, Natal instead of Radial]; father: an unwashed mutator; mother: Moscow!'" And she would laugh out loud.

Later, when I used to play hooky from school, I would take the metro to this station as though the decorations, two-thirds brown—my color—were painted with my mother's waters. I would walk the station from end to end, thinking that this place could have been my birthplace—or the place of my stillbirth, the place of my death. It was here that my pulse disappeared during the labor pangs.

As they arrived at the hospital, the midwife rushed to tell the doctors with my mother shrieking, "No, anything but that!" and within five minutes surgeons and nurses and orderlies with carts came scurrying out of the train, and Irina Rodionovna gave the order: "Let's operate!"

In the far corner, opposite the escalators, I smelled the drugs that put my mother to sleep, and when the crowd dissipated as quickly as those nurses and orderlies had appeared; throughout that whole echoing hall, I felt Mommy's immense, cold loneliness, left with the lifeless me.

"Quick! Operate, operate!" she whispered with slow lips, like the gradual braking of the train approaching on the iron rails. And suddenly a cry rang out, a child's cry, jolting me as if I had just been born. I looked around, confused, as a young mother with a howling child appeared from the next archway.

"That started out as a night of two deaths," Mommy would tell me. "First I was sure you'd died inside me and then, when they started cutting me open, I was sure I was going to die too."

"But it turned out to be the night of two births!" I said, trying in my childish way to be clever, and Mommy would always grin.

In reality, I was born in the maternity ward of Pirogov Hospital, the one on Lenin Prospekt. But that's beside the point...

Shabolovskaya Station
KALUZHSKO-RIZHSKAYA LINE

A few years after my birth, my Mommy took me through that ill-fated station to the kindergarten choir near Shabolovskaya, where—thanks to my blackness—I was the best-known face among the children, all dressed in white shirts. They put me right in the middle as a kind of axis for the others, and I thought this was my true role in the choir, since my voice was pretty rough.

"The scars of long tears," as Mommy put it.

But it wasn't the choir I wanted to tell you about—it was Shabolovskaya Station. "This is where I buried my father," Mommy used to say.

No, he didn't die from the stab wounds; they operated on him at Sklifosovsky Hospital, got him back on his feet quickly, and discharged him a day before Mommy and me. The retired Colonel Rzhevsky's gentlemanliness prevented him from staying at a women's hostel. Irina Rodionovna lived alone and, with all due respect to her savior, neither her manners nor his would allow him to spend a night at her place, so she set him up for a night in a cheap hotel near Shabolovskaya.

After Mommy and I were discharged from Pirogov, she went with Irina Rodionovna to see her father. The prudent Irina Rodionovna had arranged the meeting inside Shabolovskaya Station so I wouldn't catch a chill from the wind—and because, after the meeting, Grandpa had to get to Paveletsky Station, then to Yaroslavsky, where he would catch the evening train to Abakan, or maybe Tayshet.

There at the station, by the stained-glass window (which from a distance looks like the Iron Cross worn by the SS), Grandpa fell on his daughter with tears in his eyes. But as he held out his arms to her, a sharp pain shot through his wounded side. Lowering his arms, he asked just to see his first grandson. When Mommy opened up the thick blanket and turned my face toward him, Grandpa suddenly turned blue, then green, then red, and he screeched for the whole empty station to hear: "Ssl-luu-ttt!" Irina Rodionovna and I shrieked together, and the doctor became hysterical—probably a flashback to the attempted rape. Grandpa was holding his side with one hand and groping the wall with the other, as if searching for a crowbar with which to whack his daughter.

"You're no daughter of mine anymore! Curse you! Prostitute!" he shrieked in his throaty voice, that cellar-like hall doubling the overtones of his Siberian yelp.

Luckily, a train pulled up and Mommy, her face turned to stone, threw herself inside followed by Irina Rodionovna, fighting off fright and hysterics, and my grandpa, who was still hurling curses. The doors closed, leaving the blood-blue memories on that station.

Oktyabrskaya and Paveletskaya Stations

KOLTSEVAYA LINE

Mother never told me about that last conversation with her father, my only Russian grandfather. But at least she had a father, I thought. Even if he cursed her, he still existed. I didn't have anyone to curse me.

Once, when Irina Rodionovna took my slightly tipsy mother to church, I was amazed at how easily my non-believing mother slipped into the role of fallen and forgiven daughter, how easily she cried in the solemn darkness, at the priest's cloying voice. And as the choir took up the hymn, she covered me in tears and snot. Through the darkness I could still feel the harsh stares of the priest and congregation, as if they had discovered a little black devil inside their church.

My sanctuary, if there was such a thing, was the hall of Oktybrskaya Circle Station, late in the evening, when it was emptied of people. Here, I paced slowly in the dim blueness, listening to the boom of each step, in the depths of the hall, like an altar, where you could open the door and find yourself in the empty, fatherless twilight. The candelabras drenched the walls in a waxy light, as if lost in thought over my fatherlessness—as though it were a problem for the whole universe, impenetrable to the religions of mankind.

Christ would have understood my soul; after all, he didn't have a father either. Zarathustra and Muhammad would have understood me. With these thoughts I reached the altar of eternal twilight and made an awkward pleading gesture. I looked around to make sure no one had seen me and added, just in case, "Christ is risen" (though what kind of Christian would I make, a Khakass-Negro?). Then I took the first train to Paveletskaya.

On the train, I would sometimes pick an old gypsy-like southerner from out of town. I'd get as close as possible, trying mightily to implant in him the notion that we were father and son. And he would sense my strain, give a fleeting, awkward glance, and turn away, clinging tighter to his suitcases—or else give a forced, toothless smile. But either way, he would exit the car first, leaving behind a void. I would inhale that emptiness deeply; and then, a moment before the doors closed, I'd fling myself onto the platform as the old southerner walked away, glancing back in pity or anger. I would go in the other direction, past the mandalas staring out from the walls, their deathless eyes spread over me. As I grasped the railing, I would pause for a moment over the same thought: even in the underworld, there is always a road that leads lower...

1985 Model

see how the winter sunset is pointless...
All this is not invented by us but
all this is lived out by us as an ailment, as a disease...

Turgenevskaya Station

*F*athers and Sons... but for me it was *Fatherless and Orphaned.* Until the end of the world, until doomsday, I would have the whole of eternal darkness to think over my twelve years of life. It has always seemed strange that there is so much more darkness in the universe than light, and humanity grasps at the tiny dots of stars as though equating an infinitesimal day with the vast, fathomless night; forcing light to overcome darkness. Why do we do that? Take a look around you. Well, that binary just isn't there! Only the isometric letter *M* glows, with its ruby zigzag, in the Moscow darkness above me, and smothered in neon, even that now goes out, now flickers, or, crackling, flares up anew...

O mother of mine—Moscow, Mara, Marusia—how did she suddenly turn from a limitchitsa at the car factory into a model? What part is reason here, what part is memory? Very vaguely, I remember a place by the neat name of Clean Ponds. I don't remember the ponds themselves, just a boulevard in May bloom where, from time to time, a brass band would play and curious drivers on either side of the road would slow and roll down their windows. And despite the breeze and faint sunshine, I remember most of all a stuffy studio in a dilapidated house crammed with frames, pictures, plaster, teapots, smelling of everything from lime to resin.

Mommy and I and were greeted by a bearded man with a pipe between his teeth. Without taking the chomped stem from his mouth, he greeted us and sat me down by some lumps of multicolored clay. He led Mommy through some cluttered corridors "for a séance." I was afraid of that word, lisped by the bearded man with prickly eyes, but Mommy would tie a smock around me, kiss me on the forehead, smile and, as she always did, spit on the ground, whispering, "I'll be back before it dries!"

From that clay I would mold my dismay, my loss, my abandonment, my fears, hatred, jealousy—but usually all that came out was either a small, dark, asymmetrical star or a sexless stick figure without a face.

But one day, when my hands were all smeared in that worthless clay, I heard—not with my ears, but with my empty, rumbling gut—a nervous laugh from my mother. I threw off my little shoes and went in my little white socks toward that laughter. At the first turn, I stepped on a nail sticking out from a frame. It punctured me and the pain was chilling, but my fear was even greater and the pain dissolved into it, like the blood soaking into my sock. I was getting closer to the twitching laugh, and when I peeked around the screen I saw my naked mother crouching on all fours on a platform and that awful artist hanging over her with his pipe between his teeth. One hand was resting on Mommy's bare ass, and with the other he was adjusting her breast. At each touch she gave a dirty laugh, and he lisped through his teeth and his pipe: "Wait, wait, now I'll touth your tittieth..."

"Mommy, I need to poop..." I said, and they both shrieked—twice, because the pipe fell from his stinking mouth onto Mommy's back, and he began smacking the burned powder from her startled, exposed body. Those yelps made me forget that what I really wanted to do was cry and throw up at the same time. And later, having been soundly smacked at the dusky Clean Ponds, I, limping because of the wound on my foot, burst into tears along with Mommy at the smoky, faceless Turgenevskaya Station, and I vomited up some sort of clayish mass...

Ploshchad Nogina Station

KALUZHSKO-RIZHSKAYA AND
TAGANSKO-KRASNOPRESNENSKAYA LINES

But that was not the most degrading scene I witnessed that May in Moscow. One stop farther was the Hotel Russia, where Mommy and I went to pick up a package her mother had sent from Siberia. After all the phone calls about where to go, what the box looked like, and so on, Mommy took me with her, and it turned into a treasure hunt; the first clue—after the rusty aquarium-like station, look for a bell or a church cupola, growing out of the ground right by the exit—was rich in promises and secrets.

Out on the windy street, passing the little church, we went up to one of the hotel's entrances where uniformed flunkies were showing Soviet courtiers into Soviet chariots-cum-yellow taxis. Mommy called somebody from the lobby, and, after a while, a swaggering, burly guy wearing officer's pants and a white T-shirt came down. He kissed Mommy three times and gave me a flick on the nose. We went up in the elevator, then walked down long corridors. The man bought a bottle of wine, a bottle of vodka, and some sweetmeats from the buffet in the corner, and we went into his room.

The television was on, though there was no one there. I should explain that, as we were making our way here, it seemed like we were still on a treasure hunt. "And there is the Kremlin!" The man opened the heavy curtains, the way you would pry open a treasure chest. Mommy let out an exaggerated gasp, like she had never seen it before; I marveled at how the view looked like a postcard.

He struck a warrior-like karate pose and showed off some moves: a fist thrust and a block, turning smoothly. Then he kicked his feet, in their patent leather officer's boots, right up to the ceiling, hung in the air, and then landed in a split. Mommy clapped and said he was still just as sporty as he had been in school, at which point he stood up and bowed.

I looked around. Two armchairs had been pushed toward the coffee table where smoked fish, an open jar of pickles, some sliced sausage, and some peeled boiled eggs were laid out.

On the way here, Mommy had promised we would just grab the package and be on our way, but now she was asking about her mother or other people they both knew but I didn't know. He invited us over to the coffee table; Mommy took me on her knee. He opened the bottle of wine and the bottle of vodka, poured some wine into Mommy's glass and some vodka into his own, and proposed a toast to Mommy and me. At first Mommy protested. He said he hadn't seen her for so many years but remembered her from when she was so high—he gave a nod in my direction—and she was still just as pretty! Mommy picked up the wine and the spicy smell hit my nostrils. I turned away, and they drank.

The man told Mommy the latest news about her mother, about her father—Colonel Rzhevsky was his former boss—and she asked about her classmates, her words getting ever louder and hotter against my ear. The man poured them each another glass and suggested sitting me on the bed. He bent over us, exhaling his vodka and sausage, and having for some reason gathered up my mother's legs along with me, he forced both her and himself to laugh.

I didn't eat anything. I was waiting for him to finally hand over our package, my secret treasure from my unknown Grandma. But the man kept eating and drinking, and—strangely—it didn't bother my mother. They drank a third round, and the man looked over to me, and, as if suddenly remembering something, asked, "But why isn't that little brunette eating anything?" at which Mommy just waved her hand and, through her laughter, replied something unintelligible that sounded like: "Thasshh's jussh the way he issshhh!"

"I've got a toy for him!" the man said and made his way on unsteady legs to the door of the closet opposite the bathroom, where the suitcases were. I was sitting with my back to him and so could only hear him shuffling around. Then he called Mommy by name: "Mossshcow, won'cha give me a hand?" Mommy planted a wet kiss on my forehead and walked over to him on her own wobbly legs. A suitcase skidded and fell with a bang. He said: "Thissshh waay, in here..." a door slammed, a key turned, and for some reason only the sound of running water could be heard.

My heart began thumping harder, the blood was pounding in my head and, no matter how hard I tried to block it all out with the sounds of the TV and the gushing water, certain noises crept into my bare consciousness: smacking lips, faint gasps, heavy panting, and suddenly, a dull, rhythmic thumping, as if my heart had fallen out in the commotion and was now pounding on the floor, the walls, the bathroom tiles...

Petrified, I somehow got to the bathroom door; all those noises were coming from there. With all my desperation and childish strength, I banged on that door, screaming: "Mo-ommeee! Mo-om-meee!" The door opened. I was hit by the smell of a thousand dirty men's socks, as if the whole bathtub were full of them, then Mommy, tousled and swollen, poked her head out and said drunkenly: "Wacchha sshhhhouting about? We jusshh can't get thisshh sshhuitcassh open... Gimmee a mmminit to finisshh wasssshhhing!" All sound stopped, except the intermittent rush of water, and Mommy came out, freshly washed, her blouse and skirt soaked. After a while, the man came out, too, dragging a suitcase behind him. He had completely forgotten about the promised toy but handed us the box that Grandma sent. I don't remember what was in the box; I don't remember how we got out of there, out of the Hotel Russia just opposite the Kremlin... I don't remember anything... I don't want to remember...

Kuznetskiy Most and Dzerzhinskaya Stations

TAGANSKO-KRASNOPRESNENSKAYA AND SOKOLNICHESKAYA LINES

N o, no, I remember what was in the box. Because, as I said earlier, no matter how low you descend, there are always steps leading even lower. Or as my mother, with her characteristic Siberian love of proverbs, would say: "You fall into a puddle but have to get yourself out of a pit." It was Saturday, and we took the metro to Kuznetskiy Most Station, which I have already mentioned. There, in the middle of the bathhouse-like hall, sat two benches, their fat, marble backs leaning against each other. By those benches, with her little scissors, Mommy cut through the sticky tape and pulled out a pile of books. Under the books were books, and under those books—more books. She put them all back, and we went up to the surface, heading—or so I thought—to the same cozy bookshop I had visited with Uncle Gleb that winter.

But in front of the shop, a crowd of people of all stripes were blocking the whole street. They all carried bulging briefcases or huge bags slung over their shoulders. Many of them clutched little sheets of paper, scribbled with notes. We entered the crowd together with our box, and I heard strange whispers going from person to person:

"Do you have Faulkner?"

"No, but I do have Sartre."

"How about Pikul?"

"Yes. What exactly are you looking for?"

Everyone was searching for, or offering something, mysterious. It was only after I saw a man rummage through his briefcase and pull out a big, fat volume wrapped in plastic that I realized where we were: the flea market for books. And I also suddenly understood why Mommy had brought me here. She set our box right in the very middle of the crowd, just as they stood me in the center of the preschool choir at Shabolovskaya, and pulled out a pile of books, setting them out in a row.

We hadn't been standing long before the curious started to approach. Those with bags and briefcases threw slippery glances at the books but mostly stared at Mommy with sordid eyes: *where, pray tell, had this one come from?* The few people with empty hands or cellophane packets leafed through some book or other, but no one asked the price. And so time passed. Then suddenly, like iron filings to a magnet, everyone around us abruptly turned to passersby, pressing onto the pavement and going about their business up or down Kuznetskiy Most. Only a few empty-handed people—and, of course, Mommy and I with our box—were left in the middle of the street. And while I was wondering what that could mean, two policemen loomed up in front of us and, saluting Mommy as she crouched down to the box (which brought her to exactly the same height as me), they demanded to see her papers.

She didn't have any papers with her except for her factory pass, and then when one of the policemen took her pass and said, smirking: "Look! She's called Moscow!" Mommy suddenly shrieked for all on the street to hear: "And you? Do you have papers? Well let's see them, maybe you're some kind of werewolf!" The policeman was at a loss. The second rushed to help, flipping open his ID and holding it close to Mommy's face. Mother started wailing even louder: "And that's my son. Don't you dare lay a finger on him!" And at that I, too, started bawling for the whole street to hear, either from fear or from shame, because my still-not-fully-sober Mommy continued with a volley of frenzied cries: "Yes, Moscow! Yes, imagine that, I'm Moscow! Unlucky Moscow!"

Panicking, the first policeman radioed for a patrol car, and the people began to hiss and hoot, either at us or at the policemen, and someone from the depths of the crowd said: "Let the woman and child go!"—to which the policeman who had flashed his ID replied: "Well, we'll see about that. Maybe she pilfered the little Negro!" Then I bawled at the top of my voice: "No! She's my Mommy! Mommy!" and latched myself onto her skirt.

Lights flashing, the patrol car pulled up and two police officers lifted Mommy by the arms. I flattened myself against the pavement and started to howl with all my strength. An officer grabbed me around the waist, and I affixed my teeth to his sleeve. He yelped: "Aha, you little animal, so you bite, too?" He slapped me on the cheek and grabbed me so tightly that I couldn't even squirm. Mommy threw herself at me as an uproar broke out, whistles and whoops, but the cops finally shoved us into the car. We drove off under those scandalized glares, as the people with their bags and briefcases were already regrouping in the street. They took us to the nearest police station, which turned out to be by a pie shop. The policemen, following protocol, confiscated our Siberian gift. After threatening to write a letter to her boss, they let her go, a mother with a young child—but just in case, they asked her, timid and conciliatory: "You never worked for any of the ministries, by any chance, have you?" After that, the first thing we did was to go to the pie shop and, with the rubles hidden in her bra, Mommy bought a bunch of cabbage pies and two cups of cocoa...

Prospekt Marksa and
Ploshchad Sverdlova Stations
SOKOLNICHESKAYA AND ZAMOSKVORETSKAYA LINES

Sometimes the maggots get bored of digging into my decaying body, and they abandon me, burrowing tunnels to the surface to take a breather after it rains. Then within the cavities of my body I feel an emptiness, into which water sometimes gushes like metro trains, or ants, waking up to May, file through like the people pouring into the subway cars above.

As for us, in that distant May we walked uphill slightly through the never-ending maggot tunnels of the connecting passage between Marx Boulevard and Sverdlov Square, my sandals slipping on the shiny marble floor, and I thought about what would happen if you filled this pipe with water or sewage from all of Moscow...

My mother, sober by now, stopped in the middle of that rib-cage-like passage, and, not finding anything to sit down on, leaned her elbows against one of the granite arches. As she was perching herself more comfortably to catch her breath, her handkerchief slipped from her fingers and spread itself out at her feet. She merely waved her hand, as usual, not having the strength to bend down for it.

But when I bent down to pick it up, two coins fell onto it, right under my nose. While Mommy yelled something after someone, others, persuaded that the woman wasn't satisfied with the coppers, began throwing ten, fifteen, or twenty kopek coins as they passed. Mommy looked at me, perplexed, and burst out laughing, and I started laughing too.

We didn't bother to gather up that money or the handkerchief but just flushed ourselves away unnoticed, as though carried upward by a stream of water or shit. We clambered out, pretending that we needed to dry off, at Ploshchad Sverdlova Station, and, after sitting for a bit in its waffle-like hall, stood up, dived under the low arch that resembled a marble bench, and vanished onto a train heading north.

Gorkovskaya Station

But I certainly don't want you to think my Mommy was a perpetually half-drunk bitch. Not at all, and not just because she was my mother. I've almost spent, above and under this earth, as many years as she lived, and I would like to say that she was an amazingly beautiful woman. You simply have no idea what a beautiful half-Russian, half-Khakassian girl looks like. Such a girl is much more beautiful and expressive than a pretty Russian, Jewish, or French girl—prettier than anyone! My first stepfather, Gleb, used to say about her straight, slim little nose: "Like the *Lady with an Ermine*..." Anyone whose eyes met my mother's could never forget them; their clearly defined almond shape, fine eyebrows traced on a milky face—they were like a laser that consumed, glued, hooked, emptied. And their color was like autumn, enticing, but fading, inevitably...

There are two or three photographs of Mommy left: one belongs to my first stepfather Gleb, the second to Irina Rodionovna, and the third to someone else. Not one of them hung those pictures on the wall. Those eyes were so piercing that the owners of the portraits guiltily lay them down, under the pretext of preventing them from getting dusty or fading in the light—and so those photos are still looking down, into the depths, at me...

I often think that I don't look at all like my Mommy, but then at other times I notice how she looks out through me, smiles, wrinkles up her forehead. But seeing my reflection is enough to make me wonder gloomily: how could she consider this mysterious creature, whom no one recognized as her relation in any way whatsoever, to be her son? What was it like for her, so pretty and extraordinary, to have a little nigger boy? Many thought it was a whim, an extravagance: So a pretty woman decided to adopt a monkey? Well, people keep all kinds of pets— cats, hedgehogs, crocodiles... She would get really angry when people made those jokes in front of her; I remember one day a small squirt of blood shot out her nose in her fury. Really, it was just the opposite; she possessed me so completely that I sometimes felt suffocated by her motherly attention.

The paradox is that in trying to prove to everyone that I belonged to her, she turned me into a doll, a pet, a toy that sings and dances and ice skates better than everyone else, and learns French at home with Marina Borisovna...

But now I'm getting distracted. Vaguely, these thoughts also came to me that distant May when, after arriving at Gorkovskaya Station, we stood by the far wall opposite the escalator down to Pushkinskaya Station (no matter how far you descend into the deep, you are always on the brink of another abyss), and I didn't look at those stairs, but in the other direction at the thick wall where Maxim Gorky stands alone on a disintegrating stone yacht. He was chiseled from brown stone, so the color of his face was similar to mine, and I was happy about this likeness. One day, I thought, I, too, will be tall and fine; one day I, too, will grow my hair down to my shoulders and stand on a yacht; one day I, too...

But just then my stepfather, Uncle Gleb, came up behind us and kissed us both loudly on the cheek, saying: "So how about we hit the town?!" At first I was worried that Uncle Gleb knew all about what had happened that day, but as he led us to the surface of the city, my child's brain understood that he had just been paid...

You may remember that, near the exit from Gorky's stony intestines, on the other side of Gorky Prospekt, there is a trendy café on the corner called Lira. Uncle Gleb took us there. Places had been reserved for us right by the big glass windows that opened onto the scene outside. After an urgent inspection of the bathroom, I sat down at the table to contemplate the mouth of Tver Boulevard as twilight descended that May evening...

Everyone has something to hide, I thought, looking out into the night, and Mommy questioned my stepfather about his day, about his successes. Even I have secrets, and I've been hiding, until now, what may be my most painful secret: starting from kindergarten, people didn't nickname me Blackie or Black-ass, not Monkey or Macaque and not even Chocolate, but... Pushkin. I thought often about that man, whom I hated—or maybe loved—for all my torments and now there he was, his statue darkening across the square, and I thought, just as he was an Abyssinian by his great-grandfather, Ibrahim Gannibal, so I was a Russian by my grandfather, Colonel Rzhevsky of the ancient Rzhevsky clan, who once gave his daughter to a Negro. And who knows, I thought, if God had let me be born in Abyssinia and not here, I might have become their Pushkin...

They brought us chicken noodle soup, and I was distracted from the street, but threw a glance at the people at the next table, a French couple (it wasn't for naught that Marina Borisovna had, for a whole week, drummed into me the phrases: *les muttons et les chevres* or *des carrots et des betteraves*). They were smiling at me as only foreigners can smile. I suspect that my father conquered my mother not with gifts of foreign blouses and jeans but with his smile: pearly white teeth in a black face...

My mother was purring with my stepfather after a glass of Georgian Saperavi, and while I picked at my noodle soup the couple winked at me three times. *Il est mignon? Ne c'est pas?*

Their phrases that would never fit into Marina Borisovna's classified world of flora and fauna, but I felt something warm and pleasant from their tone.

For the main course they brought Kiev cutlets for me and my stepfather, and some Tatar *azu* for Mommy. My stepfather described scenes from his next novel, set around the tragic love between an author and a prostitute. Mommy was basking in what God had created her for: to make her a beautiful woman, to be loved, and to love herself. She was listening absently to my stepfather and savoring sips of her Saperavi. The French couple kept smiling at me. At some point Mommy sensed that my eyes were wandering toward strangers, and she turned around briefly, nearly knocking her handbag—into which she had already managed to stash away my stepfather's wages, or was it royalties?—off the back of her chair. Seeing a respectable couple she turned back, the smile not yet faded from her lips, which angered my stepfather. He threw a displeased glance over his shoulder, but after a minute or so moved on to the description of the final scene...

When we had finished our supper, that wonderful French couple was no longer there. But neither was Mommy's handbag, which had been hanging on the back of her chair. They had also taken all her makeup, my stepfather's wages and royalties, her pass for the car factory. Mommy wept, stamped her feet, shouted at me that I'd attracted the thieves; my stepfather cussed about his hard-earned money; the waiters called the police and soon a patrol car zoomed through the night with its flashing blue lights. Two policemen saw my tear-drenched Mommy with my stepfather and me; almost as one, they shouted: "Moscow! You again?!"

My youthful Pushkinesque skills are insufficient to recount the rest of what happened that evening, and later that night at my stepfather's house, but I will certainly tell you about it once I gather Gorky's bitter strength...

1986 Hysterics

*I've gone around all death's dark alleys,
in search of my fear... There a cracked street lamp...*

Oktyabrskoye Pole Station

KALUZHSKO-RIZHSKAYA LINE

When your body is buried, it no longer matters where you lie: in Silver Forest Station or Belokamennaya Station or Bittsevsky Park Station. All distances become equal to the distance of eternity. I have heard people say: "Well, the last stop is Eternity."

"No," I would say. "It is Oktyabrskoye Pole Station."

That autumn we lived on Marshal Zhukov Street, not far from Khorezhev and Mnevniki streets. Mommy was renting a room in an apartment belonging to the Ministry of Communications, and I went to the Ministry of Communication's departmental kindergarten, although none of us actually had any contact with that ministry. It was just that, quite simply, my first stepfather, Uncle Gleb—we had moved out of his place but we hadn't fallen out of touch—sent them a letter from his journal *Friendship of the Nations* and, as the living embodiment of the friendship and love between nations, they had accepted me into their kindergarten, located somewhere in the depths behind the apartment block.

Ours was a nine-story block right on the street, directly opposite the post office (and that, by the way, is what our streetcar stop was called). There was a big billboard with a sign, which I read aloud as "Kuchernenko." But if you went the other way, further in, toward the Ministry of Communications' kindergarten, and behind a couple of blocks like ours and a troika of Khrushchev shacks, a silver birch grove began, where Mommy and I would walk after school. There was a grocer's there, too, where she would buy a carton of the best creamy baked milk made by Mozhaisk, which she forced me to drink every night before bed. I refused as best I could, not because it didn't taste nice—far from it; it reminded me of sweetened condensed milk, which Mommy warned could give me the mumps. No, not because of the taste, but because of the... color. You see, I thought that when people spoke of someone's "peaches and cream" complexion, it meant they drank a lot of cream, but my face would never get even the slightest bit whiter from that brown Mozhaisk creamy baked milk...

Later, when the huge "Kuchernenko" billboard disappeared and—as if for drivers—they wrote "Acceleration," that same shop began to sell vodka on ration cards, and the age of creamy baked milk was over for me because the hordes that gathered made it unreachable. But it was there, opposite that shop, that I saw a sight I would remember all my life.

It was seven o'clock on a frosty October morning, the first snow of the season had fallen, and Mommy was taking me to the singing teacher who lived on the other side of the silver birch grove. When we had reached the little grocer's, already under siege, three people came swiftly toward us: two women and one man. The women were Russian, obviously mother and daughter, but between them, holding hands with both, walked a Negro.

But the strange thing was not that a Negro was walking between these two women, who at that early hour were already tipsy, or maybe still tipsy from the night before, but that his eyes—his huge, lilac eyes—were just as empty and senseless as theirs. They were hollow as that gray morning, that irrational crowd, that pointless road from nowhere to nowhere...

Mommy was preoccupied by the slippery road and didn't notice, or pretended she hadn't. But for me, that image of a Negro who had become even more Russian than the Russians penetrated the very depths of my naked soul, as though my future had passed by me as a morning apparition...

But I had wanted to tell you about Oktyabrskoye Pole...

Polezhayevskaya Station

TAGANSKO-KRASNOPRESNENSKAYA LINE

That night my drunken stepfather chased my Mommy with a knife while I attached myself to his legs and squealed, maybe in fear or maybe in hatred. Or maybe I was just asking him to take pity on us.

Mommy locked herself in the bathroom. My stepfather banged on the door with his knife until the tip flew off, leaving little craggy scratches on the door. Meanwhile, already hoarse, I was afraid to slip behind him to the stairwell to call the neighbors. My step-father shouted and cursed, Mother was shouting something back at him from the tiny bathroom, and I prayed to God that she would be quiet and wouldn't make him angrier. My next thought was to shout to the neighbors, but who would call back? Or maybe I should tie a sheet onto the balcony and try to climb down to the floor below? But what if there was no one out there in the sub-zero October weather? Or maybe I should just run out onto the balcony and throw myself off? But who would notice? My drunken stepfather, ready to kill Mommy with a knife, or Mommy, locked in the bathroom? And what would I do if he broke down the bathroom door?!

There was no end to my misery, and all I wished for was a neighbor, coming home late and sober, maybe just back from his shift, or maybe just going out for a cigarette... But which of the neighbors was ever sober?! Perhaps someone would deliver warm bread to the baker's below our flat for the morning? But that wouldn't be until nearly daybreak... How long would I still have to wait? *If we can only keep our stand for the night and hold out for the day...*

When would it end? My stepfather hacked and banged on the doors, then grabbed the handle and, with all the strength he had left, tug, tug, tugged at it rapidly like a pneumatic drill. It ripped off, leaving a hole in the door behind it, and he went along with it, thrown into the coat rack. The coats and hats muffled my stepfather's curses, he tossed them in all directions—*now I definitely won't be able to make a run for the door*—and he hurled himself at the bathroom again with the knife, thrusting the stub into that hole, like he was stabbing my Mommy in her solar plexus. With an unbearable screech, the knife stuck between the door and the screws. My stepfather yanked it back out and suddenly leapt back, yelping: a stream of blood running down his hand. Terrified, I threw myself at him, crying, "Mommy! Momm-meee!" He shook his hand and blood splattered off, sticking to my face; a little stream hit my lips, too, and against my will I tasted a bitter, salty, stranger's taste on my tongue... My stepfather rushed to the kitchen, and only then I realized it was him, not Mommy, who had been stabbed by the knife, now half sticking out of the door. Mommy rushed out of the bathroom and grabbed me, tripping over the bloody coats and hats, crying, "Help!" She opened the front door and ran out barefoot into the hall, past the elevator, knocking on every door...

Begovaya Station
TAGANSKO-KRASNOPRESNENSKAYA LINE

What a name! Like our night flights from the drunken stepfather, the writer who transforms into an intellectual in a tweed jacket, from which Mommy wipes traces of puke or caked blood before he goes to work.

He would travel as far as Begovaya Station and come back unexpectedly, before Mommy had time to take me, unrested and crotchety, to kindergarten. He would get down on his knees at the doorstep, usually with a bouquet of cheap flowers or just a bunch he'd picked himself, begging Mommy to forgive him and come back with him to the Left Bank. He would grab me, all dressed for kindergarten, and announce: "We're going to Silver Forest." The little radio in the kitchen would strike up some *perestroika* bravura, and my stepfather—the smell of last night's smoking bout still coming through the thick, woody layer of aftershave—would fling open the metal doors of our antediluvian elevator, as though he were welcoming us into a limousine.

We would get on streetcar number twenty-one, which stopped a little way from the apartment block, watching, as the late October sun rose behind us over Moscow, how the hoar frost melted, the ice turned to puddles and autumn once again showed its soft, merciful face. We would get off at the end of the line. There, the sandy earth, springy with a lot of dry grass, could unexpectedly throw up a tussock, or in other places, your foot could suddenly disappear into a hole left in the grass by a replanted sapling or a little burrower's burrow.

And then the pine forest proper began, at first only glimpsed through the secretive railings of generals' country cottages, then in all its glory, surrounded by wind, water, and sky. I would hop, skip, and jump around on the sand, fashion some swiftly disintegrating figures, and where the water was darkest, would look to the left once more, where, downstream, like a little badge, a sign pinned to the far-distant earth at one end and to the even more distant sky at the other, Moscow University twinkled on Lenin's Hills...

"Moscow! Moscow!" I would shout out, at which Mommy, laughing, would always turn back and come running to me to spin me around in the air as a carousel spins its ponies, as the wind whirls its leaves, as a whirlpool draws celestial images into itself.

But most of all I liked the huge, impenetrable hawthorn bushes and the dog roses on the little islands we saw when we hired a rowboat and would glide through the autumnal backwaters toward the unpeopled, sunny glades where Mommy was happy and at peace...

At other times, Uncle Gleb would take us in the opposite direction, on streetcar number twenty to Begovaya Station, although from there we would go right to the platform for the elektrichka, which runs from Belorussky Rail Terminal to Naro-Fominsk, and that elektrichka would carry us away via Golitsino right on to Pioneer Station, some two hours from Moscow. There, a tiny bus would meet us at the station square and carry us through a village, a field, a wood, over a ravine, a gully, and a stream to Maleevka, to Writers' House, where everyone already knew Uncle Gleb, and then soon got to know Mommy and me.

There, in that stately country house, where the sister-housekeeper—who met all new conscripts with tales of "the Germans who quartered here during the last war"—allocated us a room with an extra folding bed, and, after a sumptuous lunch of baked potatoes à la Maleevka, we would go up with Uncle Gleb to the billiards room on the first floor where he would teach me to put the balls in the pockets with a tapered cue, and most certainly "with a crunch."

"Now, this little ball can be persuaded like this," he would say, most probably to himself rather than to teach me, and would slowly roll the ball into an inconvenient corner, waiting for some provincial Hero of Social Labor so he could chuck at him all the pretensions and complexes of a capital-dweller. Then, in cocky spirits he would strike up a whistle and go to his room to hammer away on his yellow German typewriter while Mommy and I would go out to play.

Ah, those October Maleevkian strolls! If you go to the left, down behind the little garden and the little bridges leading to a tongue of woodland flanked by a vast field, and walk the length of this field, then after ten minutes you will lose all sense of direction and you can spend hours wandering around until you chance upon one of the locals and, in reply to your question about the House of Creativity, he or she will lead you in a direction diametrically opposed to the one you had supposed, returning you in half an hour to those very same little bridges, those very same little waterfalls, the same neglected garden, and the same unassuming of the house where you'll find the windows are already lit for the night...

Ulitsa 1905 Goda Station
Tagansko-Krasnopresnenskaya Line

Mommy and I were sitting in the *pelmeni* canteen, just by the exit of the 1905 round tower—you just have to cross the street and there you are—when Uncle Gleb arrived, half an hour late. He came over to Mommy, without a smile or a hello. We had almost finished our pelmeni with a double portion of thick sour cream, leaving some bouillon in our bowls so they wouldn't throw us out before my stepfather arrived. But instead of ordering himself a double portion and a bottle of beer, he put his arm around Mommy's shoulders and whispered something in her ear.

Mommy's face suddenly turned as pale as the sour-creamed bouillon, her lips pursed and knotted together, and she hardened like stone. I was most afraid of Mommy when she was like that. Let her yell, let her spank and beat me with her belt, let her make me kneel with bare knees on coarse salt in the corner, anything but this. No words, no emotions; even if she moves, it is as mountains move...

My stepfather came around the table to me and whispered: "Your Grandpa died..."

I didn't know what to do. What do people do when their grandpas die? Cry? Howl? Scream? I looked over at Mommy, at a loss, wondering what people do when their fathers die, but Mommy's face was still stony, if you didn't count the slightest, slightest twitching of her lips. My stepfather hugged me, and then I started to cry. It was the first death of my life, the death of a person I didn't remember, who, it was said, I had seen only once, and who, even though he had cut himself off from me, had a direct connection to me, contributing the Russian quarter of my mixed blood. I wept with this quarter, feeling sorry not so much for the deceased, but so much more for myself, orphaned by a quarter, maybe my best quarter...

My stepfather stroked my back, and Mommy sat there, staring at a distant point, as though she wanted, with her gaze, to bore through that fairytale mountain that had closed up behind her. It was that death, which, I suppose, didn't change my world in any way, but, more important, it confirmed that life is essentially senseless, that we drag sense into life, clinging to the mad rush.

And Mommy sat as still as stone. And that is precisely why everything became so scary. The whole of your life is built on the assumption that something will always distract you: maybe Mommy takes you to kindergarten; maybe at school you run, jump, eat, then sleep with your little eyes closed; then wait for Mommy; then go home; then eat, sing, go to the potty, and sleep...

But when your mommy turns to stone, and there is nothing external in the whole wide world, then you find yourself face to face with yourself, beyond demands and duties, in spiritual weightlessness, superfluousness, uselessness... what do you do then...?

Surely any person fears, above all, this abyss, when he sees into his own emptiness, his own lack of belonging, his own uselessness, this greatest trial of a person's robustness: will he survive and stand firm when no one and nothing needs him, neither to survive nor stand firm?

Mommy was still as stone, and I tried to attach myself to her stoniness, without success. Who can bear themselves when there is nothing to do for more than five minutes? I feared that, if I slipped down into myself as a stallion tied to a rock slips down into a ravine because of his own prancing impatience, then none of the child's thoughts I had been floundering in would help me, and I would be buried under an indifferent current with neither beginning nor end.

Barrikadnaya and Presnya Stations
Tagansko-Krasnopresnenskaya and Koltsevaya Lines

I remember another time Mommy turned to stone, at my school, when Dashka's brother Goshka pushed me with all his might while I was talking to Dashka, and I fell flat on the concrete playground. It grew dark in my eyes, in my soul, in my body—and when I came to, our teacher Valentina Fedorova was waving a wet cheesecloth towel over me, and I was already lying on a bed.

Mommy came in with exactly that same face. She didn't say a word to our teacher or to the night warden, Nana Martha, who chased everyone away with the same phrase: "Get outta here!"

No, Mommy just picked me up in her arms and carried me off, without uttering a word to them, or to me.

The ambulance was already waiting near our house. We didn't bother to go home but climbed straight in, and it took us toward Begovaya Station, sirens wailing, and then to the right, past Vagankovo Cemetery toward Barrikadnaya Station. Somewhere along the way it turned off to the right again and I lost my catlike sense of direction. Looping through the side streets, the ambulance brought us to the hospital where, after having my temperature taken at reception, they immediately rolled me off on a gurney to the fourth floor. They didn't let Mommy go up, and she was left at the doors with her face of stone, only now two drops of moisture appeared...

They drove me on that same gurney to the ward, changed me into hospital gowns, and I was suddenly frightened beyond

79

all the curiosity I had felt. In those state pajamas I lost all sense of myself; was I still me or someone else? Who could tell me? Second, I was afraid of having an operation; I had learned a phrase along the lines of "trepanation of the skull," though I didn't really understand it. Now I was afraid of the trepanation of the skull that no longer belonged to me. Third, I was afraid of my aloneness: if they hadn't let Mommy come in (and they always let her in everywhere, no matter where I was), could I be the only one in this ward, and was I about to become the subject of some cruel experiments?! And fourth, I was frightened because there were just so many things to be frightened of...

The nurse put me on an IV, and measuring time by the drips, I had time to calm down and think. A drip slipped slowly down the tube, followed leisurely by another. Time was riding on the backs of those drips. My head was spinning and I felt a bit queasy.

"Maybe we should put him in with those two?" one of the nurses whispered to another one by the ward's massive doors, and I half cheered up, realizing there was someone else here besides myself, but at the same time I was also scared, out of habit: "But what are they whispering about it? What are 'those two'? People? Animals? Children, monsters, aliens?" Everything was like a nasty, nightmarish-fairytale dream...

Without having overcome my thoughts, or my fears, or my bewilderment, I very soon fell asleep.

When I woke up the next morning, it was as though the night, now left behind, was peering with its half-closed eyes from behind the doors. Some dim flashes of nurses shoving tablets under my tongue, turning me over onto my stomach through the sleep of the dead—for an injection... The late autumn sun was shining through the window of the fourth floor, and the old panes shattered the rays into stars and rainbows on the wall.

What I had thought to be the night, staring with sleepy eyes from around the corner, turned out to be two striplings, slightly older than myself. One of them asked in a commander's voice: "Are you Russian?" I nodded. He announced: "Now they're going to bring us breakfast!" Distant doors creaked, and the two ran off to their rooms as fast as their legs could carry them.

On the first day I found out their names and, on the second day, when I was allowed to go to the toilet by myself, I peeked into their ward; they seemed to be having more fun together than I was having on my own. On the third day, after the nurse had brought me fruit and candy and had me stand by the window and wave to Mommy, I went over to Kozma and Dmitry with my offerings.

They accepted the fruit and sweets, then jammed the doors from inside with a mop propped between the twin handles and pushed a chair in front of one of the beds. I thought that now we, the three *bogatyrs* Dobrinya Nikitich, Ilya Muromets, and Alyosha Popovich, or the three musketeers, Athos, Porthos, and Aramis, would begin to feast: "It's time! It's time! It's high time for the good times in our lifetime!" They ordered me to sit. As soon as I did, Kozma threw his hospital pajamas over me from behind and before I knew it, they had tied me firmly to the chair with the sleeves. I couldn't move. If I wriggled, the chair would topple over, and I would have banged my injured head hard either on the ribs of the iron bed or on the floor of coarse tiles. I sat there, petrified.

"Now we'll pass lynch law on you!" said Dmitry. I didn't know what lynch law was and so was all the more terrified.

"Name?" asked Kozma.

I didn't understand him and just turned my head.

"I'm asking you your name!" he repeated, icily.

"Kirill," I mumbled.

"Louder and clearer!" Dmitry pronounced—loudly and clearly—from the other side. I answered him "Kirill," but my voice trembled, and I had to gasp for air.

"I'm asking for your real name!" Kozma insisted.

"Mbobo," I replied immediately.

"Age?"

I said the year of my birth.

"Age can only be given in years," Kozma corrected.

I replied, almost crying.

"Address?" asked Kozma. Maybe he was the leader—maybe I should give him my answers, maybe he was more compassionate.

I forced myself to state my address on Marshall Zhukov Prospekt and now it was Mommy that frightened me: what if she found out I had given our address to these two? After all, didn't she absolutely strictly forbid me from telling our address to anyone, no matter who they were, even policemen...?

"Parents?" Dmitry continued, coldly. I got confused and started to cry. It's hard to cry without your hands—the tears rolled down my face and under my collar.

"Douse him with water," came Dmitry's voice, either a question or a command, and one of them threw a glass of water at me. I started to choke, either on tears or air or water, and began to cough. I coughed non-stop, gasping, until I threw up on myself, in weakness and despair. White vomit of rice pudding sprinkled with apple ran over Kozma's pajamas, and he shouted at me: "Aha! Spoiling socialist property!"

If they had untied my hands, I would have licked up my vomit, I would have washed those pajamas, but they decided to continue questioning me.

"When did the Russians beat the Swedes?"

Through my tears, my vomit and sobs, I was grateful that they had dropped the previous question, so I asked for clarification:

"At ice hockey or for real?"

"In the Ice Battle," Kozma replied generously, but Dmitry quickly butted in.

"That was the Teutons."

Now Kozma turned to Dmitry and, in the same chilly tone, said: "You always mess everything up!"

"Not in front of the accused," Dmitry said, trying to out-maneuver him.

"Let him hear!" Kozma interjected.

"OK, then, let him wash the pajamas instead, and we'll continue tomorrow," Dmitry recommended, and Kozma declared: "Lynch law has been adjourned until tomorrow. The accused is sentenced to restoring the socialist property to good order and will appear in court tomorrow with his confession. Are there any questions?"

I shook my head, bits of vomit flying in all directions, and Kozma untied the pajamas while Dmitry got the mop from the door handles. I was humiliated but free. Maybe it was the cold tap water I used to wash out my sticky vomit, or maybe it was lingering fear—either way, my temperature rose sharply that night, and for the whole next day I had to lie on the IV drip again, with a nurse sitting beside me, contemplating time as it slowly passed...

Belorusskaya Metro Station

Koltsevaya Line

I tried to imagine how my grandfather might have felt, in his coffin—dead, washed, and anointed with aftershave—as he was taken off to the frozen Siberian graveyard. The gravedigger beat the earth until his hands bled, his pickaxe and shovel breaking through the icy crust of snow, the lumps of frozen, crumbling earth, until finally he reached hardened soil. The twenty or so people who'd come along on the bus—mainly veterans—began to drag the coffin, first from the wrong end, then turned it around inside the bus. Grandfather's body shifted inside his coffin, knocking against the sides and nearly falling out. Finally, they got the coffin out and rested it on the frozen earth, but it started sliding down into the pit too soon. The gravedigger, along with a few younger officers drafted for the occasion from the local military commissariat, grabbed the coffin and felt, for the last time, the involuntary weight of the lifeless body inside it.

And again came the muted knocking of the dead body against the coffin's wood as the young officers began slowly lowering their end into the black pit. Then the others in attendance walked past, awkwardly throwing the so-called handful of ash (actually a clump of earth or bit of ice, whatever was on hand). And then the gravedigger took his spade and began to shovel big lumps of earth into the grave. Those most pained by the absurdity of their presence—the young officers—again lent a hand and the pit was filled up. Several people—Grandfather's brothers in arms— made speeches, the others listened, and the procession moved back to the bus. The gravedigger, having received his money, stayed behind to smooth over the grave. But as soon as the bus had driven off, he picked up his tool and headed home for lunch...

And Grandfather—Colonel Rzhevsky—was left alone in the ground.

What should he have felt, free from everyone, yet abandoned by all? That man who had named his first daughter after what he held most dear—Moscow—yet who had beaten her so badly that the poor thing would wet herself in fear, despair, and helplessness. The man who had limitless faith in his own power over his children, who had cursed his daughter when she gave him his first grandson. What could he feel in that lonely frozen earth, he who had abused everyone close to him and died friendless, who had lived by his principles and didn't believe in God?!

Rechnoy Vokzal Station
ZAMOSKVORETSKAYA LINE

We traveled on the green line right to the very end, to Rechnoy Vokzal Station. On that ride, I had plenty of time to wonder if Mommy was taking me back to Uncle Gleb's place on the Left Bank. That same Left Bank, with all its sprawling, natural beauty, was where pedophiles lurked in the apple orchards, and a little farther on, to the left of the bookshop, the patients stared forlornly out of the little barred windows of the mental institution.

In the black-and-white sequence of the tunnels and stations—a kind of extension of the chessboard floor—I thought about the fact that my Mommy has her Mommy. Admittedly I had never met her mother, but I knew that my Mommy believed that she was the root of all problems—not only with her own father, sister, and brother, but also with her husbands, including this present one, Uncle Gleb.

Even though Grandfather had cursed her, Mommy didn't hold it against him. Grandma, on the other hand, she saw as a puppeteer, turning Grandfather against his own children. Two weeks earlier, as Grandfather lay at home in a half-comatose state, I'd eavesdropped on a telephone call between Mommy and Grandma. "Well, you've got him completely in your hands, at long last!" Mommy had said. "Now you can do with him as you please. And with no complaints!"

I guessed that Grandma was crying into the phone and showering curses on Mommy.

"Don't listen to any of those doctors, just follow the blessed knowledge you've scavenged from the newspapers!" Mommy didn't let up, free-falling into hysterics. "After all, you know everything better than everyone else; you've read about everything in your stupid papers! You ruined all our lives, pitted us against each other, and so now you're left all by yourself, like a spider caught in its own web..." Mommy was already crying but she just couldn't stop herself. "So now if you like, you can pour moonshine into him. If you like, you can starve him to death. If you like, you can bathe him in triple-filtered eau de cologne. If you don't like that, you can roll him around in your own shit! Be bold, Mother!"

Two laments processed along thousands of kilometers of wire toward one another and, like two metro trains on a double stretch of track underground, they tore past each other with a roar. I stared at my reflection in the dark glass where only two little star-tears shone sharply in the darkness, already plummeting back to Earth...

Why is there so much cruelty in the world? I thought, but found no answer within myself; I only felt, as we walked out of the terminal, the strange sense that in all that collapse I would never get out of this succession of identical stations and into the clear, white light of the world...

1987 Longitudes

among the living I grow older
than more and more people and so patriarchal
is becoming my soul...

Arbatskaya Station

Of all the seasons, for me winter, especially the December evenings, is the bleakest—cold, short, and dark, like my life. If I simply pause and glance at the black Moscow trees, pushing starkly into the dark blue, agonizing sky, it seems that life itself is all in vain, and I pity everyone.

At this hour, almost everyone else is picked up from kindergarten; sometimes Arkasha Strugatsky, whose parents are splitting up, stays behind with me, but he keeps quiet, too... Mommy doesn't come and doesn't come. She might just not come at all today, and then I'll spend the night here with Nana Martha.

The toys are back in their drawers, and even those lying on someone's chair or on someone's bed bear the imprint of uselessness, but that is not what nags at my heart. Today I broke a little mirror belonging to Aleshka Mokaseev, and his Mommy is a judge in the People's Court. He said he would tell her it was me who threw the mirror onto the blacktop and broke it in two, each half reflecting a snapshot of my brief terror. And now, in this twilight hour, Aleshka Mokaseev would be sitting in the backseat of his mother's Volga, shifting all the blame onto me. My fate was surely being decided, and tomorrow I would be arrested like a hooligan for "spoiling a citizen's socialist property." In the morning they'd take me away in handcuffs, and Mommy would never know what happened... Then she'd be sorry...

I cried in silent self-pity. The teachers had already all gone home and Nana Martha, who had taken over, was sitting in the kitchen with her supper: "Food feeds the head," she would say to herself. And even Arkasha Strugatsky had nodded off in his little chair, but I just kept looking out the window, wondering when Mommy would come. Martha, grumbling, went to open the door, but I recognized the voice of Arkasha's grandmother. The two old biddies oohed and aahed on the doorstep for a long time, letting in a cold draft. Then Nana Martha came into our room and woke little Arkasha, throwing a glance at me as she did: "An' this poor li'l nigger boy, you're still here, huh?"

I heard how they made a joint effort to dress the whimpering Arkasha and hassled him; how they scolded, dragging the senseless youth of today over the coals; how—finally—the door banged shut behind Arkasha's grandmother, dragging him across the snow against his will, breathing the cold street air out again; how steps crunched on the snow; how the gate creaked; how Nana Martha again shuffled back to the kitchen to finish up her raspberry *kissel*, and once again I was left all alone.

I don't know how to describe that sense of abandonment, so unbearable even with toys, while we are talking about a living person... No, I didn't wholly understand, but I sensed that even if I were to give Aleshka Mokaseev a brand new, whole little mirror, I would never manage to stick my shattered reflection back together in it, as though today that wholeness had been lost forever...

I was waiting for Mommy...

Nana Martha finished eating and went to watch television in the principal's office. Some idle sounds came through the walls, from behind the door, but they didn't interest me. Beyond the black window, snowflakes were whirling, crazed, in the light of a squinting street lamp. A stray dog whimpered somewhere, freezing, and I thought my simple thoughts.

A few days earlier we had gone to the Arbat, to Mommy's new friend, police captain Uncle Nazar. I don't know why, but everything was festive that day, as if New Year's had come early. The metro station was glistening like a frosted cake. The white, low-ceilinged chambers of the mansion gave off a pink glow, thanks to the red granite below. The stucco bas-relief of flowers; the patterned ribs of the beams; the lamps, like straw bouquets—all this was a backdrop for Mommy, dressed in lace and frills under her fur coat. And as Mommy paraded me extravagantly from the station to the street, it was as if even the crown chandeliers at the top of the escalators were waiting for her wedding.

As we walked along the Old Arbat, she spoke in a whisper, like we were in Lenin's Mausoleum. We went into one of the old, greenish little courtyards and from there into one of the old, greenish buildings, where on the darkened first floor none other than Uncle Nazar opened the door to us.

It turned out that he lived in one of the buildings condemned for demolition, though God only knew when that would happen. He was studying at the Academy of the Ministry of Internal Affairs, so he managed to get a permit to live there and keep an eye on all the buildings in the block. His apartment was a shabby studio with a miniature kitchen and an even tinier bathroom, which I set about inspecting while Uncle Nazar and Mommy exchanged pleasantries. The walls and ceiling were cracking, but a kerosene stove was burning in the kitchen instead of an ordinary electric one, and that made the whole place seem more cheerful.

To tell you the truth, once I got used to that new apartment, I spent the whole evening feeling possessive of Mommy—being secretly, sadly jealous of Uncle Nazar. I was not feeling my own jealousy, but Uncle Gleb's. And I think Uncle Nazar sensed it. He gave me all kinds of trifles—his old army stripes, a cockade, and some metal trinkets—but I didn't give in, so by the end of the evening he had pulled out not one but *three* medals for "impeccable service" and pinned them to my breast, one after the other, pro-claiming me a Triple Hero of the Soviet Union...

And now, sitting by the dark window and watching the snow-flakes settle quietly on the ground in acquiescence to the night, I thought: what if tomorrow, when Aleshka Mokaseev's mommy comes to arrest me at dawn, I offer Alesha all three of those medals in exchange for his broken mirror? But even now, hav-ing solved the pressing concerns of my school day, Mommy still didn't come, and didn't come, and my heart kept plodding and plodding toward her...

Smolenskaya Station

There is one sneaky thing about Moscow's metro stations that I noticed a long time ago. Each one may appear unique—but the same rows of spindly square pylons are joined by the same beams, marching in the same parade in the form of the Greek letter pi: ΠΠΠΠΠΠΠΠΠ. And not only that, but one station's pillars are taken from this-or-that other station, the lamps from another, and that bas-relief from yet another. The stations maintain only a pretense of individuality, and I saw right through this at Smolensk Station. If you take a look yourself, you'll notice the pillars pilfered from Belorusskaya Radial, the lamps lifted from October Circle, and that stony family (this time with weapons in hand) filched from Belorusskaya Circle. Or am I just hallucinating, from the lack of oxygen in winter's stale air? Or out of the sameness in my one-dimensional life?

But sitting on the stone bench with Mommy, waiting for Uncle Nazar, a Central Asian, I'm thinking about how, all in all, a policeman like him isn't better or different than my yet-unseen father or Uncle Gleb, who Mommy had a fight with. And probably just as I assess the stations, so Mommy sees something of my father in Uncle Nazar, something of Uncle Gleb, and even something of herself. But, in my opinion, they are all the same: they all just take Mommy away from me; one with his absence, one with his beatings, and one with hopes.

Mommy was already tipsy, her eyes no longer signaling anything. I wondered with a burning despair what I could do to make her mine again. Run away from home? Get lost? Get sick? Die a slow death? What would make her forget all those Uncle Glebs and Uncle Nazars, all those painters, artists, philatelists she talked to and drank with and kept company—and then dropped. So many uncles stopped by our house for a day, for an evening, for a night. They played soccer with me, sat me on their knees, and let me drive their cars; or just stared down and hid out in the kitchen, leaving behind a bestial smell of stale tobacco and wine...

My gut burned there in that station, made up of scraps from three or four other stations, as I thought about my own powerlessness to intervene in this relationship of my Mommy Moscow with the stallionesque Uncle Nazar, new, yet just another repetition of the last...

I wanted to cry from powerlessness. I wanted someone to let go of the station's heavy glass door as he passed, smashing his head to smithereens. If not that, I hoped he'd be squashed by the turnstile, or that he'd roll head over heels down the escalator, or that the mass of people seething before the arrival of the announced train would trample him, pushing him onto the rails under the train car. Or a bandit in the car—who the policeman Uncle Nazar would of course try to apprehend—could stab him with a knife! And let that bandit even be Uncle Gleb!

Using different scraps, I sewed him one and the same death, which would leave my mother in peace without him. Let them bury him here at this station where the cold slaps your legs with every approaching train, right under those armed people, as though he were one of them...

I don't want my Mommy to disappear with these men into the mountain and for the stone curtain to be drawn in front of me, my hot tears falling as I whisper: "*Yaril tas... Yaril tas...* Open sesame!"

Kiyevskaya Station

FILYOVSKAYA LINE

I was never so jealous of Uncle Gleb, probably because he was hollow inside and tried his whole life to fill himself up with drinking binges, or chasing Mommy, or keeping himself busy with me. But I could see that, deep down, he was indifferent to it all. His apathy was like December snow: it falls because it falls, because it cannot *not* fall. Even if everything is already as white as white can be, the flakes still keep on falling. Maybe that is why my happiest—and maybe also my unhappiest—hours of family life were spent in his company.

We meet up just by the clock tower where you come out of Kiyevskaya Station, and he asks me: "So, Pushkin my boy, what's the metro like this morning?"

I try to remember the station we just left and chirp: "Like the operating theater in the Parthenon?" I remember the forest of pillars, the narrow passageway between them; the upturned tubs on the ceiling that conceal the lamps—maybe that's where the sense of an operating theater comes from. I remember the whistle of the cold in that narrow avenue and the tatters of snow falling from boots or clinging to them at every other step...

"Bravo, Son! You've got a good eye for things!" Uncle Gleb praises me, but he's already testing my IQ: "OK then, Pushkin, tell me which elektrichka will take us to the writers' village." And I answer right away: "Take the Petushkovo train as far as Peredelkino." He is holding Mommy by the arm as she slinks around in her fashionable Czech boots, and we make our way to the ticket office. While Uncle Gleb buys tickets, Mommy orders pies and pastries from a stall.

Oh, hot cabbage and mushroom pies on an elektrichka in winter! For these trips, Mommy always had a flask of hot tea, and we would take turns drinking out of the lid, blowing on it and trying not to let our lips touch the burning metal.

The ticket inspectors go by, someone hawks newspapers, frozen wheels knock on frozen rails. Mommy tells some made-up stories of Siberian life, Uncle Gleb learns them carefully, and I delight in the view from the window. And so we arrive at Peredelkino Station, get out onto the snowy platform, go down the stairs to our familiar path, which is, sadly, buried in snow. We have to walk along the road, glancing back from time to time, looking out for a drunk driver who might skid and plow into us. Mommy wobbles on her boots, almost falling over, but Uncle Gleb catches her each time. Where the graveyard suddenly gives way to fields, they fall over together and, for some reason, start laughing heartily. I make the most of the distraction and slide down the bank on my smooth, thick-soled boots.

It takes us an hour, but we come to the Writers' House, freezing and "ringing-cheeked." (Uncle Gleb made up that phrase on the spot, just for me; Mommy he called just "red-cheeked.")

All the staff and servants know me here. They call me "our little Michael Jackson." Sometimes I have to moonwalk in front of the communal television or act out his numbers in the canteen. Incidentally, they call Mommy by her real name here, Moscow, and this sends Uncle Gleb into special rapture, and he says: "*O, my bosom Russia, O, my Moscow*"... or "*Moscow, how much that word holds for a Russian heart!*" The old biddies start scolding him, and that is just what Uncle Gleb, drunk, is after...

There's one thing I don't like about Peredelkino: the blood-sucking bugs. "They've been here throughout history, since the time of Mayakovsky," said Uncle Gleb as he drank glass after glass before bedding down, so that the insects—which had sucked the blood of Platonov and Tarkovsky—would choke on the puke running through his veins. But I knew that his veins were hollow. He had tried to slit them twice but nothing flowed out, and only scars were left, bulging up under his watch.

Yes, Uncle Gleb was a hollow man, and if I had to compare him to anything at all on this earth, I would compare him to the whistling cavities of the dark metro, their grayness occasionally lit up with bursts of uncommon beauty.

Park Kultury Station

As I told you earlier, Uncle Gleb often took me to readings and artists' salons, to his "December evenings" or "December chitchats" or "December lectures." The code word "event," on the other hand, I'd supposed was devised by him and Mommy to confuse me when they planned to leave me all night with Nana Martha.

But that evening they announced, "We are going to an event today," and took me along. As usual, I embarrassed Mommy with my awkward, inconvenient questions. So as soon as we had come out of the Park Kultury Radial Station, I asked, "What's that? The Sanduny porch?"

"Where did you get that from, Pushkin?" Uncle Gleb asked curiously, but by then Mommy had already managed to fling me over to her side away from him and was already twisting my ear so that I would be quiet and not make a peep. We went out of the round building that looked like a bathhouse and headed in the direction of the Crimea Bridge, me puzzling all the while as to why Mommy had treated me so badly at the metro station.

That evening, one of Uncle Gleb's friends called Yerofeyev was giving a reading, though Mommy told me—much to Uncle Gleb's annoyance—that it wasn't *that* Yerofeyev at all, as though "Yerofeyev" could be "non-Yerofeyev." They even managed to fight as we walked along the windy riverbank to the huge exhibition hall where the lecture was to take place. Then Uncle Gleb went to have a chat with Yerofeyev, the non-Yerofeyev, while

Mommy and I sat ourselves down in the back row in the darkness, farthest away from the floodlit podium.

I was, of course, burning with curiosity to find out what exactly an "event" was because the term still stood for something otherworldly, like that word you meet in Greek myths: "libation." So I sat solemnly, waiting for some mysteries, but instead, the artificial Yerofeyev set about reading a book out loud. "Dora Iosifovna's vagina had the power of speech..." he began, muddling me with yet another unfamiliar word.

"Mommy, what's a vagina?" I asked innocently at the top of my voice. Everyone around turned toward us with curiosity, and Mommy—who had already put her hand on my ear to twist it as usual—grew flustered under those intellectual looks and began distractedly stroking my little head, whispering, "Keep listening and you'll understand." Those around us now looked with curiosity not at me, but at Mommy. Because of that misunderstanding, we missed part of what that make-believe Yerofeyev was saying, and I regained my concentration only as he read a word for which Mommy had already once given me a good beating: "prostitute."

I really liked this word because of the way it sounded. Our neighbor, Oleshka Simov, had told me a joke about a girl with a strange name, Tute, and a boy who had behaved badly toward her and then said: "Prosti [forgive me], Tute!" and Oleshka, who was a whole year older than me, laughed for a long time, but I felt sorry for that girl with the silly name and felt as though I were that guilty boy, so on the way home from Oleshka's I sadly and pensively muttered, "Prosti, Tute... Prosti, Tute..." When she heard me, Mommy asked me to repeat out loud what I had been saying under my breath. Not suspecting anything, I fulfilled Mommy's wish and said loudly: "Prosti, Tute!" and before I could finish the phrase, let alone tell the whole story about that poor girl,

Mommy took a full swing at me and slapped me in the face, not once but twice, saying as she did so: "I'll show you a prostitute! I'll tear your little tongue out!"

With this memory still very much alive, I got really frightened that Mommy would jump up from her chair and start a fight with that false Yerofeyev, and I shrank into a little ball, but for some reason an embarrassed little laugh rustled through the hall and Mommy, in marked contrast to her previous reaction, even smiled. I didn't understand a thing.

Fake Yerofeyev read monotonously and for a long time. I fell asleep, tangled up in Mommy, who was now listening to him with all her strength. When they woke me up, right in Yerofeyev-who-was-not-Yerofeyev's place was standing a tall man with a nasty face, and everyone was applauding him. That means that there wasn't any Yerofeyev at all, which means that I'd just dreamed it, I thought as I rubbed my eyes. As I was thinking these thoughts, Uncle Gleb brought that tall, nasty man over to Mommy and introduced him: "This is none other than Vanya Zhdanov." Vanya Zhdanov smiled biliously at Mommy, looked nastily at me, and was immediately surrounded by a crowd of noisy maidens.

Uncle Gleb then steered us to the buffet where we sat down with two already-tipsy poets who Uncle Gleb introduced to Mommy. One he called Yerema; for the other he gave a complicated surname, impossible to pronounce.

"You know, Sasha, my old chap Pushkin knows your work by heart. You wanna hear?" Uncle Gleb winked at me and prompted: "OK, Pushkin my boy, regale us with 'In the dense metallurgical forests...'"

I knew that poem by heart and really liked it, but because I'd learned it after "Autumn's Architecture," I thought for some reason that it was by someone by the name of Zabolotsky, whose house near Begovaya Station had been pointed out to me by Uncle Gleb. But it turned out Zabolotsky wasn't Zabolotsky at all, but Yerema.

> *In the dense metallurgical forests,*
> *Where the process of the creation of chlorophyll preceded*
> *A leaf has crashed; autumn is already here,*
> *In the dense, metallurgical forests.*
> *There, stuck forever in the heavens*
> *Is a fuel tanker with a little fly drosophila,*
> *The power presses them equally,*
> *And they are bogged down in the beaten out hours.*
> *The last eagle owl is scythed and sawn up,*
> *And, pinned up with drawing pins,*
> *Is hanging head downward,*
> *Shaking his upside-down head.*
> *He is hanging and thinking to himself,*
> *Why with such terrible force*
> *Have field binoculars been mounted in him?*

When I had finished reciting the poem, the drunken man by the name of Yerema silently picked me up, tossed me in the air, and kissed me on the forehead. Then everyone set to drinking, and they bought me two red caviar canapés.

The man with the complicated surname pulled out a pile of papers, called them a literal translation, and suggested splitting them in three parts to be translated into Russian. "Well, there's plenty of blood here," he said. "How we gonna translate... in red lead or carmine?"

He handed all the poems over to Yerema, leaving one for Uncle Gleb because the poet's name—he was named Belg—was made up of the same letters as his. I remember that very translation (with the same dualism as I remember that whole evening, because after all, how can you translate into Russian what has already been said in Russian?!)—or more precisely, the end of it was so forceful that even now, lying in the frozen December soil, I repeat it over and over as though whispering it with my own nonexistent lips:

> *Bedding down in the evenings I think that one of these days*
> *When my soul flies away, leaving this flesh, these bones*
> *I'm sorry for this body, mixed with earth, because*
> *These bones ached so for you, these lips dried out for you...*

Kropotkinskaya Station

If I'd ever wanted a tomb for my dead body, I would have picked the Kropotkinskaya Station. That is my vault: elegant and airy, impractical and absurd, standing all by itself, in the middle of the road, like an arch from nowhere to nowhere. If you find yourself on Volkhonk Street and pass under this frilly gape of an arch, should you turn left, you'll end up in my underground hell, the very station where I, the stoker-imp, am covered in soot. There, fountains of flames spurt up toward the hot ceiling from the torch-like pillars, where the light of day is never seen.

It was from there that Uncle Nazar steered me to the right, toward the Moscow swimming pool. It was such a freezing December, even your spit hit the snow as an icicle, but Uncle Nazar was testing my mettle. I badly wanted not to go to that swimming pool, and not just because I didn't like getting undressed in public—a black face is one thing, you can half-hide it in your hat with earflaps or your scarf, but a whole black body is quite another. But I was really just terrified of the cold; I got the shivers just thinking about it and my teeth were already chattering. Uncle Nazar, unafraid, was full of police wisdom: "Take a good lungful of air and don't breathe for exactly a minute! You'll get warm then!" I reluctantly obeyed and, taking in a lungful of freezing air, a coughing fit overcame me, and I went blue. "Don't worry, you'll warm up in the water," said Uncle Nazar, chasing after me. I was already shaking, but he took me firmly by the wrists and led me to the steamy pool.

I remember that moment of fiery anguish when he shoved me into the water, guffawing. I couldn't breathe or make a sound; my lungs were blocked. "Swim!" he shouted through the icy canopy. My whole life flashed before me and went quiet, and everything seemed peculiar and distant, like it had been in the tar...

When I came back to life, they were rubbing me with vodka in the changing room. Several tipsy, red-faced men were towering over me, along with that hateful Uncle Nazar, and each had his own theory:

"A Negro's skin's too thin!" said one, but another countered:

"What?! Their skin's as thick as old boots; they've just got no layer of fat under it."

A third suggested that Negroes are strangers to water: "Just think," he reasoned, "they have all the champions in running, but not one in swimming!"

Only Uncle Nazar, sensing I had some consciousness back, whispered: "Maggot... no guts..." and I closed my eyes again, imagining for a moment my hot hell, with the empty vault above it...

Biblioteka Imeni Lenina Station

No, even if he beat Mommy black and blue and chased us with a knife when he was drunk, Uncle Gleb was still better. Or am I being unfair? Maybe, even given all of Uncle Gleb's lessons and kitchen table chats, his readings and his theater openings, I learned more about life from Uncle Nazar's nasty lessons? But, biased or not, I fondly remember both Lenin libraries, one on the Left Bank where Uncle Gleb lived and worked part-time, the other in the center of Moscow, just past Manezh.

Mommy and Uncle Gleb had a funny story about Manezh, and both of them—especially Uncle Gleb—liked to tell it in public. Once, when they had only just met after a writers' evening in the car factory's House of Culture, Uncle Gleb invited her to meet him by the columns of the Bolshoi. Mommy (who at the time was still a limitchitsa) left me with Irina Rodionovna on Grand Tartar Street and skipped off, half an hour early. She stood by the columns and waited. Half an hour passed, no sign of Uncle Gleb; another five minutes passed, another ten, another fifteen, and Uncle Gleb still didn't show. All sorts of thoughts passed through her head. Then, coming out a bit from behind the columns, she looked around and saw the famous statue of Apollo's chariot was missing. At first she thought someone must have stolen it. But she asked a passerby, who merely shrugged his stooping, genteel shoulders and said: "Manezh was indeed a stable, but the horses to which you refer, my dear, were never here. Are you mistaking Manezh for the Bolshoi?"

"This isn't the Bolshoi?!" cried Mommy, now realizing she had been waiting all that time under the columns of Manezh...

No, in those days, Uncle Gleb didn't punish Mommy at all. Just the opposite. When she trotted up to Bolshoi—its God, horses, and chariot intact—an hour late, Uncle Gleb was standing there, frozen, with a bunch of roses, waiting for her.

I always wondered what happened to that Uncle Gleb, as he drank away the December evenings, his silence audible from the other room. Then he would become aggressive, banging his fist on the table for no reason, or he'd grasp a glass in his hand until it shattered, his hand splattered with blood, or he'd suddenly shout something incoherent like, "Coup d'état! Fuck." Then, all hunched down like a little mouse, I would sense that we might not make it through the terrible night.

When Mommy drank with him, she would try to calm him, but he was already untamable. Then Mommy would drunkenly wave her hand, as if to say, "Whatever will be will be," and that, usually, was the signal to act.

My stepfather would snatch a plate and let it fly at her, or yank the corner of the tablecloth and tip everything onto her with a roar, or simply fling himself at Mommy and start strangling her. I would always spring into action at such moments, forgetting my fear: I would latch myself onto his arms, his legs as he swatted me to the floor, and then my mother would start scratching and biting, like a wounded animal. My demented stepfather, foaming at the mouth, would wallop her with anything handy until, covered in blood, she scrambled out of the room...

My heart trembled each evening when she picked me up from school and we went back to the three-roomed apartment on the Left Bank, buying some wine on the way. I was glad when there was no wine, or when Uncle Gleb, sour but sober, took me to work in the mornings, to Lenin's Library right here on the Left Bank.

We would walk along the street—in two deep and icy tracks—past the supermarket, past the bus stop for Rechnoy Vokzal Station and Long Ponds, past the long, nine-story blocks that stood at an angle to each other like an open newspaper, and went up to a building where the doormen knew me and gave me the odd nickname "Glebich."

Uncle Gleb worked as a consultant but, instead of sitting in his office, as a rule he would reserve himself a stack of ancient newspapers and sit in the public reading room with a view of the forest. The withered papers gave off a smell of autumnal decay, which I had to bear for half the day, drawing my drawings or just playing with the table lamp that turned my paper a slightly greenish hue when it was switched on or a slightly bluish one when switched off.

I loved the Lenin Library on the Left Bank because of its simplicity and because of the modernity of its canteen, where Uncle Gleb and I used to have lunch and where, with no one else to talk to and while he was, technically, speaking to me, calling me "Pushkin," he would deliver a monologue on raped and ravaged Russia, poor and prostituting herself. I would for some reason imagine my Mommy Moscow, as he spoke, beaten and battered by him, but I was afraid to give voice to this, so I silently chewed my cutlet or Kostomskoe cheese sandwich instead.

I fell in love with the other Lenin Library because of the lavish view of Pashkov House as we came out of the vast, waffle-ceilinged hangar of the underground station. But I also loved it for its second staircase, just inside the building, where Uncle Gleb, maybe joking or maybe serious, told the guard: "This Abyssinian is our guest from Africa. He's been sent as a spy to gather intelligence."

We ascended the staircase solemnly, slowly gazing around us, and turned right to cross a landing, finding ourselves in a vast hall with cupboards and balustrades around the walls. Still solemn and orderly, we crossed that hall where rows and rows of lifeless people were sitting surrounded by stacks of books under greenish lamps. At the far end of the hall we emerged onto a staircase which rose even higher than the balustrade, and where Uncle Gleb opened a mighty door and I saw dozens of slide projectors like the one Mommy kept at home to show me fairy tales on the ceiling before I went to sleep.

Uncle Gleb spoke in a whisper to one of the women in overalls and, having received his bundle of reels, sat down to play them on his personal screen. They were drawings, maybe by Pushkin, maybe by Dostoyevsky, alongside their texts. I looked at those sharp drawings and I, too, wanted to become Dostoyevsky or Pushkin so that 100, 150 years after my death, some new Uncle Gleb would sit down and pore over my strokes, without a thought of finding something better for himself in life...

When we went out through those mighty doors an hour later, I felt like I'd emerged from a steam bath: tired, but full of power, and I looked down from above on all those people sitting in rows, surrounded by stacks of books. Not one of them noticed me, and that gave me secret pleasure and reassurance.

Track from Park Kultury Circle
to Kiyevskaya Station

Koltsevaya Line

That, it seemed to me, was where Mommy got stuck between Uncle Gleb and Uncle Nazar, until everything finally resolved itself in a sea of tears, late in the evening of December 31.

After a whole day off in the park, when both hands on the clock at Park Kultury Station had dropped to the very lowest point, Mommy and I went right down, obediently taking directions from those hands, to Park Kultury Circle Station. Uncle Nazar met us there. He was working as "reinforcement" today and was guarding the red line, walking from the end of the train to the beginning and back again, removing all the citizens who got drunk and fell asleep. Uncle Nazar handed Mommy a squashed bouquet of nearly wilted flowers, having pulled them out of the armpit of his gray overcoat where he had been carrying them all day. Mommy invited him to see in the New Year with us. But Uncle Nazar, all stuttering and red, had to march up and down in the metro until the end of the shift, at half-past one, and then... maybe tomorrow. Mommy gave him a peck on the cheek and said: "Oh, OK, then, we'll be off..."

I couldn't see it at the time, but Uncle Nazar was being sliced up inside. His uniform was telling us one thing but the man under that uniform wanted something quite different. I understand that now.

We got on the Circle Line and Uncle Nazar, waving to us, dragged himself off with passive steps to fight alcoholism and its enthusiasts on his Frunzensk-Preobrazhenskaya line, his face red like his cap-band.

Traveling clockwise, we got out at the next station, Kiyevskaya. A slightly tipsy Uncle Gleb met us in the middle of that station. Probably because of my bias, I suddenly felt the magnificence of this station, a true mansion, decorous, majestic. *Comeliness*, that was a suitable word for this station, like a Gzhel figurine or a lacquered Palekh miniature, like the golden piety of icons; in short, the very nature of Old Russia that should, after all, be associated with Kiyevskaya Station...

And here in this temple of beauty, Mommy suddenly got the idea to confess everything to Uncle Gleb and admit that Uncle Nazar the policeman had appeared in her life. She was going to marry him, since he was not only able to protect her but also to provide for her and was sound not only of body but also of mind, and so her relationship with Uncle Gleb would come to an end today.

At first Uncle Gleb tried to make a joke, saying that it was especially pathetic to be dumped today, on December 31, New Year's Eve. He tried to poke fun at "Uncle Steppe policeman," but Mommy didn't laugh. She stung him instead with contrast after contrast in which Uncle Nazar always came out a head taller and cleaner than Uncle Gleb, which enraged him, and he started cursing foully. So Mommy said she could now see how right she'd been, at which Uncle Gleb fell silent and suddenly, for the first time in his life, burst into tears. Mommy was at a loss. Uncle Gleb got down on his knees and begged her not to leave him. That made Mommy cry too. Through his tears, Uncle Gleb kept repeating the phrase: "Do you remember, wife... Do you remember?"

The passengers were hurrying off to their New Year parties. To any well-wisher who looked in our direction as we sat on a bench under one of the naive paintings, we must have made an absurd tableau: an Asiatic woman with a black child sitting on a bench, a deacon-like Russian with long hair and a thin face kneeling, like Chernyshevsky at his civil execution, not knowing what to do...

Finally Uncle Gleb went too far; he tried to convince Mommy that the policeman would treat me like a mongrel, and Mommy jumped up. "How dare you say such a thing in front of the child?!" Bundling me into her arms, she darted across the empty magnificence of that station, under the chandeliers like carriage wheels, past the festive throng in multicolored clothes and flared pants. Uncle Gleb just barely managed to thrust a pile of papers into my arms and then he fell flat on the slippery, cold floor like Ivan the Terrible after the murder of his son, the Crown Prince Alexei.

And so it turned out that on that New Year's Eve we rode to Mommy's place, to welcome the New Year in her room, without a feast, and we read those papers that my former stepfather, Uncle Gleb, handed me, his little Pushkin.

The Apartment

"Do you remember, wife?" I ask, searching for a certain formula, a certain warm and homely tone, a certain standpoint, and I know that right from the outset, this search is related to another search, the search for my own point to stand, a certain warm and homely comfort, some formula for an acceptable way to live in this vast city, amidst whose chaos I whisper once more: "Do you remember, wife?..."

"Do you remember, wife?" I say, and all that passed before becomes a sort of formality, as when, after several years of happy life in the apartment we'd rented together, the landlord had appeared at the beginning of August and said: "Well, here I am, I'm back..."

You remember, wife, it was the beginning of August, and my work hadn't quite panned out. Should we leave forever or stay? And so we persuaded the landlord to give us a couple of extra weeks.

Our little boy was just about to start school, and that was our greatest concern. I suggested sending him to Grandma the Beautiful, to your mom in Siberia. Let the boy start school there, then we'd see later. You didn't agree and asked me to figure everything out as quickly as possible. "If we're staying," you said, "then we have to find a place urgently and set the boy up in school. If we're leaving, then..."

The only thing to do was look for an apartment.

You remember, wife, how we began calling all our friends and acquaintances. The best thing, the experienced renters told us, is to buy the classifieds in the Evening Chronicle *and to call fellow apartment hunters—someone might have found a place they didn't want.*

The first real lead I'd gotten was from the fifth or sixth fellow apartment hunter, the first who wasn't baffled. Typically, people who have advertised in search of an apartment in the city center will slam the phone down after my first words. By the time I'd called that number, I'd already gained at least some experience: I had the number of a place that had been rented out long ago. It was a fantastic prospect; the landlord had gone off to the North somewhere and left his dog.

I spent a long time getting used to the idea of that dog and our life together with it, although at least one problem would be solved: writing every day in my diary, "Tomorrow, I will get up at six and go jogging!"

That in itself was a strong argument, but the relative ease with which this possibility had manifested itself made me feel I could talk to the landlord as though we were equals, and it seems that he was rather taken aback at this and asked me to call back later, telling me he ought to talk to a girl at work just in case, because she was looking for a flat too...

After that, unfortunately, no one ever picked up the phone. I decided that the landlord had taken his dog with him, leaving the place under lock and key. There was nothing for us to do but put on a brave face and laugh.

Then there was another possibility, a writer's possibility, a gift from Peredelkino. We chased it for several evenings: a friend of a friend was supposed to ask about his neighbor's dacha; she was an old and sick author who was going to live in the city for the winter—would she rent us her summer place? Well, Peredelkino's not so far away, we thought, especially since there is a school there and what's more, we could come to some arrangement with the House of Creativity about food...

A week before on the TV program Travelers Club, *they had described the little town of Sokol as a masterpiece of residential building within a park, and seeing as it was only a stone's throw away, I had decided that I would like to live in that stately paradise.*

One day I went to that little town, which turned out to be not just reminiscent of Platonov, but shrouded in the constant feeling that it had just rained. Here, for this town, summer was rain, warmth was rain, people were rain.

There, in the State Residential Property Office, I waited for the boss, who was holding a never-ending meeting with the plumbers and road sweepers. His voice, coming through the doors in a demonstration of all its shades, had grown almost dear to me, and I used it to try to form an image of its owner and our imminent conversation.

Do you remember, wife, I wanted you to sign up as a road sweeper, but it would have been me who swept the dry leaves in the mornings, and we would have lived there in that little town, just as I imagined... But only the memory is left now, etched in the voice of the State ResProp official: "We already have too many poet-road sweepers..."

1985 Languor

and what I couldn't say about the mid-Russian summer
the trunk of a violin said

Domodedovskaya Station

By June, Uncle Nazar had definitively replaced Uncle Gleb, and we moved into his place on the Old Arbat (the one condemned to demolition) for a while. But first, we all went our separate ways. Uncle Nazar—Mommy asked me to call him "Daddy" now—and I took Mommy to Domodedovo Airport, from where she was supposed to fly to Siberia, to Abakan or maybe Tayshet, where her mother had fallen ill. On the way to Domodedovskaya Station, Mommy told Uncle Nazar her mother's whole life story. I was pretending to read a book by Eduard Uspensky.

My grandmother, it seemed, was not a human but an outright monster. Though she might call up at three in the morning just because she'd had a bad dream about Mommy or me, in actuality, she was the worst manipulator ever born, controlling her husband as if he were a marionette.

"It was her who turned my father against me!" said Mommy. "It was her who stirred things up between me and my brother and sister, and between them, too! My brother's gotten married for the third time now—she hounded out the first two—and now my brother's left and gone north to keep his family intact! What drives her to it?" Mommy asked, and then answered herself. "Her soul is somehow too depraved, godless. Other people get softer, obliging, meek in their old age, but not her...

"If you only knew how she treated her own mother. Grandma had a notoriously bad back, cramped with rheumatism, and could no longer walk. She spent most days alone in her room, which my mother didn't even enter, blaming the smell. I cleaned Grandma's sheets under her, washed her every day, spoon-fed her, read *One Thousand and One Nights* out loud to keep her entertained, until one day she was no more. Even that day, when she passed away, mother did not come to the room. I washed her myself, wrapped her body in clean linen, and put her into the coffin. How can I love my mother after all that?"

I noticed that, although Mommy was glancing at Uncle Nazar from time to time, she was really talking to herself, and that frightened me a bit.

"And you know what, when my father was dying, my sister says even when he was only half conscious he croaked at her one day: 'There you go again, whirling and flitting about in front of my eyes! Go fall to the fallen!'"

I was more and more horrified that Mommy was saying those things about her mother and thought to myself: "Could I ever feel so cruelly toward Moscow, toward my own Mommy?" I tried with all my might to bury myself in *The School for Clowns*, though my burning red ears probably gave me away.

"By my seventeenth birthday I was ready to run away, anywhere, to take any job, and so I came here, as a limitchitsa." Uncle Nazar was sitting in his captain's uniform so he merely nodded politely to her occasionally, thinking increasingly about those around us and what kind of impression we might be making on them. Of course, everyone—as everyone usually is—was busy with their own business, and no one apart from me was paying any attention to my Mommy's story.

We rumbled on to Domodedovskaya Station, and it was there, at this unremarkable station, that Mommy suddenly turned on me with anger.

"You think I didn't notice you listening to everything I said? Why don't you read your shitty book? Do you want me to leave you here?! That's where you're heading!" She bashed my head against one of the unremarkable pillars.

"Will you behave yourself?!"

I didn't know how I should behave. As soon as I'd started to nod in agreement with her first question, I found myself suddenly ensnared in her second question, and my nod only served to wind her up more.

"Oh-ho, like that, is it?! You will, will you? Well, that's what you get for it! That's what you get..."

Uncle Nazar didn't interfere in the slightest and if the next train hadn't shot noisily out of the tunnel, Mommy would have probably bashed my brains out.

I cried silently as they led me upstairs, crucified between their two hands. We got on a shuttle bus that took us to the airport. Now Mommy was silent; now it was Uncle Nazar who occasionally spoke up, telling her not to worry, assuring either Mommy or himself that he would send me off to the Zosimova Pustyn monastery for the summer and that he would visit me there and call Mommy...

In childhood you don't describe landscapes, you live them. The road, like a black ribbon, is unfurled across the middle of the endless green Russian plain, and suddenly, the road rises, and your stomach leaps as you fly over a hill. You inhale deeply, and you see how the black ribbon is flanked by a forest, mist, a river, and you count the telegraph poles on either side, delighting in the way the transmission towers disappear off into the distance like loaded caravans. Sky, plane, woods, June...

Mommy flew away that afternoon, and from that night on I dreamed of airplanes.

Kashirskaya Station

For some strange reason, we took the bus back from Domodedovskaya to the Kashirskaya metro station. It's another typical station—why do they even bother giving them different names? They could have given them numbers, after all. But if you sniff the air, you'll find that station has the faint smell of a Laundromat. I've been to that station so many times since that distant June, but I will never be able to dislodge that scent from my nose.

For the first time in my life, I was in the city without my Mommy, left with a stranger. Mommy may have thought he was her next husband, but I didn't like him and didn't accept him. Uncle Nazar sensed my cold distance but hid his anger. Where Uncle Gleb had vast indifference, in this man everything occurred clearly and distinctly: if he decided to hide his hatred, he knew how to do it.

On the very first night, I burst into tears, tired of pretending to be asleep. I couldn't hold back my sobbing. He hung over me and asked with careful softness: "What are you blubbering for?" The gentleness of his voice frightened me even more, and I dived into the pillow. But he switched the light on, turned me over to face him and, like an interrogator, asked me: "Are you going to answer me?"

I didn't know what I could say: admit my simple fear, my orphan's defenselessness, my sense of being abandoned... What could I admit to him, as he flexed his lazy muscles over me?

Tears choked me; I had a coughing fit. He started to hit me on the back with his heavy hand. That stopped the coughing but enlarged the tears. He held off for a long time, but then he simply picked up his policeman's belt from the ground and, waving it slightly, whipped me on my back through the blanket. I howled at the top of my lungs. He threw the blanket off me and whipped me on my back and bottom repeatedly. The pain from the wide belt was colossal but dull, not the sharp, stinging pain from a thin ladies' belt or a switch of fresh willow.

Now my fear and pain overtook all reasoning, and with all my might I shouted, "Mommy! Mo-om-meee!" As if I were able to shout all the way to Siberia. He smothered my mouth with his huge hand and began whipping me harder and harder. Then he threw me back, shamefully, onto the pillow. I felt emptied, exhausted from my tears, damp from the blood coming through my back, from the urine flowing unhindered under me, and I only wanted one thing: death, so that Mommy would fly back to bury me and cry...

In the morning, he took me to the Laundromat where, unable to sit, I stood in front of the washing machine where my blood, urine, and tears all spun, first in one direction, then in another, then again, and again. Suddenly I threw up yellow bile and blood clots. Ladies rushed around, shouting for an ambulance. But Uncle Nazar showed everyone his red ID card and gathered the damp sheets in his rucksack. Then he led me underground, where the station still smells like the Laundromat...

Paveletskaya Station
ZAMOSKVORETSKAYA LINE

Everything is mixed up in the empty box of my skull. You have probably sensed that from my poor speech. You see, they don't talk here... We don't converse. Maybe the maggots are crawling along the wrong tracks.

I remember Paveletskaya Station, with its pillars, plodding like elephant legs. I come out at Novoslobodskaya Station, past its stained-glass panels of peasants in their *kokoshnik,* enter a hall like the Parthenon, and in Uncle Nazar's iron grip I get hauled along to streetcar number three, which will take us to Savelovsky railway station, where we get off. I looked upon all those cosmic flyovers there with horror, with Uncle Nazar dragging me any old way to the elektrichka—past the old station building, along the platform and, struggling against pain in my body, I force myself to sit down on the slippery wooden lattice of the seat. The carriage of the suburban train starts to jolt about, distributing not so much the pain itself, but rather its echo, its memory, through my back and thighs. We ride for a long time, dully, and I count the stations.

At Timiryazevskaya, an old lady got into our car. She had a basket with several kittens sitting inside. They meowed ceaselessly and smelled like cat pee, filling the whole car. At Okruzhnaya Station, two tipsy soldiers got on and gave a teasing salute as they passed—not to Uncle Nazar, sitting in uniform, but to me. They sat down behind us, conquering the cat pee with their stench of alcohol.

The old lady got off at Degunino Station, but the smells did not leave with her. A young family got on with a stroller. The sound of the closing doors woke their baby, who started to wail, but neither mother nor father picked it up; instead, they rocked the stroller with all four hands, against the rhythm of the jolting car. The child howled for four minutes, until a group of teenagers piled in at Bezkudnikov Station and, in the commotion, the baby just shut up. Or maybe we just couldn't hear it any more. After another three minutes, all of them—the older kids and the young family—got out at Lianozovo Station, but their place was taken by a horde of traders from the local market with their morning goods—potatoes, or onions, or early apples...

At Lianozovo, the drinking began for real. The smell—not vodka but perestroika moonshine—stalked the car. Next came an empty station with the strange name "Mark." With nothing to look at, I suddenly realized I was deliberately memorizing all these stations by heart, like I wanted to cram my brain, so that nothing remained except for these stations and these people.

We rode out of Moscow and once again, from the gap between two stations, the driver announced the next station, Novodachnoya. Here, the two soldiers got off, leaving their smell behind to be shared by the whole carriage. Uncle Nazar, who had from the outset taken off his distinctive policeman's cap, now devoted himself to his notes so as not to interfere in the chaos, and I was alone in observing both our journey and our carriage.

At Dolgoprudnaya, a few flashily dressed loafers got on. Seeing a policeman, they bit harder on their cigarettes and strode past into the next car. Uncle Nazar did not so much as lift an eye from his notes on the fight against crime. It was right here at Dolgoprudnaya that the smell of Podmoscovia wafted in: a blend of freshness and the scent of forest, marsh, and turf, a wood-goblin smell that grew stronger when the doors opened at Vodniki

Station. Here the River Moscow flowed by in all its breadth, as yet unblemished by Moscow itself. While I was looking out of the window, I didn't notice the dozen or so gypsies who had gotten on in the car in front of ours, but a minute later, as soon as the train had pulled away, they burst through the doors into our car. First came the women, babies in their arms, then boys and girls with dirty hair, and then three imposing men in multicolored lawn shirts bringing up the rear.

Catching sight of a policeman, they showed no fear but dashed toward us, and a woman with a syrupy voice half sang: "Ah, my handsome fellow, why have you taken that blackie? Give him to us! Set him free in the gypsy band!"

It was so startling that I grabbed hold of Uncle Nazar's shirt. You see, I was really afraid—I thought that he might just hand me over to the gypsies, lock, stock, and barrel. But Uncle Nazar raised his eyes, put his cap on his head, pulled himself up to his full height and bellowed: "So, you want me to call a patrol car to the next station? I'll inform the driver at once!"

No sooner had he made a move toward the emergency intercom, than all the gypsies began twittering, but not as much as me, now terrified that he would leave me alone here.

The gypsy men stepped forward, over their children, and pushed their womenfolk ahead. One of them said to Uncle Nazar by way of conciliation: "Commander, the woman's a fool. We don't need your Negro at all!" He scooped his offspring into his arms and carried them toward the next car. I went back to counting stations, out of fear or superstition, and with a trembling heart noted the sign for Khlebnikovo on the last plank of the platform.

Does the elektrichka fly along so fast or is space measured differently in Podmoscovia? In my mind, Sheremetyevo was so far from Moscow, but now here we were—two more minutes, and the next station, Sheremetyevo, sends two beautiful, elegant stewardesses into our car, wheeling their little foreign suitcases along the gap between the seats. I saw how Uncle Nazar's gaze was drawn away from his notes on maintaining social order, how his eyes burned at the familiar uniform, and suddenly I felt a terrible jealousy on Mommy's behalf, as though she had left me to protect her claim to this man...

The next station was Depot, which I didn't know. No one got on or off there. I didn't know that station nor did I know the next one, Lugovaya. Mommy loved the film *Never Forget Lugovaya Station*, but whether it was this Lugovaya or not, I didn't know and I didn't want to ask Uncle Nazar about it. At this particular Lugovaya Station, three drunk men got on the train with a dog on a leash, leaving the door open, and sat down without any special ceremony or shame, then opened a new bottle. Their foul language stayed between them; they didn't touch anyone else in the car apart from the dog, which one of them called a lousy bitch.

They had downed that bottle well before the next station, Nekrasovsky, and had gone quiet for a bit, but at Nekrasovsky one of them got up and started peeing openly onto the platform. Uncle Nazar tore himself away from his notes, donned his cap, and went off to re-establish social order in the wagon. He approached the man—who hadn't finished peeing—just as the train pulled out of the station, and as he swung his whole body around, he let his stream flow onto Uncle Nazar's uniform.

The policeman, infuriated, took a swing at the guy, who collapsed in a heap in his own urine. Then the one with the dog jumped up, croaking, "Get him!" With a snarl, the dog lunged at Uncle Nazar, but he countered like lightning and kicked it with his policeman's boot. The dog crawled, whimpering, under the seat. Uncle Nazar threw himself at the dog's owner, twisted his arms behind his back. The man howled drunkenly, and we all rolled into Katuar Station.

Uncle Nazar shouted at me to pull the emergency stop. I ran to him, where I could see the third man, watching it all indifferently through drunken eyes. Seeing me, he hiccuped and declared: "There's a Negro here too!"

I pulled the stop signal and told the driver there was a fight in our carriage. The train stopped at Katuar and waited with open doors until the driver managed to call someone from the station to whom he handed over the trio along with the dog. In the trio, one man was bloodied, the second couldn't untwist his arms from behind his back, and the third kept hiccuping, gaping at me goggle-eyed, quite unable to accommodate in his brain either my appearance there or my fluent Russian. Did he see me as a little black imp, one of his alcohol-induced hallucinations? He couldn't take his drunken eyes off me, still hiccuping: "Well, *hic!* A Neeegro, too, *hic!*"

After some delay the elektrichka finally pulled away, and we came into Trudovaya Station, where Uncle Nazar and I got out into the forest, no longer enemies but, as I thought, distant allies.

Admittedly, quite why I began this tale from Paveletskaya metro station, I am still not sure. Maybe I had better tell you about Trudovaya Station, where the first thing Uncle Nazar did on duty at his academy's deserted summer camp was to get drunk on that same vodka with his brother in arms, helping it down with local mushrooms, all the while trying to pour a glass down me, too, now like one of the family. Or maybe I'd better not...

Chertanovskaya Station

For all my Khakassian-Negro crossbreeding, alas, I was the very incarnation of Russian literature. And not because Uncle Gleb had nicknamed me "Little Pushkin"; or because they called me Pushkin at kindergarten; or because almost from the cradle I would furtively read all my mother's books, from *The Battle Along the Way* to *I Enter the Storm*; certainly not because life was forming out of me some "perfect organ." But because... well, I'll be damned, but I won't say why! After all, you've probably been thinking for a while now that this is all made up: after all, how is a three- or four-year-old boy capable of all this? Retelling something, sure—but to feel it all, let alone remember it...

But I tell you it was me—a three-, four-, five-, or six-year-old—who lived through all of this, down to the letter, and I felt it all exactly as I am telling it now. Maybe now that I've lived beyond my years—or rather, in the immortal age—it's easier for me to use a figure of speech here or a witty word there that might not have entered my head back then. But my jumbled delivery has its roots in my youth. But as for the feelings, please take them in good faith. I may not draw them clearly—but merely sketch them, mention them, hint at them—sometimes even to me my tale seems painfully stilted, schematic.

Were I alive now, I sometimes think, within the emptiness of my skull, I would be around twenty-six or twenty-eight, the age of genius, so I have nothing to be ashamed of, nothing to spell out or explain.

But I was talking about Chertanovskaya Station, one of the rare suburban stations not executed in the image of the columnar T or the parade of the Grecian pi. No, this station is unique, not mass made; it is stylish, special. I would have called it Snow Queen Station, a place where I could put Kai and Gerda, were I to know them better. Look at the noble coldness of the icy flooring, the crystalline embrace of the pillars, the hanging stalactite lamps—and all on a sultry summer's day!

But step outside and you wonder what has happened to that feeling. You'll find yourself in a typical Moscow suburb; it could be Teplii Stan or Altufyevo, Yugo-Zapadnaya, Yasenevo or Belyaevo.

I was taken out there by two of Mommy's friends who were supposed to keep me while Uncle Nazar was on duty at his Academy. Escorted by them, like that Negro I'd glimpsed walking between two Russian women by the vodka line, I did feel like I was in the Snow Queen's realm, so neat and tidy was their seventeenth-floor apartment, and so splendid was the view of the heavenly Moscow suburbs from their windows and balcony.

I had always dreamed of watching the sunset from the roof of some building and, as though they'd known my wishes, they led me, just like that, just before sunset, onto the roof. The wind rustled our hair, and the sunset was indescribably beautiful and pitiful, and it lasted a long, long time, as it can on cloudless June evenings. I thought of Mommy; after all, she was on this earth, under this same sun... I never missed my Mommy so much as I did during that Moscow sunset on the roof of a Chertanovian apartment block.

By the next evening, as I was waiting joylessly for Uncle Nazar to pick me up and take me back to his decrepit apartment, the weather had already turned foul. Auntie Irma was sitting with me while Auntie Lira went to the metro station to buy vegetables for dinner.

It was the hour of day that seemed so fleeting and ephemeral in fair weather, but in foul weather it was a burdensome thing, stuck between day and night, not twilight at all. Auntie Lira didn't come back for a long time, and Auntie Irma got impatient. But to my delight, Uncle Nazar hadn't arrived either, and it seemed like once again time got scrambled up between our opposing desires.

Auntie Irma gave me a bundle of vegetable peelings and sent me to throw it down the trash chute, right by the elevator. I went out and, after I had successfully pushed it into the chute's ever-hungry mouth (with a whoop, the peelings had flown down from the seventeenth floor to the depths below), the devil prompted me to turn toward the emergency stairs: was it that I wanted to look down at foul-weather Moscow from this height? Whatever it was, I yanked open the door to the stairs and saw Uncle Nazar and Auntie Lira panting away. They were standing with their backs to me and, of course, they didn't see me. She was bent over double, supporting herself with her hands on the wall, her skirt hitched up over her back, her panties cuffing her ankles, and Uncle Nazar, his pants halfway down, was inculcating her backside, time and again, time and again...

I carefully closed the door, burning with the shame of what I had seen. That shame was mine alone. I was not ashamed of them or for them, but of myself, for watching all that. Blood was throbbing in my temples as though I had been caught red-handed, and I retreated like a coward to Auntie Irma's, where I locked myself in the bathroom and flushed my face with cold water.

When I came out, everyone was sitting around the table, pouring wine brought by Uncle Nazar, who for no apparent reason gave me a conspiratorial wink. But I felt so bad for Mommy, so bad that I ran back to the bathroom...

Dobryninskaya Station
KOLTSEVAYA LINE

W ere it not for the serpentine lamps, Dobryninskaya would remind you of a wine cellar, but with them the station gives off the lingering impression that the Georgian wine of the cellar has been somehow revamped into some sort of Russian moonshine; the air here is always tinged with the scent of stale alcohol. Or was it Uncle Nazar who brought that smell with him, when he took me here one June morning to send me on my way to the distant countryside beyond Moscow—to Zosimova Pustyn cloister. The buses were leaving from Dobryninskaya, although the departmental nursery was a long way from here, but maybe it was the proximity of the department itself that dictated we should gather here at the monument by the exit of Dobryninskaya?

Now even I notice that all my memories connected with Uncle Nazar are somehow linked to moving, journeys, or—as is more often the case—running away. Well, I didn't like that Akhal-Teke stallion; I didn't like him and I kept out of his way. Even being sent off to that former nunnery—where they'd made the summer nursery for us while the visitors were gathering in Moscow for the festival—was preferable to staying in Moscow waiting for Mommy to come back. Funnily enough, before we left we all had to shave our heads completely, supposedly to avoid lice infection, but in the back of my mind I think there was a correspondence— or perhaps just a coincidence—with the shaved nuns.

Mommy had never shaved my head, because, you see, if there was anything at all respectable in my mixed appearance, it was my curly hair, giving me the air of Pushkin-cum-Angela Davis. But in just one hour I was stripped of my glory, my helmet, left stunningly vulnerable for the whole of the first week.

The drive to the cloister took a long, long time, a very long time. Through lanes and streets, city roads and country roads, through village ruts, forks, and forest tracks, and finally to a place that was so quiet that your ears rang, creating a playful sound for their own amusement. They settled us into a stone building with metal bunk beds screwed to the floor forever and a day, and we began to live our quasi-monastic summertime life.

We were woken at seven by a horn and a drum roll, which was repeated at the morning flag-raising ceremony. One day, when my turn to raise the flag had come around, as I was gradually, rhythmically drawing the rope toward me, through the circular block, it jammed. With all my might, I tried to pull the rope in time with the horn and drum, but it sprang back and wouldn't surrender, the flattened flag dangling almost under my flattened nose. And then our teacher, Tamara Fillipovna, who had been standing eyes front, rushed to my aid. Noticing the commotion, first the horn player and then the drummer fell out of rhythm and trailed off awkwardly. A gasp of horror went up from the ranks, or so I thought in my fright. Then Tamara Fillipovna tugged at the rope so hard it burned my hands, and shaking its heavy head, the flag suddenly woke up and leapt to its post without any horn or fine drum roll, but under Tamara Fillipovna's stinging whisper, right in my ear: "Your hands, Mbobo, are growing from THE WRONG PLACE!" But there, at that moment, I thought she had announced it over the camp's loudspeaker, and the echo rang through the ranks, with their eyes on the red of my disgrace, now quivering on high for all the world to see...

Then, after a breakfast of hateful semolina, or even more hateful pearl barley porridge, washed down with watery juice, we would go out to work in the fields, to gather Saint John's wort, which the teachers first dried in their quarters and then sold to the local pharmacist. That yellow-eyed flower hid behind distractingly blue cornflowers (it was so tempting to pick them!) or behind prickly, hairy burdock, threatening to hold you at bay with its violet eyes. We went out to gather Saint John's wort in our vests and knickers, and returned scratched and bleeding, after which the director would haul me out before the group, turn me around in all directions like a doll, exclaiming: "Look, children! Not a scratch to be seen on the boy! By the end of the summer, each of you here in this nursery should get a tan like this African tan! Understood?!" And everyone would answer, unwillingly and untogether, "Understood..."

Whether I should have been proud of my skin in that situation or not, I don't know, but each and every time the director singled me out from the herd of pale skins and held me up to show that my skin didn't blush red, but purple, like the prickly, fleshy stalks of the burdock, I wanted to sink all my prickly teeth into the hands that were turning me around and around, this way and that...

After gathering Saint John's wort, we would wash and be led in single file to lunch. For the most part we were fed macaroni and sauerkraut, along with some sort of disintegrating burgers, which left a stinky, sour aftertaste that pervaded your whole mouth and fostered burning, sour burps, especially in the horizontal position they'd tucked us up into for our after-lunch nap. During our nap the nannies paced between the beds as though they were guards on duty, interrupting even the tiniest sneak at talking, and so we lay at attention, screwing our eyes up with all our might until the measured hum of the sun in the sky or the summer fields beyond the window bored through that blind man's bluff of our screwed-up eyes with a true, wakeless sleep, from which we were rescued, sweaty and swollen, by those same guard-nannies (or was it the midday sun, bristling in the window?) who chased us off for a snack of burned-oat biscuits with stewed fruit.

Then they would read books to us about a brave traveler with the strange name of Miklukho-Maklai and his Papuans, who we, for some reason, all called "Papa-u-whiskers" after our teacher, and at that point, to show everyone what those "Papa-u-whiskers" were really like, Tamara Fillipovna would stand me in the center of the circle and ask me to dance around the bench and, still sleepy and crotchety, I would jump around, doing something akin to a sailor's jig, and everyone would squeal and suffocate with laughter...

On other days we would use colored threads to sew vases out of the postcards sent by our parents, but seeing as no one ever wrote to me, I would sit in the sticky afternoon, waiting for one of the children to prick his or her finger, when I would be called to their aid to skewer someone's loving letters with the slippery needle, and then I would again see that same prickly, hairy burdock with its fleshy purple stalks, and I would of course prick my own finger, and my purple blood, almost invisible against my skin, would come out as a small teardrop, unseen by anybody...

There in this summer camp I met a lonely, mouse-like girl my age, by the un-Russian name of Zulita, Zulya.

The story of our meeting went like this. After a visiting day for parents (on which everyone had parents visiting except for me), Tamara Fillipovna organized a celebratory picnic. One after another, she unwrapped all the edible goodies that the parents had brought: Dasha got a cake, Arkashka got pies, and this very Zulita's father had brought her a real rarity—an enormous pineapple. Tamara Fillipovna then called Zulita out to the middle to give her the very first piece of the coveted fruit, but as she sliced it before everyone, the pineapple turned out to be thoroughly rotten. For a moment the girl stood there, lost for words, and then she burst into tears and dashed out of the room. Tamara Fillipovna chose not to draw attention it, quickly disposed of the disappointing fruit, wiped clean the knife, and cut into Dasha's cake.

Perhaps I was the only person in the room who could have understood how this girl felt, because at this celebration I had nothing that was mine.

Later, when the evening roll call was taken, Zulita was still missing and Tamara Fillipovna raised the alarm. Everyone took part in the search, combing through the entire area of the camp. I was the one to find her, crouching in the bushes of gooseberry, which only my thick skin could take. She sat there on the dusty earth, still tearful, whimpering from time to time. I don't know what came over me, but I brought her out of there on my back, and was praised for this selfless act by Tamara Fillipovna, on the way having managed to confide in Zulita that though I hadn't received anything either on that day, I found I was still OK.

As it turned out she had recently moved to Moscow with her parents from some small town in Dagestan. She lived with her dad, stepmother, and her old grandma. Two non-Russian outcasts, we quickly felt an affinity and grew closer. Once Zulya showed me an old photograph of a woman and a girl taken in Dagestan and explained, pointing to it, "this is me as a child." Confused, I wondered aloud: "But you're still one—" She cut me short: "Kirill, why don't you get it! It's me as a *young* child."

She was right to describe herself as a young child at the time, because her mom had passed away when she was only six months old. She remembered her mother only through photos and her grandma's stories and, as she once told me, she still remembered her smell. "What kind of smell?" I wondered. "Of warm fresh milk," she replied, and grew quiet.

She was disliked by her stepmother, and her dad would always side with his new wife. Her grandmother was the only person close to her, but she was so old that she was pretty much immobile, and Zulya had to look after her and read her fairy tales, because her stepmother would never set foot in Grandma's room, saying it stank. (And just to think that my mother had told me a similar story, before she left for Hakasia, going to visit her mother...)

When I confided in Zulya how my stepdad Uncle Nazar beat me with a belt, Zulya admitted that she too got beaten by her father. "At least you have a real mom," she would say with a note of either envy or sadness in her voice...

From Kashirskaya Station to Kakhovskaya Station

I have already lived through more death underground than I lived life on the surface. You lie there, and when the emptiness in your bones begins to whistle with cold, a certain music manifests itself, as though Orpheus had come down to us with his reed pipe (or is it made of bones grown thin?), and barren memories interrupt one another, as though the long-awaited Festival had been put on for them...

Artists from all over the globe came for the World Festival of Youth and Students that summer. Moscow, my Mommy, perhaps expected to discover my primeval father among them because, despite the ban from the departmental nursery, she took me back to her place in the city, and every evening we would go together, usually to watch the Afro-Caribbean shows (luckily, Uncle Nazar was away all this time on "reinforcement"). From one point of view it was uplifting to see such a huge number of my fellow black skins around, but at the same time as soon as they began to fawn over me, and via me, over Mommy, I felt ashamed and disgusted because I myself was one of them, one of those who had come here, as Mommy put it, "hunting happiness and a bit of skirt." I had never experienced such simultaneous joy and shame. But how I loved their shows!

And that is how the Festival passed for Mommy and me: day-night, day-night, day-night. Another evening we went to watch a Khakassian tale about the realm of the underworld. Was it merely a coincidence, or was it Mommy's choice, knowing or foreseeing something? Now with the wisdom of the years I have lived and the years I have been dead, I can guess, but maybe that is how the art of the Soviet underground expressed itself?

* * *

Once upon a time, there were three brothers: the god of the heavens, Tengeri; the god of the Earth, Khudai; and the god of the under-world, Erlik. One day Erlik—that old man with eyes and brows as black as soot, with a forked beard down to his knees, with mus-tache-like tusks, with horns like a dungeon full of twisted roots— came out from his underworld and asked Khudai for some earth. Khudai gave Erlik just as much earth as would fit under his staff.

Then Erlik made an opening in the earth and planted a black larch. The larch grew up from the earth, and at night a black rooster would fly to its very crown. He crowed long and loud, such that ev-eryone in the audience grew uneasy and fearful. The cock would crow, and on stage the person nearest the larch would die. It would crow again, the next person would die. The people ran to Khudai, the god of the Earth, to complain.

Just then Khudai was forming a new person from black clay. He dropped it, still unformed, and ran to look at the dead. The black rooster transformed into an aina-*devil, flew to the unformed child, and began spitting on it. He spat and spat until there was no living spot left on it, then turned back into a bird and flew back to the larch.*

Seeing this, some of the people ran once again to Khudai, while some snatched up their weapons and went to shoot the rooster. They fired once, and as though nothing had happened, the bird crowed so loudly that the terror of his crowing covered the whole hall. They fired another volley, but it crowed again, even more piercingly and eerily. Just then day dawned clearly, spreading like a rooster's tail feathers, and the creature faded into the darkness.

Those people who had gone to seek out Khudai found him resuscitating a dead person. With horror, they told him of the bespittled boy, still unformed from the black clay, and then Khudai, seeing his creation's unhappiness and misery, decided to send the person he had just resurrected into the underworld of his brother Erlik after the rooster. On coming back to life, this person transformed into a shaman and set off on his journey. He walked around the stage (which was spinning like a carousel) until he reached the black trunk of the black larch and sang together with the whole audience:

> The black stump,
> A table for divination.
> The earth where you know
> of life and death.
> The black path
> Into the depths of the universe,
> The path trod
> By elders and devils...

The first gate was opened for him. The stage spun again, and again the shaman set off on his journey with his echoing drum. He reached a black field with a black burial mound and sang in a threatening voice:

> The black field
> Of the clatter of horses' hooves,
> Which beat as a hammer on the anvil,
> In black tongs
> Shards of experience
> Blow into the bellows
> Together with exultation...

The doors of the black burial mound opened, and once again the stage spun and whirled. The shaman made his way with his songs and cries through the gates of the black ravines, through the swamp of black frogs, through the black forest of the black bears, through the black vat of boiling hell and finally came to the place where nine rivers flow together, where the palace of black earth stands with its iron tethering post and hordes of black shooters. And here he sang his last song:

> On a black tray
> My head
> I offer to you, lord of shadows!
> The black cockerel
> I need in exchange.
> It is Khudai who demands it
> Ever more strongly.
> Hoop upon hoop
> Is hiding me.
> The hoop of the whirlwind
> Over my head.
> Give Khudai the cock,
> Erlik!
> And I will depart
> Forever from you!

But Erlik, that disheveled and black old man, didn't want to simply hand over the bird for nothing, and demanded in exchange the soul and body of the unformed boy bespittled by the cock. After all, now he will never escape from scorn and sickness, Erlik assures the shaman-messenger. "As soon as they bring him to the larch, I will release the rooster and reveal to you the secret of its vulnerability..."

The scenes spin again, in the opposite direction, and the sha-man-messenger returns through the nine gates to the people and to Khudai, bent over his weakening child. The shaman tells him what happened. But now Khudai refuses to hand over the black, unformed boy.

Night fell, and the evil cock once more spread its wings over the black larch. The riflemen carefully closed the circle around him, so that no one would be left nearer the tree than another, and in their midst stood the shaman. But just before dawn broke, just before the rooster's most blood-curdling cry, the little black boy—seeking revenge or craving sacrifice—tore through the chain of shooters just as the bird crowed. The boy fell dead, and his body tumbled to the roots of the larch, going deep under the earth. At that moment a volley rang out, each bullet marked with a cross as the shaman had ordered, and the cockerel's feathers flew into the sky, splattering blood, a bloody sunrise spread over the earth, and the shaman's song rang out, a song about a boy who saved the people from the ill-omened rooster...

* * *

When, by some indirect route, Mommy and I found ourselves at Kashirskaya metro station, with its typical little glass coffin above ground, I sensed with horror that we would have to go down into the underground kingdom of the unruly Erlik. It was a fleeting feeling, both familiar and unfamiliar, which made it all the more confusing. It seemed that I was that unformed black boy while, without telling her, I gave Mommy the role of Inanna, the goddess beginning her descent to the underworld. My mind nodding off, I followed each of our downward steps, noting the glass doors into the metro station, then the second gate, where Mommy paid the fare, then the turnstile followed by the entrance into the hall itself. The light marble arches stood for the missing gates, and then finally a corpse-like voice announced: "Mind the closing doors! Next station is Warsaw."

The doors of the ninth gate slammed shut, and the train carried us through the underground kingdom. In each window, where occasional faces were reflected in the darkness, I thought I caught fleeting glimpses of either Erlik or Ereshkigal with hair trailing behind, like the thundering darkness behind the train. Those locks somehow reminded me of the long hair and disheveled beard of my first stepfather, Uncle Gleb. As I was getting used to those ideas, the train suddenly pulled into Warsaw Station, where we glimpsed a lone policeman on the platform; the sight of him gave both Mommy and me a shudder, but it wasn't Uncle Nazar in a rooster's cap.

My thoughts wandered to my stepfathers and to my father, as though they were that trinity of gods—from the unseen heavens via the gloomy earth to the black underground—and I skittered between them, but the train sprang up again through its dark realm; once again the locks of Erlik and Ereshkigal streamed out toward themselves before it, and with an animal's fear I knew that it was not just this late-night journey from God-knows-where to God-knows-where, but my whole life in those theatrical parables, incarnated into reality, and suddenly yet another station with those same pi-shaped arches, gate after gate, flashed before my eyes and a fear that we were not moving at all, that Erlik and Ereshkigal had rushed past, took hold of me for a fleeting moment, but my sharp eyes spotted that the pillars in this station were no longer grayish white, but bloody-brown, the color of the civil war. And the announcer, with a shaman's voice, confirmed the difference externally: "Kakhovskaya Station. This train is going no further. Please vacate the cars..."

1986 Wanderings

I forgot the word and there in the subway of my sleep
my tongue gets bitter and fails to pronounce it

Prospekt Marksa, Ploshchad Sverdlova, and Ploshchad Revolyutsii Stations

Sokolnicheskaya, Zamoskvoretskaya, and Arbatsko-Pokrovskaya Lines

There, in that September...
like a little amber-colored spider trembling in the air,
the song sways
There, in that September
a maple leaf glistened like a star,
There was I happy, as I will never be, never

Like that little spider, trapped forever in September's amber, Mommy and I simply can't see the forest for the trees, lost among them forever. But what have I said? Not trees, of course, but those three stations, linked to one another in a semicircle. How did we end up there—or, rather, first of all—in the ancient Hunters' Row?

Had we entered via the red granite of the Moscow Hotel into her subconscious, confusing the capital with the hotel, and both the capital and the hotel with Mommy? Around that time Mommy was reading the *Bardo Thodol*, the *Tibetan Book of the Dead*, as though she were preparing herself—and, as it turns out, preparing me, too—for a new journey. I knew how important it was to maintain consciousness—not only as you enter death, but in the far more routine preparation for dreaming.

But this was no dream, so how could I have missed both the entrance gates and the ski-slope trajectory of the escalators, finding not only myself but also Mommy next to me, sober (which was so rare that spring and that summer or earlier that September), and in her sudden sobriety, she didn't know why we were here, where we were headed, what we were looking for...?

And that book of the dead, given to her by a friend, Masha Arbatova, from the Society of Professional Playwrights, was with Mommy. Following its advice, I was jumping from one white square on the checkerboard floor to another, thinking meanwhile that maybe we were here on account of Auntie Masha and her two twins—Peter and Paul—but this wasn't the Arbat line, was it? The checkerboard floor, like the twins who flashed into my thoughts, was reflected in the waffle-like ceiling that shone with a dull light, and as the *Bardo Thodol* said:

> *beware of the dull light...*
> *The city has woken from winter's ice*
> *Suddenly grown bright, like a picture postcard,*
> *Only don't think that all this*
> *Has made me oh so glad*

The song flickered from some unknown place, as if one of the gloomy announcers had forgotten to switch off the public-address system when he turned on his radio, or as if some madman were following close on our heels, his transistor radio, or more likely, a tape player, hidden behind the massive pillars, which were not really pillars but rather buttresses.

We had nowhere to live. My Mommy Moscow, torn between a writer and a policeman, docked with neither, just as the sportsman—my father—had run away from her earlier, and I did not so much understand as guess (after all, a guess is better than knowledge!) that we hadn't lost our way among those three stations, nor among three trees, but among our lives: among body, legal codex, and spirit. And thus I was guessing about the Sportsman, the Policeman, and the Writer. As though running away from something, my mother led me confidently to the transfer station, and without a single word we hurried along the slippery tube, where behind our backs the song still wafted:

I only need to remember how, lowering your face, you tell me you don't love me. And September returns, and the leaves are falling again.

Mommy had been coughing terribly for months now, since we went to Gorky Park on the first of May, and it was raining there, and we didn't know yet that the clouds came from Chernobyl. Mommy had taken off her light jacket and thrown it over my unruly curls, leaving herself with nothing but a chiffon blouse. So now she was coughing, trying to hurry, trying to run away from that drawling, treacly, cloying song. Mommy was so faint that as soon as we reached the hall of Ploshchad Sverdlova Station, she sat down in the alcove of a pillar under a bright lamp.

The light, cool marble soothed Mommy's cough. We sat there, breathing in that primordial smell of Moscow's swampy dampness, mixed with creosote, the smell of Moscow's metro, and Mommy's lungs were calming down after the radioactive alien intrusion. The *Bardo Thodol* spoke of falls, of transits, of tunnels, and I was sitting next to Mommy and arranging our stations into a certain order, as other boys my age, boys in their first year of school, would arrange building blocks: from Marx, the flaming theoretician of the revolution; to Sverdlov, its cheerless and common practitioner; and then to the Revolution itself. No matter how you place them, no matter how you toss them, it's all the same—these three stations fall into a certain logic, flickering unattainably ahead; but *beware the dull, flickering light*, the book said, and the tacky song seconded it:

I am left there, where water quivers in the puddles,
Where any moment is a celebration,
Where you and I cannot be one without the other

The route, the book, the swaying...

I know that there is nothing more absurd than the dream,
That you will suddenly muddle up Septembers,
That you will suddenly muddle up two Septembers...

Having caught her breath, Mommy led me by a third route: from the middle of the hall in Ploshchad Sverdlova Station up along the bridge over the tracks and from there, beside the long, echoing tunnel to the butt-end of the third station, where the vaults were supported along their length by two dozen trimmed pillars that disappeared, skipping, into the distance. Each arch here was guarded by a bronzed gatekeeper: the disheveled old man, half-kneeling, leaning against his shouldered rifle—Erlik! I recognize you! A little farther on, a lady balancing a little dish in her palm was hiding away like a lynx. Her other hand was sticking out in the strange, primordial gesture of a temptress: her thumb and middle finger touching, her ring finger lightly resting on her palm, and her little finger and index finger turned upward. Ereshkigal could not disguise herself in that girl, and so we kept going farther and farther, past the confused idols of the underground realm until we reached an arch where my Mommy Moscow sat down and looked into the emptiness in fear, holding me against her naked shoulder, having left her shrouds at the previous gates...

We stood face-to-face with our primordial forms, a mother and child, frozen forever, and all at once it seemed like the snatches of that song were floating out of me against my will, leaving behind my heart, empty and hard as stone:

And so you'll come to me...
There, there I am left there where water quivers in puddles,
Where every moment is like a celebration,
Where you and I cannot be one without the other,
Forever, do you hear, I am left,
In September, that September

Where there is still half a day before
You stop loving me

It was there, and then, in that September, as we wandered aimlessly back and forth between those three endless stations that I first guessed (isn't a guess better than knowing?) that one of us would soon die...

1987 M

Some April—these nymphs will walk away
taking with them the shadows, as though walking on grief,
past the windows of oh so empty ambulances
so that you will feel me with your tightened throat,
you will remember, and drop a knife of spoon...

Novogireyevo Station

SERPUKHOVSKO-TIMIRYAZEVSKAYA LINE

In the year of her death, still out of control, my Mommy lived between Uncle Nazar and Uncle Gleb. Through it all, I kept going to the same school on the Left Bank I'd started when we had moved from Goncharova Street, and while Mommy found reasons to go off to Uncle Nazar's, to that apartment block still condemned to demolition, where aside from him only phantoms were left, I would get picked up by the neighbor or the lady from the post office below our balcony, or by a drunk but conciliatory Uncle Gleb, now turned churchgoer.

That March, Mommy Moscow had a visit from her younger sister, who had the artless name of Emma. (Mommy simply called her "Em.") I knew that all names beginning with *E* carry within them the echo of the other side: Erlik, Ereshkigal, Enki... Worse, in her youthful splendor, Em was more beautiful than Mommy, so every evening more new admirers would call her on our tinkling phone. This one she'd met on the elektrichka, that one on the escalator, another in the GUM department store; she got to know the fourth at the theater. Mommy was angry, but there was something in the sisters' relationship that stopped her from forbidding or meddling, as an older sister might. Mommy blamed my Auntie Emma's allure on their mother's hocus-pocus. I say "my auntie," but frankly she never acknowledged me, and I was embarrassed by her vulgar makeup, her hips swiveling from side to side, the clop of her high heels that could be heard throughout the universe when she clattered up the stairs at night, rousing all the neighbors and their wives, albeit for different reasons...

Sometimes during her visit, I thought: well, what haven't I seen in Mommy that distinguishes her from her sister? And calmed by that thought, I stuck on two points. Auntie Em smoked, and she swore terribly. One night when Mommy had decided to confront her about the phone calls and nightly clopping, Auntie Em simply locked herself in the kitchen and, just as we were getting ready for bed, she stuck her head out and said, loudly, "Fuck all of you!" Then she closed the door again.

Taganskaya Station

TAGANSKO-KRASNOPRESNENSKAYA LINE

And suddenly Mommy wasn't there...

Ploshchad Nogina Station

TAGANSKO-KRASNOPRESNENSKAYA LINE

... and Mommy wasn't there...

Ploshchad Nogina Interchange

KALUZHSKO-RIZHSKAYA AND
TAGANSKO-KRASNOPRESNENSKAYA LINES

....

Ploshchad Revolyutsii Station

Arbatsko-Pokrovskaya Line

Somewhere, something didn't connect. I don't remember how I ended up at that station in the kingdom of underground shadows. I don't remember how I discovered—no, not disheveled Erlik with a rifle, nor Ereshkigal tempting us with her dish and gesture, nor even myself with Mommy, gazing beyond into the darkness—no, I searched out what I had noticed last time but was afraid to look at because of the deep superstition that had taken root in my fertile fear. Yes, that's how it was: the figure that represented my Mommy Moscow, sitting in her dark alcove, bent over a black rooster under whose feet, distracting our gaze, a hen was entwined. The rooster was all bespittled, some recent, snotty spittle was still drying on him, and the mother's iron hand, despite her kindness, could not reach out to clean him before the night cleaners—those other disheveled old men with mops instead of rifles, their talkative assistants with brushes instead of pistols—came.

I started to cry. I felt such pain for Mommy, for her present absence, for myself, not only bespittled (as if that weren't enough) but also forsaken by her. Now I'd been left alone, all by myself with this world. Why, I thought, did you give birth to me if you couldn't raise me, couldn't defend me, couldn't protect me? Even that piece of iron was looking with more mercy at that cursed black rooster than you looked at me, when instead of a lullaby you would sing:

Poor old cat was blacker than black
From his tail to his whiskers, from his belly to his back.
And so, in short, my song's about that:
How horrible it is to be a little black cat...

I have never cried so deeply or so wildly as I did at that terrible metro station, that omen of that world we all go to at our preordained time: my lungs let loose with gasps, the torrent of tears left my innards dry; they became taut, like the skin on your face when it's dried by the wind, trembling, like a drum skin, or rather, like the skin on milk that has just boiled and cooled. And I remembered what I heard last summer from the lonely mouse-like girl Zulita, who lost her mother at just six months old: "I still remember her smell. The smell of warm fresh milk..."

Why did she drink with Uncle Gleb that evening and go and sleep in the bedroom without saying goodbye to me? Her snores woke me in the night. She had never snored so loud. Muttering, drunk Uncle Gleb went to sleep on the chairs in the kitchen. I assumed the snoring was due to drunkenness and went into the bedroom to turn her over onto her side.

"Mommy, turn over, do you hear me?"

But the weight of her body did not yield. I tugged her hand, but she still didn't wake up. "Dead to the world..." I supposed, but then scared by my own thought, I tried to wake her again. No, she wouldn't wake up. With difficulty, I turned her to the side and her snoring eased slightly. It was a strange snore, not the usual nasal one, but somehow deeper, as though bubbles were in her lungs.

I went and lay down in my bed in the living room. In the morning I got up before everyone else, quickly had a sandwich for breakfast and hurried to school, leaving the house with its heavy smell of last night's drinking...

I don't know why, but that day in shop class I thought I was quite grown-up when the mail lady Auntie Lina, who sometimes used to pick me up, looked in the window. She waved her arms, then disappeared for a while and then reappeared at the door, but she didn't come up to me; she went to our shop teacher.

He called to me over the noise of the electric tools, and then Auntie Lina said: "We're going home. They took your mommy away in an ambulance."

I can't say I was shocked or anything... At that age, you are glad for anything unexpected, any chance to break rank, to distinguish yourself, even if it's because they have come for you because your mommy's been taken to the hospital. So I triumphantly attached myself to stout Auntie Lina in her ancient flip-flops.

The first tremor ran through me when I saw our apartment full of neighbors, although hardly anyone paid any attention to me, with the exception of Auntie Olesia, Mommy's friend from the same hall. As soon as she laid eyes on me, she asked:

"You know the address of your grandma in Siberia?"

I nodded my head.

"Then run over to the post office and send a telegram that your mommy is in the hospital with emphysema. She should come quick!"

I dropped my school bag and ran with Auntie Lina to the post office, around the other side of our enormous building, under our rear balcony. The March sun was shining but not yet giving off any warmth; the snow had no intention of melting and the trees no intention of sprouting. It was a strange time of year and a strange time of day. Time stood still. We ran, and I tried to pace myself to stay with heavy Auntie Lina as she slipped on the shadowy dark-blue ice at the end of the block, holding onto the wall now and then.

When we got to the post office, Auntie Lina walked in first and commanded:

"We need an urgent telegram."

I went up to the cashier's desk, where the girl was already waiting for me by the telegram machine and began to dictate the Siberian address. When the typist had finished spelling out the surname Rzhevsky, Auntie Lina dictated the message itself.

"Come urgently. Stop."

"Co-me ur-gent-ly," I repeated, just in case.

"Mommy..."

"Mom-my ser-ious-ly ill..."

"Write: has died."

I turned around at that familiar voice, coming from behind. There was Uncle Gleb, smelling slightly of yesterday's alcohol.

"Write: ha-as di-ed."

Teatralnaya Station
ZAMOSKVORETSKAYA LINE

And so I went home from the post office while the utterly useless sun was hanging overhead, while my breath was floating unnecessarily upward, with last year's withered leaves refusing to yellow, still hanging on the trees, simply rustling loudly for no reason whatsoever.

And at that station, where I'd cried my fill, where my Mommy Moscow and I had gotten lost last September, the lights were on in broad daylight. Despite the bustling crowds, it was an exercise in futility: the lights were on in broad daylight; the glazed images of Terpsichore and Melpomene, squashed into their diamond-shaped hoops and frozen in foolish, ugly immobility; the black-yellow field of the marble floor like stained teeth...

When I returned to our flat, where our new cat, Mikki, frightened by the influx of strangers, had hidden herself in the shoe cupboard, the sour smell of yesterday's drinking still hung in the air, aggravated by a generous helping of Troynoi eau de cologne. For some reason the kitchen radio was playing and someone was mumbling dispassionately about perestroika and *uskoreniye*. No one was paying any attention to it. I still had not shed a single tear. I saw how fearfully Mikki picked her way across the hall, how, glancing left and right, she opened the kitchen door a crack, and came in to me, meowing pitifully...

And suddenly I held back no longer. Hugging this small, warm, dear creature, I sobbed, long and deep, while she just meowed and stroked my cheek with the tip of her wet tail...

How do people get over the deaths of their mothers? Once again I remembered that girl Zulya, who was with me in Zosimova Pustyn. Is it not better to lose your mom young, when you don't realize the depth of your loss, when she remains only a distant memory, known only through photos and a distant aroma of closeness... Where is Zulya now?

A train pulled in, surplus people poured through its doors. I went in through the last door so I could squeeze into the corner. "Watch the closing doors! The next station is Gorky," said a sepulchral voice. I didn't look around, but I could sense with all the pores of my body that everyone around me was dead: their stiff expressions; the foolish, ugly rigidity of a person bent over a book, scratching his head or staring at the metro map, mouth gaping; another simply fixing her eyes on her own suspicious reflection in the window...

They floated by me, as I moved through hospital corridors in a ward I was not allowed to enter, or was the way simply barred by a crowd of dead bodies? I just stood and stood there until the ward transformed into a morgue and through the dirty, dusty glass that separates life from death I tried to catch a glimpse of Mommy's features as she lay on the table under a sheet with strips of bandages fastening her lower jaw to the rest of her head—an apparatus which I saw as some kind of pair of headphones or protective spacesuit for her journey into those regions she had studied in the *Bardo Thodol*...

A bitter station on the way from nowhere to nowhere...

Domodedovskaya Station

ZAMOSKVORETSKAYA LINE

My Grandma—whom I spoke of earlier—arrived then, to take Mommy's body and bury it in Siberia. Uncle Gleb and I met her at the station, having made the following arrangements with her by phone: "You'll recognize me by your grandson. I'll be standing by the central notice board with a Negro."

Grandma turned out to be a stony-faced old woman without a headscarf, her flat half-gray hair scooped into two tangled plaits. She walked, swaying from side to side, and because of her gait, her boots took on the air of slippers hastily thrown onto her feet. She was carrying a canvas bundle that was both stuck together with tape and tied up with a clothesline.

I didn't know how to behave as she approached, and so I stood, hiding slightly behind Uncle Gleb, but she gazed at me with penetrating eyes as she came and finally exclaimed, "Well, you said you'd be with a little Negro—you must be Gleb!"

Uncle Gleb obediently stepped forward to greet her, snatching her heavy bag away, and I remained where I stood, until Grandma asked:

"And you, do you speak Russian?"

I nodded. Then she laid her heavy, fleshy hand on my head and said, as though she'd just remembered: "Ah, you're an orphan!'"

Uncle Gleb was fawning all over her now; I had never seen him so ingratiating.

"We have to take the metro, Mom, and then the bus... It's about half an hour... Hope you won't get too tired."

159

She didn't respond, but she ruffled my wiry hair with interest and continued: "Maybe I should take you with me. There's never been a Negro in our Siberia."

I shrank under her hand, but even more so under the weight of the decision. I didn't want to go anywhere, to leave Moscow, the city with my Mommy's name, where she gave birth to me, where she brought me up, and where, finally, she died without me...

"Well, let's go. Lead me to this metro!" The old lady took command in a familiar way, and I slipped out from under her fat fingers. Crossing the square in front of the green Aeroflot building, we hurried off to the underground. I walked in front without glancing back at her as she waddled beside Uncle Gleb, bent double.

Across buzzing Leningrad Prospekt, I saw my ruby letter *M*, like a good-luck charm, spreading its legs wide, like Grandma, for eternal stability. It was as if the letter was standing with its arms folded across its chest, asserting the city's right to me, despite whatever this old lady might think, and I hurried toward that spaghetti junction.

It all began when the station doors, after a sudden gust of wind, swung back and whacked into Grandma with all their might. As she clutched her bloody nose, Uncle Gleb, playing the simpleton, was more overcome than anyone. Sensing he had overplayed his eager helpfulness, he now tried to be rather more detached and intelligent, which only made him all the more absurd.

"I hope you haven't hurt yourself... Here's a hankie..."

Soon enough, Grandma tripped again, this time on the stairs leading into the main hall, and once again she took a tumble, cursing that cursed Moscow and its accursed underground...

And down on the platform, where people who had flown from all corners of the Union were bustling around the Aeroflot counter, Grandma didn't manage to squeeze herself into the train car in time, and the doors squashed her so that Uncle Gleb and another two men had to try to pry them open and drag the whole of her into the car while the train was already moving. Sweaty, out of breath, in her increasing fright, she looked like a real witch or Baba Yaga in her long coat.

It was then I realized that this kingdom was mine, that it was on my side, and if need be, it would protect me, defend me, avenge me...

Vodny Stadion Station
ZAMOSKVORETSKAYA LINE

I would like to tell you a story, completely unrelated to that day or to my grandma, which was told to me by Uncle Nazar. He had studied, as you may remember, at the MVD Academy at Voykovskaya Station, and as I have said before (and as he never failed to remind me), he was an excellent sportsman. But that day when Mommy and I went to visit him at Sheremetyevo Airport, in that restaurant, in the secluded police corner, he told Mommy a story that changed my perception of him and I felt truly sorry for him.

It went like this. At the Academy there was a midterm competition, a police triathlon: pull-ups on a bar, pistol shooting, and cross-country skiing. Well, in shooting and pull-ups no one even came close to Uncle Nazar, but it turned out he had never in his life stood on skis. He was from an arid region where snow was only a fable. But the captain calculated that if Uncle Nazar did as well as he should in the first two rounds, and simply showed up on the ski run, he would still bring in more points than the most experienced skier. So Uncle Nazar grabbed a pen and paper to work out how long it would take him to cover the distance even if he just tucked the skis under his arm and ran those five kilometers of the track. Not more than an hour! "Well, that's exactly the required time!" exclaimed the captain, and so the matter was settled.

The next day, Uncle Nazar excelled on the bar and on the shooting range in the morning, and in the afternoon they were sent off from Voykovskaya to Vodny Stadion Station, where the course had been mapped out along the frozen canal.

The contestants suited up in the changing rooms, where they were told to wrap their groins particularly well so they didn't freeze their "manly worth" (which, Uncle Nazar commented, happens quite often) and were called to the starting line on the river.

Uncle Nazar tried to stand up on his skis, copying the others, as they lined up on the flattened snow, which tapered into a single-file track. And you know what happened? His feet didn't slide apart, and the skis didn't slide one on top of the other, but Uncle Nazar figured the skis would right themselves as he went along. Everything pointed to success.

"Ready! Set!" The gunshot rang out and the skiers lurched onto the run. Uncle Nazar lurched too, but it was here things went awry: either one ski would slide over the other; or they'd slide off in opposite directions, his legs in a split; or his poles would get tangled with his skis, or his legs, or each other...

So Uncle Nazar threw off his safety catches, tucked the skis under his arm, and set out spryly over the trampled snow. He set off at a good stride—might as well, he thought—but no sooner had he reached the track than he began to sink into the soft snow. With a squelch, his leg plunged down into the snow up to his knee, and when he tried to pull it out, his other leg, with the same velocity, submerged to keep it company. Uncle Nazar realized he should lean on the skis, and somehow or other he scrambled out to fasten the safety catches to his boots again. Struggling to keep his balance, he stood up straight and tried, very carefully, for half a step, to slide one ski forward. "OK..." he told himself. "Now, bring your center of gravity over that ski, and do the same with the other ski..."

And so, half a step at a time, he moved forward. The other competitors had long since disappeared from view, just as the judges had disappeared into the changing rooms to thaw out over coffee, and only lone Uncle Nazar remained, moving slowly ahead to meet the piercing wind on the snow-white desert of Vodny Stadion. The cross-country contestants soon began to reappear, one after the other, already on their way back. "Is it far to the turning point?" Uncle Nazar asked his classmate through frozen lips.

"A couple of kilometers..." one called out, as he hurried back toward the finish line. To be fair to Uncle Nazar, I have to point out that he didn't cut corners, but honestly grappled right up to the flag at the turning point (and by then the long, blue shadows of dusk had set in), where, undaunted, either with a second wind or maybe out of fear of staying on the ski track over night, he charged out on the way back.

By that point, he wasn't doing too badly on his skis, and even when one of them glided a bit too far ahead, he managed to hang on, lifting his second ski over the snow like a white heron. After spending another hour on the way back (and by then in darkness, guided fortunately by the flattened single-file ski track), he finally made it to the finish line.

Of course, there was no one left. There was no one in the changing rooms, as everyone had already finished their showers and beer. The judges had left a note on the door, though, with instructions on to how to lock up and where to leave the keys. One of his good-natured classmates had left his unfinished bottle of Zhigulevskoe, but Uncle Nazar was drunk enough without it. He had just enough strength to get changed, without washing, and it wasn't until he was sitting on a bench at Vodny Stadion Station, not remembering which direction to go, that he felt once more that he was alive, and that he was in Moscow...

And now, passing through that station, where we stopped for a moment, I peeked out of the open doors and into a gap between the wood-grained pillars that looks like a long ski track. Isn't that Uncle Nazar, walking along or sitting down, left behind and abandoned? Uncle Nazar who I always thought of as the Akhal-Teke stallion...

Rechnoy Vokzal Station

But that's not what I wanted to talk about. I wanted to change the world of the Moscow metro, my kingdom, which belonged to me. I wanted to change it so that every time you were there, you would look at every station through my eyes, you would smell the smell of each station through my nostrils and know by heart where I cried; where I threw up; where my grandfather, Colonel Rzhevsky, cut me off; where my insolent grandmother was punished; where I am still sitting in my Mommy Moscow's arms, coated in black bronze that doesn't tarnish...

The metro is my innards: my thoughts, my experiences, my life, my cavities, my veins, my arteries. If you cut me open on the operating table, you wouldn't find blue veins and red arteries, but the multicolored web of the Moscow metro stations.

These were my thoughts as we came closer and closer to the final stop on our journey, Rechnoy Vokzal Station, and I regretted that I couldn't admit this to my Mommy, the late Moscow. But then, I thought, what would have changed if I had told her all of that? What could those secrets change in the old lady, my so-called grandma, who had plopped down on the seat and fallen peacefully asleep to the rhythm of the wheels, another echo of my heartbeat. If she wanted to, she would take me, together with the body of my dead Mommy—still lying in the morgue with a bandaged jaw—to her Khakassian lands, not understanding that I might be more Russian than the most deep-rooted Russian; after all, it is as if these lines were dedicated to me, the very lines that I have recited ever since I was a baby, by saying a prayer and shielding spell at bedtime:

> *My hour of freedom, is it coming?*
> *I call to it: it's time, it's time!*
> *Above the sea, forever roaming,*
> *I beckon every sail and clime.*

(*Eugene Onegin*, I:50)

1988 Assonance

suddenly feeling that you won't be
in this world any more, but that this fir tree
will still be alive in ten years time and in the depths
of the earth, into which, year after year,
this one tree is growing and is crowding
toward the cut in its rings;
the warmth of your hand will be left...
so it seems...

Medvedkovo Station
KALUZHSKO-RIZHSKAYA LINE

There is a certain unrealness, an irreality, in a Moscow summer. The green of the leaves and of the grass is somehow tinged with the chill of forest bogs, and because of that the shadows of the limp lime trees are fudged as though the sun were only halfheartedly pretending to shine, incapable of painting the shadows clearly. The heat remains somewhere high up and far off, on the sidelines, so that only a cheerless light reaches the ground. You can recognize this pretense of a Moscow summer particularly if you go to the true south—Koktebel in July, or Pitsunda in August. Those were my sunny Africas, where Uncle Gleb took me as an orphan on a free trip organized by Ada Efimovna from the Litfund; she still remembered my Mommy Moscow.

There the sun shone without shame, and my skin sang like a red-hot drum.

"Mbobo," said Uncle Gleb, forgetting that I was still "Little Pushkin" to him.

"Mbobo," he called me, by the tender nickname left as an inheritance from Mommy.

"Mbobo, now you're a real Negro! Blow me, but I'll bet all those old farts will write about you in their repor—no, no—books!" Lying on the red-hot Pitsunda sand mixed with gravel, he spread his arm and traced the whole seaboard: all, all!

I told you, didn't I, that although the name on my birth certificate is Kirill, ever since I was a baby Mommy had called me

Mbobo, because of my fat lips, the color of my skin, a certain prenatal nasality, and that's why in my own eyes I was much more a Mbobo than a Kirill. When someone called me Kirill, in keeping with my papers, I always had the feeling they were trying to goad me.

All the members of the Pitsunda High Society—Fasil Iskander, Anatoli Pristavkin and the Chiladze brothers—called me Mbobo, although Tamaz Chiladze very politely called me Mbobo Glebovitch. Between us, I would have preferred either simply Mbobo, or Kirill Glebovitch, but it's not polite to correct an elder. The Chiladze brothers and Nodar Khundadze took us on the local bus one day to a wine tasting at the Cherkesski gorge.

Ah, that road, snaking up the gorge! There was hardly room for the bus's wheels, with the wall of the tree-lined mountains on one side of us and the sheer drop on the other, where a stream bubbled and gurgled below. It was as though all the Caucasian poetry of Pushkin and Lermontov were entwined in one braid here, like the Aragva and Kura rivers, and a tiny little bus joined them, crawling beetle-like, higher and higher. At last, a scooped-out valley opened up beyond a turnoff. There was a small farm with little wooden houses, and we sped into a green woody yard where the beetle's buzzing engine choked. In the deafening silence, a Georgian lumberjack, a shiftless loner, came to meet us and without further ado, he led us straight to the huge wooden table that stood in front of his cabin in the dappled shade of a nut tree.

"Well, well, well. You've brought the god of wine with you, I see," he said, eyeing me, and the elder Chiladze introduced me: "This is Mbobo Glebovitch!"

"What a Georgian name!" said our host, waving his arms and spreading his hands as Georgians do. He proposed a toast to the Georgian in each of us.

Still breathless after the journey, everyone drank his special wine, which went by the name of Isabella. We drank to Isabella, then simply to Bella, then to Gleb Mbobovitch, to Fazil the Abkhaz, to Otar the Georgian, to Akhyar the Tartar, to Iva the French—in short, to everyone, including the driver Datiko, his dog, the roasted sweet corn we were eating, the nut tree we were sitting under, the earth where we lived...

We drank, saying, "Now we're mocking old Gorbachev." We drank a lot but it was a happy kind of drunkenness, like that sun-dappled forest high in the mountains, not the heavy drunkenness of Moscow. Remorseful and confessional, Uncle Gleb cried on the shoulders of the Jews or Gorbuntsov the Russian, all of whom nodded their wise heads in understanding.

We spent the night there in Cherkesski gorge and, early in the morning, after a breakfast of hot flatbreads and salty cheese, when our beetle had started snaking down the mountain road, just as we were coming to the main road, we were stopped by machine-gunners.

Then another group stopped us, just one kilometer farther along on the River Bzib, then another... I didn't understand a thing: they would just make me get out, shout something in either Georgian or in Abkhazian, and then for some reason they would make Iva the Frenchman say something in French, and for some reason they'd let us continue on to the next group of armed people.

We didn't reach the House of Creativity until nightfall, and the next morning we hurriedly packed our suitcases and drove off to Adler, and from there we took a plane to Moscow.

No, none of those famous people wrote anything about me. Now, sitting at Medvedkovo Station with my classmates on a summer Moscow evening, I realize that they used me, a black boy, as their white flag... but at least we got out alive...

The buses and streetcars are going in the direction of Bibirevo, but we still sit here under the station sign, swinging our legs, and watch the slow, indigo sky over the two nine-story blocks of apartments—one sideways, the other lengthwise—across the street and watch as a light goes on here and there, and I think the Russians keep Pushkin as a mascot only because he played neither the clown nor the holy fool, and in that respect he was unprecedented: ideal, as no Russian could be. Maybe that's why, I thought, broken Uncle Gleb kept me as a mascot—an unprecedented Russian because I cannot play a part either, although—like it or not—as far appearance goes, I am plainly a monkey, Mbobo...

And not only is there something surreal in the Moscow summer, but in the Russian character too. And so it was that Uncle Gleb—who was quite unlike Pushkin—became friends with Uncle Nazar after the death of my Mommy, who had belonged to them both and at the same time...

Rizhsky Railway Station
and Rizhskaya Station
Kaluzhsko-Rizhskaya Line

I probably didn't read the *Tibetan Book of the Dead* attentively enough when I snuck it from my dead mother's bedside table. Or the blackness of my forty days prevented me from joining with the light and saving my soul. It was not that I chose the dull light deliberately, but rather that I simply failed to put any effort into uniting with the pure, bright white light.

It was as Annensky had written: "because with her, there was no need for any light..."

And so I lie here now, forgotten by the light, in the crumbly Moscow earth, waiting for what shall befall me, the disregarded one. And what will? Will it happen according to the *Bardo Thodol* that governs my mother's bloodline, or shall Erlik mold from me—the bespittled one—a cockerel who he shall release up to the surface at night to tease the machine-gunners?

Or maybe my father will pay back with interest what he couldn't give me on this earth: instead of some civilized Ereshkigal, an unknown African god will possess my dry little carcass, until it dawns on someone on the surface to swap, let's say, their freedom for it? But the earth here is neither Tibetan nor Ethiopian after all, but Moscovite, so who knows? Maybe I am—given my late Grandpa Rzhevsky's heritage—under the jurisdiction of the Slavic queen of the underworld, Marena, the wife of the Black God Chernobog, the ruler of Nav, which stands against both Yav and Prav?

In short, it's a complete muddle, and the godless maggots and insects of the deep earth make the most of it to dig around in my emptied bones and scraps... One thing gives me pause, cause for concern: that in the muddle of my homelessness, my unbelonging, I might somehow not be forgotten, left behind for eternity, like an unregistered person, a person off the books. But against the advice of my Mommy's *Bardo Thodol*—and I remember now that Uncle Gleb never called her Moscow but always Mara—I cling to my earthly memories, hoping that, somehow, someone will notice me in this empty and lonely Nav...

Since this morning I have been remembering Rizhskaya Station in minute detail. Maybe because the inside of that station is the most like the inside of my coffin, whose walls have begun to give off a dull yellowish light with time; phosphorous particles, having left my bones, linger in the red silks of the internal upholstery. Rizhskaya glows with the same dull yellowish light. In its pillars and arches was the false simplicity of a Catholic cathedral, not a Baltic one, but a Prussian or German one. Banned from the world above, in the realm of Yav, temples and synagogues, mosques and churches, chapels and cathedrals rose in the underground realm of Nav, and people prayed, recited poems and hymns, and belonged to themselves and to God, despite what was going on up on the surface, in that other world above...

The benches in Rizhskaya Station were set into cell-like alcoves, ready to receive confessions, and the lighting on the ceiling was arranged in such a way that the shadows fell onto the carriages, turning darkness into something sinister, urging the poor flock to sit a bit longer in their loneliness and alienation, under the lights of the underground cathedral.

I remember the icy marble of the floor, deadening the footsteps, echoing solemnly, as though each one trod on you, along with your fate, and then passed by...

But maybe I am remembering Rizhskaya Station on this August morning because that is where we left from that June, coming out of the cupola of the underground building, crossing the square with its hawkers and going right up to Moscow's most Russian building, Rizhsky railway station. We set off to Mikhailovskoe for the celebration of Pushkin's anniversary. That year has remained in my memory as the year Uncle Gleb took me with him on all his trips, like a pet or an appendage, like a...

I don't know why he became so attached to me after the death of my Mommy Moscow; did he love his magnanimity or was he competing in kindness with Uncle Nazar? Or did he consider himself the Master, fashioning an apprentice, a new "Pushkin, old chap" by the name of Mbobo? It could have been anything, but surely it wasn't in memory of my late mother, nor out of attachment to me. Of that I was certain—like any sober apprentice of a drunken master.

Kolkhoznaya Station
KALUZHSKO-RIZHSKAYA LINE

That August Uncle Gleb—and I with him—moved from the Left Bank to within the perimeter of Moscow, on the other side of the Ring Line, to Leskov Street in Bibirevo. Now it was not my school or the yards and woods on Green Street that I missed most of all; they had those things here in Bibirevo, too. No, it was the River Moscow that I missed more than anything. Nowhere in Moscow, or the Moscow region, can you find banks to match those we'd abandoned, so much fun to sled down in winter, such joy to roll though the grass and flowers in summer, to walk along the river to the very last sluice in autumn...

But now, all that was gone. That August we would go for a walk in Lianosov Park (where, by the way, Stalin once had a dacha) or we would wander through the Bibirevo Woods to the Pioneers' House (where Voroshilov had once resided), but there was always something missing. And I realized that the breeze had no river freshness, no barge ever tooted, no one ever waved from a passing steamer... Our street was no longer Green, and we traded our green metro line for orange, arid and alien. But maybe I just missed my Mommy?

Her presence was everywhere—in each station, each interchange, each tunnel. It was as though, if you stared a bit, she would come out from behind the haystack-like pillars of Kolkhoznaya Station. I circled one, then a second. A third, a fourth... tied tight in the middle, the sheaves stood tensely, either hiding or revealing. A fifth, a sixth... but she was not there. Not there.

Uncle Gleb and I would go up to the surface and out into the emptiness of the street where we would be met by lonely Uncle Nazar, who was also missing something. After handing me over to Uncle Nazar, Uncle Gleb would take himself to the *Literary Gazette* office, while we would take our place on the street, lining up to buy fruit.

Even out of uniform Uncle Nazar couldn't bear disorder; he was constantly driven to control the line, though no one ever authorized him to do it. He would vigorously drive away the merely curious: "I wonder what they're selling here?" They would push their way closer and then—God forbid!—might even worm their way to the front of the line, hoping, perhaps, to pass unnoticed. That's when Uncle Nazar would swing into action. He would loudly command, "Kirill, keep our place!" and then set off to purge the troublemakers. With blessings or curses from his sweltering fellow citizens, he would lead those "sneaky bastards" to the end of the line, if they were lucky, or toss them out altogether!

Waiting in line riled him to no end. Even after filling his bag with fruit, it took a long time to calm down, showering curses and abuse on those hapless "shit bags."

I had a game that I could use for any line. I would look at the people behind and in front of me and imagine what this one or that one might have been, for example, in the court of Ivan the Terrible. That dried-up old man, with his hair carefully combed back like the academic Likhachev, would have been a deacon; the devious guy with glasses who looked like Mister Gimalayask served in the treasury; that fleshy woman would have worked in the laundry; that rascal would have done time in the prison tower; and Uncle Nazar would have been the executioner!

Everyone was given not a temporary but an eternal worth. And me, well, I would have been a Negro, a monkey, a jester...

Kirov Railway Station

My guts are being eaten away by an unknown insect with a perfectly rounded belly and uneven antennae, its little feet bristling out in all directions; it gnaws, gnaws away. I grab it by one little leg, pinching tightly on one spot, thinking: "Aha! Got you! Now you're in my hands!"

But no, the insect crawls out and starts once again to burrow into my innards. And I grab its belly, round like a circus ring, or an antenna, and again I dangle it in front of my eyes.

That reminds me of Uncle Gleb's lice hunt. One day at my new school was enough for me to catch lice, and so Uncle Gleb—who strangely enough had no women or visitors around that day—plucked the insects out of my hair and put them on a white sheet of paper, catching them with his fingernails by their round, bursting bellies, full of my blood. Having squished a dozen, he got tired of groping through my coarse curls and suggested we go to the hairdresser and shave it all off.

We went out of our block and winded our way between the other blocks, finally emerging on Muranovskaya Street where we took our place in line for the hairdresser. First, Uncle Gleb got his own hair cut so as not to arouse suspicion, then asked her to shave my head next.

The hairdresser was shocked: why shave such a mass of curls, like Angela Davis's?! But Uncle Gleb blamed the hot summer, and the hairdresser began to shear my curls with her electric razor. Having shorn half my head, she suddenly let out a squeal: "Lice!" and flung the razor to the floor.

"Lice!" she shrieked, her voice carrying through the whole salon.

"You should have stayed in Africa and not come down from the trees!"

At first I didn't understand what Africa had to do with lice or trees, but as Uncle Gleb grabbed my hand, I understood that she was referring to me, not to the lice. Everyone was shouting, scolding, chasing us out, and we retreated: with my half-shaved head, Uncle Gleb fully humiliated...

Back home, Uncle Gleb first read the *Handbook of Home Medicine*, then went downstairs to get some petrol from the neighbors who had a car. Then he made me wash my hair with that disgusting stuff and then again and again with household soap. Having dried my half-hair with the hair dryer, he started to lop my curls off with a pair of scissors. When every inch of the bathroom was covered with my hair, he once again made me smear my head with household soap, and he shaved my head with his safety razor, changing blade after blade.

If Mommy could have seen me she would have died back into this world from that other one. But fine, lice can be drowned, if not with kerosene then with petrol, and if not at the hairdresser's then with a simple razor at home. But how do you get rid of this unknown insect, crawling through the darkness, with a round belly, antennae of different length, legs that bristle out in different directions? How do you get rid of the insect growing inside me?

1989 Lota

There is a measure for everything: for words—the pay phone;
for absence—weeks, kilometers;
for poems—meter; only the faint dream of what "tomorrow" will be,
the immeasurability of death,
everything looks for a measure and finds only the dream...

Sokol Station

I remember what is, to me, one of the most beautiful metro stations in Moscow—Sokol—and instead of describing its beauty in verse, I want absolute precision in my description: a long discourse on the nature of the Soviet metro.

Looking with the mind's eye at the irreproachable geometric form of the station, at the two perfect petal-like conjugates, tying themselves in the flower of the cupola, I thought about how the metro is the subconscious of Soviet building; its collective unconscious, its archetype. What was left unrealized—or never fully realized—on the surface was achieved underground. Here, the masses are totally ordered within the bounds of time and space, and the flow of those masses is strictly regimented according to an elegant blueprint, like the robotic, round-bellied insects, moving inexorably through the darkness with a dozen little iron legs and feelers; above them, the omnipresent spider of the Party or the GPU-KGB, with hundreds of tiny eyes on each leg, on each feeler. The exit is fixed, the entrance is fixed; all loose ends are tied up.

There, in the metro, prevailed the purely communist principle that money meant nothing. Down there, you couldn't spend it on anything; there, a person was worth what he was himself meant to be worth, beyond monetary units...

But the whole of that totally controlled system could only exist at a remove from the world. It was as if it had been taken out of the equation, deleted from the face of the earth; it existed and at the same time remained invisible; the ideal was achieved, yet it remained otherworldly.

The construction of such magnificent stations as Sokol amid the maggoty darkness was a subconscious hint the heavenly homeliness of life, albeit underground, in the very place where hell is generally supposed to be—but it was only a hint. In other words, Communism was being built in experimental circumstances underground, far from the hostile eye of Sputnik, so in that respect, I would dare to venture that the best museum of Communism and the Soviets is the Moscow metro, and one of the crowning glories of that museum is Sokol Station.

Such were my thoughts in the June idleness of my underground realm, regarding with my two empty eye sockets that most elegant line of the conjugate of the station's two clover leaves, the third petal the cupola of my white skull...

Mayakovskaya Station

I know you will argue with me on this, insisting that Mayakovsky Station is the museum's crowning glory. And you may be right, but let me say it lacks the mathematical beauty of Sokol Station; as I stood on the balcony, Lobachevsky's elegant lines overcame me with their loveliness. Mayakovsky Station is simpler and grander. If you were to transpose these stations into poetry, I would compare Sokol with Mandelstam or Akhmatova (as we are speaking of two petals), although I must say that in general Mayakovsky's station doesn't have much in common with his poetry. For me, at least, his poetry is far more varied and rich than the famous mosaics in the cupolas—which are, of course, monothematic in their depictions of flight— from the airplane, to the parachute, to the ski jump, and even over to the high jump. Flight and Mayakovsky?

Well, Mayakovsky has clouds, and clouds in pants, too... Perhaps, then, the idea behind the station's ornamentation—to bring all possible types of flight underground—is predictably paradoxical and makes a compromise with Mayakovsky's more buffoonish side?

I don't know. Or maybe I am just being picky because no matter how far I dig around in my mosaic of memories, I simply cannot for the life of me remember being at that station with my Mommy Moscow.

Yes, we went to the youth cinema with Uncle Gleb, but how did we end up in the Tchaikovsky Concert Hall? After all, I remember the rustle of evening dresses, and the formal velvet of the seats, and the patterns carved around the circular hall, and the music, the music that rang out there! One day we heard Schnittke there, that piece with the banal tango-style part when Alla Pugacheva was supposed to appear, that year she was singing about birds being drawn downward...

I remember the fitful mosaic of that music, I remember Mommy uttering the intriguing phrase, "It's like I've paid off all my debts," in the intermission, and for a long time I couldn't make sense of that—at home we always had notes on the fridge along the lines of:

> *Georgii Vladimirovich—1200 (will wait till end of year)*
> *Irina Konstantinovna—500 (with the advance from Art & Lit)*
> *Masha—300 (article in "Sov. Lit.")*
> *Katya (typist)—250 (urgent)*
> *Katya (neighbor)—50 (till next wage packet)*
> *French teacher—50 (borrow from someone else)*

These little notes would change every two or three months; that is, the names would change, and the amounts, but the list remained on the side of the fridge.

If I were to compare this station with another work of Russian art, I would compare it with Tchaikovsky's Fifth Symphony, which was performed in the second half of that concert. I felt with all my soul how monotonously diverse it was, how voice by voice it soars up in an unbearably loud common movement only to hide again behind a lone voice, a melody, an instrument and then raise up again in the frenzied choir of the orchestra... It shouldn't be performed in the Tchaikovsky Concert Hall, but in the hall of Mayakovsky's metro station...

Such was our life with Uncle Gleb while Mommy was alive: in the morning we would take quiet paths either to the Art &

Literature publishing house on New Basmann Street, where it was just a stone's throw from the skyscraper at the station to the nameless little river, long since confined underground. We would spend a day or a half-day there, taking a tour of the offices or getting stuck in the iron elevator; if we were lucky, we would get some money on the first floor, cajoled, rightly or wrongly, as an advance.

Then came the ritual drinking in honor of that money, then and there in the publishers' canteen, after which everything would snowball in the usual way and would end at home in the next knife fight, with shrieking and swearing, in flight to the neighbor's with frozen feet, waiting for rampaging Uncle Gleb to fall into a drunken slumber. He would wake up to the guilty morning, washing the shame from his face with cold water, and then he would lead me along other quiet side streets to the offices of *Our Contemporary* or *Speed-Info...*

That is how the symphony of our lives sounded, in its monotonous diversity, as it rolled along on the rails of the underground and the paths of the surface.

And I remember pawnbrokers too, a word that had remained in Soviet traditions since the NEP years of Mayakovsky. Even Uncle Nazar, having taken up with my good-for-nothing Mommy Moscow, contributed his officer's boots, valued at no more than fifty rubles. How he praised them, trying to get at least seventy-five, but the appraiser heard nothing of it, showing him her price list, with its mysterious articles and stamps.

Uncle Gleb was simpler. When things got really desperate, he would open up the kitchen cabinets and gather all the empty bottles, where spiders and their spider-wives had set up house. He would wash them for a long time and then, with a canvas bag over his shoulder, he would set out for the grocer's or wherever they would take champagne and Pepsi bottles without sorting, and he would enrich himself by one or one and a half rubles so that he could continue Tchaikovsky's symphony...

Stop and listen next time you are at Mayakovsky's Station and you will hear it: keeping time with the symphony's rhythm, you will hear the lone voice of a startled passenger, then a distant beat coming closer, filling all the space right up to the mosaic on the heavenly cupola; a great number of people pour out in a polyphonic movement, the multitude gathered together as one, and suddenly it all dissolves and you are left alone, like a pause, like a cause, like the first sound of a new splash, a new sob, a new howl...

Gorkovskaya-Chekhovskaya Station
SERPUKHOVSKO-TIMIRYAZEVSKAYA LINE

In the first years after my mother's death I used to run away from home a lot, whether "home" was Uncle Gleb's apartment on Bibirevo Road or Uncle Nazar's place in that block in the Arbat, still destined for destruction. Things I could put up with from my two stepfathers while Mommy was alive now got under my skin so badly that the only answer was to leave the house. In a flood of tears I would head out to the schoolyard, where the abandoned children remained for their after-school classes, or some stubborn student who was repeating a grade played football or handball; I stayed there with my bitterness until the evening.

Then I would head to the center, to Uncle Nazar on the Arbat. It was a long journey: by bus to Voikovskaya Station, studying either Altufevskoe Chausee or Great Academic Street, Coptevsky Alley or some other; then I would take the metro and shoot off to Gorkovskaya Station, where I sometimes went outside to gaze at the black bronze statue of my colleague Pushkin, lit up with floodlights in the darkness, and after gazing at the ads outside the Rossiya cinema, I'd make my way back down into the newly renovated Chekhovskaya Station, now ashen where Gorky was granite, but otherwise painfully similar. But that June, when all the land, and all of Moscow, was living through the theater of the first Congress of National Deputies, Gleb and Nazar united in a consensus so I couldn't run away from either one to the other.

One long evening, I managed to distract Uncle Gleb away from the speech Andrei Sakharov was giving at the Party Congress, by asking for my compass, which he used to dig around in his rotten teeth, and he suddenly exploded, saying I was just a hooligan like my mother, who never thought of anyone else, and that if I kept going I would end up just like her... I walked off to my room while he was still yelling, but he yanked the door open and yelled something about my thick, black skin. Then, slamming the door, he went back to the television and his Sakharov. From then on, he became "the damned Gleb."

I cried my heart out, and when the fire in my chest had subsided—though my face was still red hot—I quietly went to the kitchen, washed my face, put my sneakers on and slipped out. I wanted to avoid the clanging elevator so I took the stairs, which stank of mice and cockroaches, and went outside.

The sun just couldn't quite set; it kept rolling and rolling along the edge of the earth, somewhere far beyond the next huge block of apartments. I wandered to the schoolyard. Sitting on the only bench, swinging his legs, was my classmate Vanka Korenovsky, who had no father. We sat together for a bit, mostly in silence, until two older boys from the senior class appeared: Serioga Demin, nicknamed Kirsa, and another I didn't know. They chased us off the bench, but just as we were about to leave the yard, Kirsa called to Vanka, and then to me. "Pushkin! Wanna smoke?" Vanka nodded because he had nothing better to do, and I tagged along for company.

"Pushkin, cover me," the second one ordered, and I was surprised he knew me or my nickname. I didn't like his familiarity, but I stood in front of him. He took out a *papirosa* cigarette and began carefully shaking the tobacco out onto his palm, twirling the cigarette paper with his fingers. Once all the tobacco had fallen out, Kirsa took a small black pellet with a sharp, spicy smell from his pocket, crumbled it into even smaller little balls and then mixed that whole concoction on his other palm. Then he stood Vanka in front of him, looked around and began extending the papirosa paper like a telescope. It expanded but didn't fall apart, and Kirsa began pushing the tobacco back in. After each push he tapped the end of the papirosa gently. Kirsa rolled the paper between his fingers so the tobacco spread evenly throughout the paper. When it was all back inside, Kirsa twisted the end shut, making a little cigar, while the other guy lit a match.

I was afraid they were playing a trick on us, maybe putting gunpowder in the cigarette so it'd blow up when we smoked it, but Kirsa took a long, deep pull on it himself. Then he gave it to his friend, exhaling smoke. It had a mild smell like the Indian incense my mother used to burn on Sundays. The second guy also inhaled to the bottom of his lungs, sleepily closing his eyes, and holding his breath before exhaling loudly: "Go on, Pushkin!"

I had never smoked before. Just once, drunk Uncle Gleb had thrust his Prima into my mouth, and I'd nearly choked to death coughing, so I hesitated. But when Vanka pushed in front of me and squealed, "He's a nerd, always gets good grades—" I grabbed the cigarette and with a sinking heart, copied what Kirsa had done. To my surprise the smoke was gentle and enveloping, like cough medicine. It wrapped my lungs in sweetness, and a warmth spread through my body, not letting that smoke go out again.

I inhaled deeply again and it sent my head spinning, making me feel light, weightless, and carefree. Something made me want to laugh, to be happy as if Mommy had returned with her incense. As though her death were only a smoke curtain that I only needed to exhale and then...

I had never felt such relief—I felt like I had on seven-league boots: one step, and I didn't remember where I had left Vanka

Korenovsky, Kirsa, and that third guy who called after me repeatedly: "Pushkin! Puuuushhkiiin!" Another step and I was back in my underground realm; one more and I was at either Gorkovskaya Station or Chekhovskaya, not knowing whether I was in the deepest of my lower depths or soaring like a seagull...

Returning to earth at the knot of these stations, I remembered that Uncle Nazar—now "treacherous Nazar"—would be unlikely to let me in, and if he did, with his cop's nose he'd sniff out that I'd been smoking, and out of goodness he would hand me over to some inspectorate or other for observation and reeducation...

There was one other place I could go: to Irina Rodionovna, who had delivered me, though she usually went away at the beginning of June to Kislovodsk or Pyatigorsk in the Caucasus for a mud spa. With these unconsoling thoughts I roamed aimlessly from one station to another, mingling first with this crowd, then with that one, so as not to fall under the gaze of either the station staff or the policemen who were already tipsy and therefore boorish. From Borovitsky Station, where the arches are bent over so sharply they're at their breaking point, to the cosmic hangar of Biblioteka Imeni Lenina Station to the elegant chambers and compressed columns of the Arbat stations and then circling around again.

The clock was already moving toward midnight: Lenin's readers had long since gone home, smelling of scholarly sweat. Following them were the cinema-goers who'd been at the evening showings at the Arbat cinemas, the late-night tourists and shoppers from Borovitsky, the night owl habitués of the Praga restaurant. The crowd was thinning, and I still didn't know where I should take myself in my condition. "It's hard for a person when he has nowhere to go," I remembered this phrase from a book, and I tasted its unbookish bitterness. My empty kingdom was pushing me to the surface.

But just then a train pulled in, its doors opened, and a re-hearsed voice uttered the customary phrase: "Dear passengers, please vacate the cars. The train is heading to the depot." The driver walked past, glancing into the empty cars, and once he had moved down two cars, I made up my mind. I squeezed through the closing doors at one end of the car, lifted up the three-person seat, and dived into the empty box under it.

I could faintly hear the doors closing, but the rails knocked much more clearly, right under my body, spreading through the metal belly of the carriage. The train traveled for a long time, the doors opened again, someone hastily breezed through with a Hoover while I hunched myself into a little ball like a little mouse on the cold, cold metal. Then it got completely dark, not a glimmer of light came through the cracks, and I cautiously raised the seat a little and looked out. The deathly silence of the night depot was all around.

I clambered out of my hidey-hole and decided to spend the night right there, on this three-person seat at the end of the car. It was a bit hard to lie on, and chilly, too. I tossed around from side to side for a long time but just couldn't fall asleep. So then I got up and dragged over another hard seat cushion, just the same as mine, from the seat opposite, put it face down on top of my lair, and burrowed my way in between the two seats. That stiff, unbending cushion was so heavy that where it touched my body (thankfully, only at a few points—chest, thighs, knees) I started to sweat, while the rest of my body froze in the un-believable draft...

I don't remember falling asleep but I remember waking up with a sudden jolt as the train pulled away and the hard cushion slipped from my body, which was stiff with cold, and crashed to the floor. I jumped up, put the cushion back in its place, and quickly flattened myself on the floor under the seat, and it was only when the train, which was gathering speed, pulled into the first station that, with a fearfully pounding heart, I sat right in the corner where I'd spent the night as the very first passenger, an old lady with a bundle, got on, and, seeing me, crossed herself for some reason and scurried off to the far end of the car. But I only traveled as far as the next station, where I went out into the light...

Kirov Railway Station and Turgenevskaya Station
Kaluzhsko-Rizhskaya Line

There are some stations that you cannot avoid; Kirov and Turgenev are two of them. But it's not as though I, or we, were in the area often—except for when we went to those shameful modeling sessions in the studio near Clean Ponds, from which a few sketches and drafts given to Mommy still remained; drawings that crawled out of hiding after her death and embarrassed me all over again. Gleb didn't know I had taken them into the yard one day, torn them into tiny pieces and burned them. Then, still unsatisfied, I had buried the ashes in the ground...

I didn't know surface Moscow at all, apart from some very limited sections. Or rather, the picture of Moscow I have retained in my consciousness I knew only in pieces: the bit between one station and another or the areas just around the stations themselves. So I never knew where Kirov Street led, but if Mommy wanted, say, some real coffee, we would emerge at a specific station, walk to the café, do our shopping and then plunge back into our metro. By the way, that very place just so happens to be on Kirov Street.

Or let's take another example: I have already told you how much time I spent with drunken Gleb on New Basmann Street at the Art & Literature publishing house, for whom he translated from the Khakassian or Altaic or Shor. But for the life of me, I didn't know it was just a stone's throw from there to those other stations. No, that was a different line, a completely different route for me, a different landscape, a different part of my brain. My Moscow glows in shreds, fragments, like a motley patchwork blanket, like a tapestry caught on the loom. I know Moscow from inside, I know Moscow from its nether regions, I know it from the metro.

The metro is Moscow's skeleton and, like a maggot, I crawl toward one of the junctions where I might be able to survive on a scrap of not-yet-rotten flesh, a shred of bone marrow not-yet-disappeared. There, as a rule, is a tiny little island of pain.

You remember Kirov Station? The one that leads into the small building in the middle of Clean Ponds Boulevard? I went there one evening when the scent of the oily, fresh, young leaves of the lime trees and the alders left me unable to sleep. I walked toward the Ponds, about which I knew nothing besides their names, and suddenly from the half-darkness of the avenue, from the farthest bench, came a dissonant clamor of voices, harmonious in their aggression:

"Hey, Negro! You, black bastard! Yeah, come on, heel!"

Without stopping, I peeked back in their direction. Rough boys, like Kirsa, were sitting on the bench, and I could see the red dots of glowing cigarettes. At first I thought that Kirsa must be there, too, and that there would be a rerun of what happened in the schoolyard.

There was no one up ahead. And I sensed there was no one behind me, either... and then I broke into a run. I don't know what drove me, but I ran with all my strength. The pack, swearing foully—"You black bastard! Think you can run?"—flew after me. And even though I was a fast runner—the genes of my African father—they caught up to me. I fell spread-eagled on the ground, and they began kicking me like a football until I curled up from the pain in my kidneys, in my back, in my shoulders. One boot blow struck me in the face, sending tears, snot, and blood spurting, and all that slush spread as my face swelled up in an instant...

They would have killed me if it hadn't been for a siren. One of them shouted, "Hold it! The pigs!" And they scattered, leaving me in a pool of my own blood to listen to the rhythm of the siren, and then the pain throbbed in rhythm, and the siren came closer and closer, somewhere right nearby, and then grew quieter, and quieter, and quieter, slipping out of my consciousness...

Toward nightfall, I crawled to those Clean Ponds and began to wash off the caked blood, hardened snot, and cold tears. My body was aching, but my soul was sniveling even more, like a beaten dog. Mommy, I thought. Mommy, why did you leave me here alone?

The Clean Ponds have long been spoiled... Look: My black blood is mingled there with hazy tears...

Babushkinskaya Station

Gleb forced me to think about Russian literature. In that verb, "forced," there is both the imperative mood and the passive voice; in other words, it's not just that he drove me in that direction with words or speeches but with the example of his good-for-nothing life.

I often wondered why Russian literature had picked Pushkin as its guiding light, its sun. I will say it again: it is because he was normal, like a non-Russian. You can't be Russian and not have a few screws loose. At best, a Russian may keep a tight grip on himself all his life, but in his final days he'll pull some crazy stunt, like Tolstoy. And so what is left is literature, a heroic attempt to balance an unbalanced life, an unbalanced soul. One such Russian was Gleb, his life, his literature. And indeed, literature was reward for his deficiencies in life, or maybe even his compensation for having no life at all.

But maybe I'm wrong. That June or July, he took me along to an evening with the poet Gennady Aigi, who was in fact Chuvash, though famous nevertheless as a Russian poet. That evening was not held in Ostankino or at the Polytechnic Museum, as was customary, but in some House Maintenance Office or other just by the entrance to Babushkin Station, or to be more precise, in one of the "red corners" of that office. We had all taken our seats in the hall when he arrived, but he energetically greeted one, then another select acquaintance and nodded in Gleb's direction.

The poet was very short, and that's why any effort to make himself grander was doomed. While telling his assistant where to put the portable tape recorder, he suddenly took an awkward step from the podium, and the whole of his puny body crashed into the audience. Some people snickered, others leapt to his aid, but the much-anticipated evening was looking like a hopeless flop from the beginning. They picked up the poet, and he went once more to the podium, very seriously. He was introduced by an unknown face, no doubt someone connected with the House Maintenance Office. Finally Aigi, arming himself with his biblical-Tolstoyan book of poems—which, as he pointed out, had been published in France—began reading his complex, uncertain, and unconnected poems.

As he read, his initial clumsiness was forgotten, even by himself. Only his glasses were visible over the rostrum, while he read that very fat book littered with bookmarks, his voice ingratiating, uncertain, and with a slight accent:

> So it was—from an unseeing visage
> And dazzling
> Resilient (in its close wandering)
> As if estranged: desperation
> (with unseeing:
> Before him:
> Abiding—this face)

So, what is Russian literature? I mused in that room, in the House Maintenance Office on the edge of Moscow, listening to a non-Russian poet who softly carried on in its name:

> No, it cannot be without words: and so I tell
> you "no." But it is not enough... and so I repeat, until the final
> "no"...

Rizhskaya Station

I like it better when they simply beat you up, be it at Clean Ponds or after your tennis lesson. At Nazar's insistence, Gleb signed me up for tennis on Thursdays, and I would make my way from our flat on the Left Bank through a couple of blocks to the sports club with a double tennis court, opposite the shop called A Thousand Trifles. But almost no one ever came to the club when I was there, so usually I would bang the ball against the wall till I was exhausted, catching the rebounds, slamming it at one wall, then the other, flinging myself around the court.

When I was fed up with hitting the ball against the walls and my hand was growing heavy from the racquet, the ball, the strikes, I would look up to the very heights of the building, where light came through the narrow slits of windows, curtained with tennis nets, which made me hope that one of those balls would rip through the net and check the hardness of the glass.

There, playing tennis—would you imagine?—I once again ran into the lonely mouse-like Zulya, who once upon a time had gone to the same summer camp in Zosimov Pustyn. It turned out that now she and her family lived not far from us. She was still intimidated by everything: passing cars, her school prospects, even the tennis balls. At the same time, she had clearly developed a motherly, bossy streak. When she found out that I'd lost my mother too, she burst into silent tears and stroked me on the head, like I was her little brother. "Cry it out, Kirill, cry it out." And then: "Look, I've got two charms against the evil eye." She stretched her wrists out, on each one was a string with a little black bead with a white drop. "I'll give you one and say I lost it if anyone asks. Keep it. It will protect you."

Her authority came through in everything. By the second training session, she began to teach me how to hold the racket correctly, and by the third, she brought along a homemade geometry book, to teach me the angles of incidence at which I must hit the ball to get the proper bounce. At the end of the lesson, she handed me the book and ordered me to solve a couple of problems, which she had thought up for homework. I don't know why, but I submitted myself to her fickle girlish will.

"Kirill, are you a friend or a stinking old boot? We've been friends, like, forever! Do you remember how you rescued me from the bushes and gave me a ride on your back? I nearly died from embarrassment that day, I was so humiliated."

She challenged me to do things that I had never dreamed of doing. Once, she brought along a bag full of paper flyers and made me sneak outside to post these flimsy notes, one on every apple tree by the road next to the sports center. "People, do not break branches off trees," the notes declared.

I quickly grew comfortable around her. I don't know—maybe she somehow took the place of my Mommy or maybe she created her own, previously unoccupied space in my life—but from then on I knew that I went to tennis lessons not just to hit the yellow ball, but to be with Zulya and her endless anxieties. "Do you know what they might call me at school?" she confided: "Daghy-doggy-baggy? Zulya-eat-a-pool-ya?" I wasn't sure how to respond to that, and it annoyed her. "Kirill, you're not applying yourself," she told me off.

"Do your parents still beat you?" she asked the next time. Again I wasn't obliging with answers, but she went on sharing: "I get beaten all the time. It's even worse now. Stepmother's always looking for something to yell about and to turn Dad against me. He always reaches for the belt. It's always like: 'you did this wrong, didn't spell that right, or you got a B.'"

"Are you a straight-A student?" she innocently asked. I was thinking again about the harshness of Soviet parents, bringing up their children to be supermen and scholars, but Zulya was already anxious about something new. "Do you think we will beat our children too?"

A throaty shout soared over from the sports center: "Zuuu-lyaaa!" It was her father.

"OK, I have to go now. Today I have to give grandma a bath," she said and headed reluctantly for the door. I had an unexpected memory of my mother, before she left for Hakasiya. She had also looked after her grandma, cleaned her sheets from underneath her, spoon-fed her, washed her, and looked after her until her dying day. And then, having thought about Zulita, about her unspoken life, interrupted with this one short hour of summer tennis, I felt a sharp pang in my heart.

I was left to wallow in my bitter solitude, so I tried to hit the ball hard, straight through the net, putting the full weight of my sadness behind every stroke. A voice boomed from the opposite corner, followed by an echo: "Hey, black boy! What the hell are you doing there?" And again: "What the fuck are you doing there?"

The echo seemed to come from just under the ceiling itself, like a falling ball. But before that ball hit the floor, something hit me between the eyes, followed by stars, and snot, and then a stream of blood...

At first I thought it was the fist that went with that well-aimed voice, but I heard more bouncing, and I realized that it was a ball, served with a masterly stroke between my eyes... I never saw who gave that lesson in applied tennis, maybe Zulya's father or someone else, as a thin film clouded my eyes. I just managed to grope my way to the locker room, get dressed, and drag myself home, not knowing how to cry, my swollen eyes hurting so much.

The next morning, Uncle Gleb took me to Rizhsky Station, where we sat on a bench barely big enough for the two of us, amid the yellowish columns that seemed violet for some reason. We were waiting for Nazar, who had promised to take me to the MVD children's hospital at Sushchevsky Val. I was afraid to look at the glowing lamps on the ceiling, because out of the corners of my eyes I could see that they were violet in color, when they should have been tennis-ball yellow, and so I just stared down at the marble floor.

Nazar finally arrived and, right in front of Gleb, cursed me out as if I were an adult:

"Fucking shit-bag of a crybaby! Can't you stand up for yourself? It's one thing to be black, but now you're all purple like a fucking eggplant! Let's go!"

And we went up to the surface and got on streetcar number forty-two right outside the metro station. We came to some factory buildings, where the hospital was, opposite a car depot.

The guard at the door knew me and welcomed me: "Don't tell me we've started beating up Negroes? After all, we're a friendly nation!" and he laughed at his own joke. I must say, everyone was quite upbeat. When the nurse at reception saw me, she sang out: "On the books there were two little Negroes, they beat up one but didn't want to get the other!" Nazar flirted with the nurse while she looked through a metal box to find my card. Then we took seats in the unevenly painted lobby, waiting to see the doctor.

"What, you again?" he would say.

"Got your little mug smashed in again?" Then, with a touch of Hippocratic compassion he would add: "Can't be easy being a Negro in this country..."

Obviously it wasn't the first time I'd been in a similar situation, at this very hospital. Several weeks before, Zulya and I had ditched a tennis session and wandered into the Lianosovo woods so I could show her the grave of my cat, Kit, who I'd been telling her about. Above one of those steep riverbanks that would normally have a wooden bridge over it, we saw bits of red tape tied around the trees leading up to it, signaling, "Do not enter." An old cardboard sign spelled out "bridge under repair" in wonky letters. But the bridge itself was missing, as if gone for renovation.

Instead of the bridge, above the three-meter drop to a shallow stream, a few boards stretched across on stilts, probably left behind by the repair crew. These boards were held in place only by good intentions, but in Zulya's presence, I was suddenly moved to show off my bravery and decided to run across. Besides, hadn't my dad been a professional runner? The moment she saw me step onto the first boards, she screamed: "Kirill, come back!" But there was no stopping me. I jumped triumphantly from board to board, feeling as light as an elf, but when I reached the middle, the old wood cracked under my foot and snapped. Only a small part of me registered that I was falling into the abyss. With lightning speed, my instincts kicked in, and I grabbed one of the boards above me with one hand. I wasn't strong enough to hold on, so I flipped over (executing something like cartwheel in the air), and went crashing into the shallow stream below. As I lay there, flat on my back, filled with shame, I caught the echo of Zulya's frantic shriek—"Iii-di-ot"—followed by loud sobbing.

Everywhere around me were bits of wooden boards from the pseudo-bridge, peppered with old rusty nails sticking out right, left, and center. How I managed to fall without hurting myself on one of these, I do not know. I saw Zulya, peering over the edge of the riverbank, in tears. I tried to get up as if nothing happened, but my legs gave out and I tumbled back into the murky stream.

"Are you alive? Stupid boy, you scared me," whimpered Zulya, looking broken, as I tried climbing out of the mud.

That day, like a model army nurse (all that time caring for her grandma had not gone to waste), she took care of my bruises and grazes, crying and whispering consolation over me, and making me promise to never, ever act so foolishly again. She put her shoulder under my arm and helped me to my house. Nazar, cursing loud, had to take me to the clinic. I found out later that Zulya got beaten with a belt that day for skipping her tennis lesson. Good thing her father never found out that she'd done so with me.

Ploshchad Nogina Station

KALUZHSKO-RIZHSKAYA LINE

Since I was little, I have looked at my pink heels and thought up all kinds of theories. We Negroes must be born white, too, but we blacken instantly, the sunlight stumbling against the cells under our skin that absorb it and respond only with darkness, like photo paper reacts to developer. After all, I didn't feel like a Negro inside; if anything, I felt like a Khakassian, especially when I recognized my mother's gaze in my own eyes. And it was only the mirror that made me into that hateful person those around me took me for, calling me Mbobo, teasing me with the name Pushkin, calling me Blackie or Chocolate or God-only-knows what other names, monikers, brands.

It was right there, in the metro, that my heart first skipped a beat at the sight of a girl who—like me—was on her own, without a mother, or grandma, or even a violin by her side. At first I thought it was Zulita, who had finally run away from her merciless parents. After that day in the woods, she had, it seemed, finally made up her mind to escape. What held her back was her sick grandma: she couldn't really leave her behind with her stepmother, who avoided the smell of grandma's room like a plague.

"Maybe I could stay at your place for a while?" she had asked at first. But then she realized that if her dad found out—which he certainly would—he'd kill us both. Lazily bouncing the ball against the floor, we explored all practical possibilities. "How about I talk about it with Nazar?" I offered. "No, he's a dictator, just like my dad," she cut me off. Gleb also didn't quite fit the role of savior. Maybe Irina Rodionovna? But she had her nephews living there, and I wasn't about to share Zulya with anyone.

"You said something about your grandma?" Zulya inquired.

"But I don't like her, and anyway..." And at this point I suddenly found myself telling her something I had never told anyone. I told her about the Moscow underground, that away from it, I am a fish out of water. She understood me and without a moment's hesitancy suggested: "How about we both live in the underground?" And I, without a second thought, agreed, not knowing what it would mean exactly, both of us living underground. But in the same spirit that stirred me to dash across the loose boards, we arranged to bring our things to the tennis lesson the next day and run for it, far from tennis and far from home.

The next day came and went, and Zulya didn't show up for our session. She didn't come the day after, either. The infinite emptiness of the underground was still mine alone.

Anyway, I got distracted. This girl I saw was empty-handed and did not belong to anyone. There was a kind of helplessness to her that made me call out to her from behind the rusty columns: "Zulya! Zulya!"

She looked around helplessly, not noticing me, as if this was her first visit to the underground realm I'd already made my home. That same way Zulita had once looked when I'd called to her in that apple grove by the sports center. Tender and vulnerable like a baby deer at a watering hole.

Sadly, it wasn't Zulita... And yet, seeing her weakness, I felt my own power. Didn't I tell you that inside I didn't feel like a fearsome Negro boy but a Khakassian? Well, here in my familiar Moscow metro I even felt completely Russian, as if a forefather like Hannibal were staring out through me.

At first I wanted to go up to her and introduce myself—as Rzhevsky, as Mbobo, as Pushkin, it didn't matter—but while I was standing, unable to tear myself away, a train pulled in and with surprising agility she leapt through the doors, without waiting for the passengers to step out, as if she did it every day.

I rushed to the other doors, but the people were already streaming out in an unstoppable flood, and I was only blocking their way. When I finally got on, I realized that she was not in that car. I pushed through to the door between the cars, but through the little window I couldn't see anything at all because some guy was leaning against the window, kissing his girlfriend.

A train had never moved so slowly. And then, in between stations, it stopped. The driver mumbled some apology for the delay, but with some animal instinct instilled in me by my African or Siberian ancestors, I felt that this was all happening to me. Then, at long last, the wheels screeched and began to turn, their gradual pounding catching up with the pounding of my heart, and when they were almost neck and neck, the train dived into the station, and my heartbeat raced hopelessly into the lead again. No, not again, I won't lose her now, the way I lost Zulya...

I sprang through the doors and darted through to the next car. The people in front of me slowly filtered out, including the kissing couple, still blocking my view of the girl I was chasing. As the new wave of passengers started climbing on, I struggled against them to the opposite end of the car, but the girl was nowhere. I hurled myself at the doors, now closing, pinning me between them, so it was not my strength but the strength of my cry that pushed me out onto the platform with bruised sides and an aching back from that last saving, shoving blow...

The platform was empty...

Tretyakovskaya Station

The platform was empty... The cold marble columns gleamed, reflecting nothing; the cold granite floor gloomily assented to them, and all that grayness gathered around to make itself a huge hole in my heart, a hole that led up somewhere toward the surface, to where the last of the departing passengers had just disappeared. Should I run after them? Should I ask those two, the kissers? But maybe I'd gotten the wrong car, looked in the wrong direction, missed something? Up? Farther? Back? Where? One station ago I, the almighty, had protected that girl in her helplessness, I had looked out for her vulnerability, I... but what about me? Now it was me who was peering about helplessly, the massive columns weighing on my heart, through which the metros bored, leaving it deserted...

Polyanka Station

I hunted for her in every station; I stood in Ploshchad Nogina Station at exactly the same time, in exactly the same spot where I first saw her, and then I would be drawn again to Tretyakovskaya Station where I had lost her... I inspected the darkness between the two stations, remembering that longest day in June when we stood in darkness on the same train, just one car apart. It felt like her image would suddenly appear in the window, in the marble, in a pair of eyes, but she was nowhere. Or maybe, I thought, had it all been a mirage? Maybe this was déjà vu. This summer, I had lost Zulya without a trace, and maybe now I was just seeing double.

Later that same day, I imagined Zulya collecting her things, gathering the resolve never to return to her cruel home, that she'd glanced around the room for the final time, kissed her peacefully sleeping grandma (cleaned earlier), and, putting her sports bag across her shoulder, jammed full of essentials for independent living, had made her way outside. She headed to the bus stop, feeling a heaviness well up in her throat, began to feel sorry for herself, for her late mother, for her helpless grandma, for her life, her family, her home. Yet, she thought, she would never again go back to that house! At the bus stop, she bumped into her stepmother getting off that very bus she waited for, totally unexpected. "Where do you think you're going, Zulya?" her stepmother inquired. "To tennis," she replied. Her stepmother responded authoritatively: "Tennis, what tennis? Enough child's play; you're already a big girl, even though your dad has misconceptions and thinks you're still a child. Come along now. I've got some housework for you to do." And she led Zulya away.

But I think she simply didn't have the heart to leave her sick grandmother behind. Even when discussing our eloping, we couldn't decide what to do about her. We couldn't take her in to live with Uncle Gleb, neither could we arrange for her to stay with Irina Rodionovna.

So in the end, Zulya couldn't betray her grandma. And Zulya really hated betrayal. Put in this situation, where she had to choose between her grandma and me, she was forced to betray me and couldn't face the shame of it and... I couldn't bear to continue that line of thought...

That hot summer, when they found a drunken Yeltsin in a country ditch with a bunch of flowers, I forgot about Mommy completely for the first time and stopped blaming everything that happened to me on this earth—and under it—on her.

That summer Gleb took me to a private premiere of some fashionable film; it started with a stylishly dressed man running through a boggy glade to a railway embankment. As he runs, a Lumière train approaches from afar: ever closer, ever louder, ever more alarming. The man runs and as he does, sliced by the reeds, he throws off his jacket, his tie, his belt. And in the train, a pen—which just a second ago was calligraphing a post-war date on someone's hand—falls upon a notebook and begins to roll from side to side to the rhythm of the train as it climbs an uphill bend. The man, slashed and bleeding, stripped naked, arrives at the embankment and begins to smear himself from head to toe with the thick, black mud of the bog under his feet. The train is coming toward him; the pen sways from side to side and that figure, black like a Negro, voluptuously smearing mud on his head, his neck, his back, then, as though drawing back curtains, with his two half-bent, arched index fingers, suddenly wipes off, skims off, the sticky black mud from his two eyelids, and his eyes open up onto to the train...

Everything got muddled up in my head, that black man and me, mud and tears, the glade and Polyanka Station, the train and the metro. Only one thing remained from that summer: the feeling of nakedness and inevitability. And that pen, swaying from side to side, would never be able to write it all down...

1990 The River of Time

the wintry little courtyard
was standing like a dog,
forgotten in the yard...

Savelovskaya Station

I will tell you something that you would never have guessed: hunger and pain—those are feelings that sting beyond the perimeters of life. If I remember rightly, in biology (which we had started to study that year) they are called the vegetative functions of the organism. "A person dies and the warm sand cools," but the enzymes are still secreted into the empty stomach, drop by drop, drip by drip, languid and forgotten, like a Tarkovsky film.

How hungry I was then, as though it were a fish Thursday, but Gleb and I had to go to the Arbat late in the evening, either to Shcherbakovsk or Savelovskaya Station, to pick up his writers' ration. From time to time, he and I were assigned different grocers, and so the route sometimes seemed like a test for a fairy tale knight: if you go to the right, you will uncover treasure; if you go straight ahead, you may never return; if you go to the left, neither Gleb nor bounty. The latter usually happened when Gleb went to pick up "the order" by himself. There, with his brothers-in-pens, he drank and ate away our two cans of sprats, a string of cervelat sausages, two cans of condensed milk, another can of Bulgarian pickles or frozen vegetables, a jar of candy, and even raw macaroni... After that, he would disappear for the evening, too, to resurface shamefacedly like a flayed dog in the morning or aggressive and drunk the following evening.

But when we went together to the sumptuous Arbat, where the sausage was meatier and the candy was sweeter, and yes, the vodka was stronger; no, even if we went to the mangy shop at

Savelovskaya Station (where, incidentally, we never met any of Gleb's coworkers, apart from the peculiar little journalist from the nearby office of *Ogonyok,* and even he was always in a hurry to file his next sensational piece), having gotten our grub, we would descend into the newly opened station that still smelled of fresh paint, drying oil, and varnish (although you couldn't see any wood whatsoever, and there was not even a single bench!) and finding ourselves like caterpillars inside a marble-concrete cocoon, determined to turn into butterflies, we would lean against the uncomfortable pillars and start to eat every edible thing from our order: a piece of Dutch or—even better—Kostromskoe cheese, some nameless smoked fish that melted in the mouth, then a stick of Finnish cervelat. And finally, just as that voracious station was filling with human meat—God forbid!—the masses returning home from work at that hour, I was no longer an empty cocoon. How I loved composing various taste-harmonies from our paltry Soviet vittles...

Mendeleyevskaya Station

Ah, if only I had found my girl—for some reason I called her after lost Zulita, though I shortened it a bit, to Lita—I would have married her a few years later at Mendelevskaya Station. Those garlands of lamps, fashioned after wondrous chemical chains, as though light were the derivative of a chemical reaction, as though if you unraveled human DNA you would be able to understand where she came from; Lita, passing fleetingly through my life like a shadow, like a phantom, and leaving me with unsolved metachemical equations along the lines of "Kirill+Lita=..."

No matter what the unknown factor, the names conjugated, and in their conjunction I led her, mentally, along the arches under the garlands of chemical light. From each archway people I knew and didn't know slowly sailed out in turn: women from one side, men from the other; in the middle of the hall, a little in front of us, they bowed to each other and, gracefully joining their hands as in a minuet, raised them in an arch over our heads. That stream of people went on and on as we walked under the garlands of light and behind us, where we had already passed by, a vortical dance began, and there at the far wall of the altar, pressing down on the mass of Moscow's deep earth, my late Mommy, Moscow, was waiting for us...

As I reminisced about my mother, unwittingly Zulya came to mind, and I suddenly stumbled upon the realization of why my mother could never decide between Gleb and Nazar. I was in a similar situation. Remembering Lita, in my mind I substituted Zulya for her, although Lita was a less painful memory, as her life had not yet merged with mine, and I could keep her at a safe distance, the distance of a dream, and not fall into the void of grief, as with Zulya.

I had realized just how much Zulya's life was intertwined with mine one day when she'd admitted that at night she would pick up an old toy phone handset and pretend to call me from under her blanket. "Kirill, is it you? How are you? What are you up to? I just prayed for both of our mothers," and just like that she would talk for hours with the ethereal me, telling me how after a miscarriage her stepmother and her dad went to a witch doctor and how he said they have evil spirits in their house and how the stepmom kept telling the father that these evil spirits are none other than her and her grandma, and as long as they live in the house, they are not to have peace and happiness. Her father guiltily tried to make excuses, saying that his mother's not got much longer to live and it will be easy to deal with the daughter after her death, not knowing that Zulya can hear it all and is telling it all to the ethereal me with tears in her eyes...

Tsvetnoy Bulvar Station
SERPUKHOVSKO-TIMIRYAZEVSKAYA LINE

And so we lived out these trifles, not knowing that this was our starry Russian hour, not knowing that this star was flaring up in the night sky, like a struck match, about to burn out forever. But now, now everyone was trying to become Russian—the Ukrainian Sasha Butovets, the Jew Deniska Abramov, the Tartar Nata Buslayeva, the gypsy Romik Gimranov, yes, and me, too, with my exotic blend of African and Siberian blood.

But they were already sitting in front of the Hotel Russia, having pitched their little tent town: the Uzbeks from Uzgen, knifed by the Kyrgyz from the neighboring mountains, just as earlier the Turk-Meskhetians had sat there, scorched out of Fergana by those same Uzbeks, just as Armenians from Sumgait had sat there, as had Azerbaijanis from Shusha, Abkhazians and Georgians, Latvians and Lithuanians.

But then suddenly everyone stopped being Russian, and even Jews, friends of my Mommy, began phoning belatedly to inform us of their imminent departures for Israel... All of them, from the first to the last, had somewhere to go, but where could I go? After all, I didn't want to renounce even my little droplet of accumulated Russianness.

It was then that Kirsa and Vanka Korenovsky formed some kind of Russian "special forces" unit, and since I had shot up a head taller than Vanka and a half-head taller than Kirsa that year, they pressed me to join and beat the hell out of the black bastards. When I blinked at his frankness, Vanka corrected himself: "I mean, the slit-eyed Caucasian assholes, not the ones like you!" And, he added: "'Cause you're one of us!"

But I didn't join their unit, no, not out of cowardice or awkwardness, but simply because that was the year Gleb became a full-time alcoholic and the House Maintenance Office sealed up his apartment, on which he hadn't paid the rent for three years—since my mother's death—and so I was forced to move to Irina Rodionovna's. That was one less chance for me to see Zulya again, who had at least known where I lived ever since she walked me home from the Lianosovo woods.

Irina Rodionovna had three nephews living with her, shipped over from the troubled Caucuses when their father—the old lady's brother—had been shot. The oldest had just gone off to do his military service, so Irina Rodionovna filled his empty bed with me. The elder of the two remaining nephews, Ruslan, was seventeen, while the younger, Akim, was almost the same age as me. Irina Rodionovna got Ruslan a place at the municipal technical high school; although he was studying in a different class, Akim went to the same school that Irina Rodionovna had managed to get me into with the help of Nazar's red ID card.

Every evening after we had eaten our dinner, prepared by the good-hearted Irina Rodionovna, Ruslan would lock himself into our shared room with Akim and begin to go through his schoolwork. And every evening, he would find some pretext to pick a fight and methodically beat his brother up, smothering him with his hand. Ruslan was fat and ungainly; Akim called him "barrel" behind his back, and so everything that Ruslan had not acted out on the cruel Caucasian streets, he vented on Akim: uppercuts, jabs to the kidneys, and knees to the face.

One day, when I happened to be in the bedroom during Akim's beating and tried to help, Ruslan pushed me away and whispered, "As for you, Mr. Negro, don't interfere!"

Ruslan beat Akim up every evening, without leaving a trace or a bruise. Irina Rodionovna knew about these beatings, but because of her spineless gentleness and Moscow genteelness, she could not intervene; to her, bad Caucasian blood and the recent trauma of their father's shooting was to blame. And so I made up my mind to look up Kirsa and Vanka Korenovsky myself—to take revenge on Ruslan for Akim.

I met up with Vanka, Kirsa, and another five or so of their crew at Tsvetnoy Bulvar Station, under the massive, stooped pillars. As usual the tone was set by the most Russian among them—the Ukrainian Sashka Butovets, the Tartar Borka Amirov, and the gypsy Romik Gimranov. We went up to the surface, circled the circus, turned off at the little bazaar and there, where Caucasians and Central Asians sold their dried fruit, I pointed to the snack bar and handed Vanka a school photo of Ruslan.

They beat Ruslan up like a true "black asshole." I stood on Flower Boulevard, and the sense of vengeance cheered me slightly, but mostly I had a gnawing feeling of foul play. The "unit" had long since gone, but I just stood with tattered regret, not knowing where to go now—obviously, I couldn't go home to Ruslan and Akim. I should have known that Ruslan would beat Akim even more mercilessly after that and would say as he did it: "There you are, black asshole! That'll teach you to live here!" The bloody times were coming...

Gorkovskaya Station

ZAMOSKVORETSKAYA LINE

Sometimes—and this is not related to anything in particular—I
want to describe a Moscow winter somewhere on the fringes. You
are sitting on a half-empty bus, leaning against the cold window.
It's snowing heavily. The road—let's take dark and gloomy
Botanical Street, which runs along the Botanical Gardens, for
example—is flooded with dark snow and leads off into the out-of-
reach blueness between the earth and the sky. If you look away
from the intrepid beam of the headlamps to one side, you'll see
obstacles along that dark blue strip, a white fence, trees looming
darkly through the snow—and to the other, white wastelands
stretching out through tongues of woodland toward weakly lit
multi-story blocks and the disorderly beginning of the housing
units from Vladikino through Otradno right up to Altufevo.

The bus stops, gulps in some steam at the doors; some late
passenger gets on, stamping the snow off his boots against the
steps; the street's cold breath breezes in for a moment, and then
the bus drones on again, warming its innards on the way...

All sorts of thoughts and poems crowd into your head on that
journey, and so you feel like saying: "Snow is falling onto my eye-
lashes, and lowers the gaze of the white vale." Or something along
those lines. It's a lie, the sort of lie that, even when you know it to
be a lie, doesn't cease to be a lie. But the bus crawls and crawls after
someone's red light on the fringes of dark and wintry Moscow...

Or take a summer dusk on Lenin's Hills, on the grassy slope
in front of Hotel "Central Committee of the All-Union Lenin's

Communist Union of Youth" (or whatever that means nowa-days) where you can lie down, staring into the yellow-green sky, or farther into the distance, at the river, at the Luzhniki Olympic Stadium beyond the river... Everything is far away, everything is as tranquil as a picture. The sun coming from the left, some-where behind the university, lends this whole toy construction a surreal, building-block air, as though in solidarity; the light breeze blowing off the river loses its way in my hair, and a horn trumpets out, either from a train on the metro bridge or from a steamer on the River Moscow, and that is the only evensong bell. You could lie like that forever, until a thin, straight crosspiece of darkness emerges, connecting the yellow-green of the still warm evening to the yellow-green of the fresh summer dawn...

And I would have traded all those memories for the shadow of my Lita in the Metro...

Mayakovskaya Station
Zamoskvoretskaya Line

Sometimes I looked at the map of the Moscow metro, especially the old one, bristling with crooked lines, and it would remind me not of a spider but of an ant. It all began when Zulita brought a book called *Ants and Anthills* to one of our tennis lessons. It had an inscription on the inside cover: "To Kirill—the hero of our times." Whether it was a joke or whatever, she earnestly handed the book to me, saying in a very adult manner: "Read and study it. You'll learn a lot."

After that, the metro itself started to look like an anthill, and I would lose myself for days at a time at the local children's library, digging through encyclopedias and collections of *Science and Life* to find out all that was known about ants.

By the end of that week I felt like an ant myself, loaded with the most intimate information about the insects, about their families, their roles: nannies and cleaners, guards and soldiers, foragers and lazy messengers. And I headed for my underground anthill where my late Mother Moscow was the eternal winged female, unseen by any worker ant.

Or maybe, just as an anthill's diaspora, its scattered individual units more powerful than a whole consciousness, is incomprehensible to our minds, so what I was and what I am still in my underground realm is considerably more than what I have just spoken of—maybe I'm taking with me, in splinters and crumbs, a whole epoch, a whole civilization, dismantling its past surface glory into little bricks, grains of sand, atomized for storage?

Maybe that's why I chose for myself the invincible underground anthill, my Moscow metro, as the place to preserve it all, like emergency rations, in the event that everything above collapses, is devastated, wiped out, as after a thermonuclear explosion?

I look at the quotes I copied from Zulya's book and I think of my Mommy: "After impregnation begins the most dangerous time for the female founder, a period of solitary existence. The female must seek out a place for her nest, prepare the chambers of the new anthill, and then after some time, proceed to the egg-laying stage. The solitary female, already shedding her wings, is easy prey for her many enemies: birds, insects, mammals, reptiles, amphibians, predatory invertebrates, and other types of ants. Of the hundreds of females who fly from the nest, only a handful will manage to build the first chamber and move on to found a new anthill. And there are even fewer whose efforts will lead to the creation of a new family..."

I have already spoken of Mayakovskaya Station as a museum of the Soviet Union. But there, too, amid all the flights depicted, dreaming or waking, you will not find the lonely flight of the winged female in pursuit of a new anthill. But I go down into that station, like an ant with its little load, and add a drawing to that museum of the USSR: a lone female with a narrow waist and transparent wings on her back, setting off on her flight—avoiding birds and insects, mammals and reptiles, amphibians and predatory invertebrates, and other types of wingless ants—to the melancholy of the dark chamber where life stirs, white at birth but blackening by the minute...

Belorusskaya Station

"Good literature is literature you can't turn into a film." Thus spoke drunk Gleb at Belorusskaya Radial Station, to which Nazar replied: "The Russian people had one chance to overcome themselves in the Soviet Übermensch, but you Russians fucked it up!" I trudged behind them in silence.

"Myths, I tell you, are the genotype of culture, while humans are the phenotype!" continued Gleb, tongue twisted and swaying. Nazar followed his thought through: "You laughed at Brezhnev; though he was the crown of Russianness, it was he who expressed the Marxist-Nietzschean idea of the new communality of people, the Soviet Nation, grown on Russian soil... and what happened? You laughed him out, pissed and shit on him." I listened to them both in silence.

"You know, there's this river in the ancient myths, the Black Currant, and in that name—just listen—there's both the Black Death and current of life..." Gleb was off on his ancient Slavonic high horse. "And now there's no communality whatsoever; now this plague of locusts will simply swallow the Russian nation, chewing it and digesting it without so much as stopping to ask its name... Give it fifty years, or a hundred..." I walked behind them dully through Belorusskaya Radial Station, and when they both for some reason asked me in unison: "How about you, are you Russian?" I answered bitterly: "I'm a black Russian..."

"Then lesshh go and knock a few back, the three of usshh," Gleb hiccuped, now completely drunk.

1991 Whirlpool

uncomfortable twilight of a winter cemetery
where there was already so much warmth
and friends...

Oktybrskaya Station

Language is so misleading! Say "October Station" and no one will think of it as they would some "August" station or "May" station; how far the word has come from its original meaning. Otherwise the station would be straw-colored like fallen leaves, and cracks from streams of rainwater would run down its walls; the wind stirred up by the trains would carry with it people like swirling leaves, and sourness, too, and the sense of the long winter ahead, worse than the winter itself. These things should also be whirling around in the station as it disappears off into the chilly, uncomfortable darkness at both ends...

I could never imagine another family as dysfunctional, wrong, abnormal as mine. I was ashamed of that fact and so never expressed it outwardly in any way. But there, at Oktybrskaya Station on a wilted October day in 1991, I suddenly sensed the nearness of that Lita, that orphaned soul with no satchel, rucksack, or violin case, no outward attachments, no school, no music, no parents, coming from nowhere and going nowhere. Feeling sorry for her, I thought of her as a gypsy.

I thought, stepping over the puddles of my station, couldn't my Zulya have tipped me off, with her life story: her stepmother, locking her four-year-old stepdaughter at home for days at a stretch; the little girl, playing until she could play no more with her single doll, which had long ago lost both arms and legs; the boredom so overwhelming that she breaks through the window and runs toward the other children; the children who tempt her into a shop for candy; the stream on the way to the shop with a pipeline over it, just beyond the bridge; her friend walking along the pipe like a tightrope and calling out to Zulya like a siren: the middle of the pipe, where the little girl's head spins, and she flies into the water; the old man who appears out of nowhere and pulls her from the stream when all her friends have fled in panic; the stepmother, coming toward her wailing and suddenly, instead of an embrace, lashes her for all to see with a thin twig, drawing blood; knickers and tights all wet again, but this time not with water but with urine...

Maybe that's why Zulya got so scared for me, as I flew into the abyss from the unsteady bridge in the woods. Or was it Mommy who told me this?

And what if Lita is that little girl years later? And what if Lita and Zulya are Mommy, years and years ago? And there is no Lita or Zulya, just as there is no Mommy any more but only the October wind blowing through the station, tattered newspapers swirling around, and I stand, supporting myself on one of the pillars at the end—or maybe at the beginning—of my lonely way?

Dobryninskaya Station

KOLTSEVAYA LINE

It's strange, but despite all the upheavals in my life, despite all the times I'd changed schools and addresses, I kept on getting good grades. I still had my insecurities about being a nerd, which I'd talked about with Zulya at the time. And at home, at Irina Rodionovna's, that monster Ruslan kept beating his brother Akim every evening, holding me up as an example, saying, "Look, even the blackest nigger can get straight As in everything, and you, who the fuck knows what the hell you're doing!" and well, then I *really* didn't want to be such a nerd, but by the next morning at school I would forget and would once again bury myself in books, lessons, studying.

Strange things happened to the teachers in those years: maybe it was *glasnost* that had such an effect on them, as they began trying out their hidden opinions on us without any prior consultation with the Regional Directorate for Education or the Municipal Department of the National Committee for Education. One of them, our geography teacher, Nikolai Ivanovich Burgermeistrov, began his class on race by establishing each of our races according to our last names and proceeded to contradict the textbooks, telling us there were three main races of human being.

He then went on to make a finer distinction, saying that Matve Sloveichik and Borya Selener were of a Semitic subgroup from the Mediterranean subtype of white Indo-Europeans. He made Slavka Maltsev—because his hair stuck up like a brush and his nose took up half his face—into the representative of the Aryan-Slavic branch of that same race, flying once again in the face of the statements in the geography textbook. But it was my race that Nikolai Ivanovich explained with greatest relish as a mix of Dravidian-African with Asian-Mongoloid. He ruffled my hair and dictated to the class: "Hair: tightly curly, coarse, and usually black or dark." Then he ran his finger over my face and continued: "The skin has a distinctive dark color, sometimes with increased sweatiness giving rise to a damp shine..."

He described the Asian-Mongol components of my racial type just as methodically, pointing with his finger instead of the marker at my slit eyes with so-called "epicanthus" instead of eyelids, and also at my broad jaw, which gave the face its triangular form... "Have you written all that down?" he asked and then, keeping me up by the blackboard, answered my fellow classmates' questions; they, of course, were just running out the clock with feigned interest.

Galia Balueva, a little know-it-all, piped up: "So why do most of the Russians in my family—and in the class, too—have triangular faces?" Nikolai Ivanovich launched into a long and complex discussion on the history of the Russian ethnicity, during which he kept pointing at me and my sweating jawbone to show the difference between the Mongoloid and the Slavic jaw, although I had inherited my jaw in equal proportions from the Russian-for-thirty-generations Colonel Rzhevsky and my Khakassian grandmother. "If white races have curly hair does that mean that Negroes were once white, too?" asked Sachka Akhtemov, a Crimean Tartar whose hair was just as curly as mine. Nikolai Ivanovich had just called him up to the board, too, to use us both to show the difference between our curliness, waviness, and bushiness, but at that moment the bell rang, and my role as a geographic mannequin came to an end.

After class, when four of us had run off to Dobryninskaya Station, right there in the middle of the hall by the bas-relief of animals, Sachka Akhtemov suddenly began to dictate in Niko-lai Ivanovich's voice: "And now look at this ram. His eyes are intelligent—doggy. But if you look carefully at this pig here, you will see that its grinning teeth are like those of a jackal or wolf—predators! But for some reason I don't see an ass here... Pardon me! What did you say?" And again, just as the bell had rung at the most interesting point, now their train pulled up, and they rushed through the low arch, laughing.

I was left alone, since I was going the other way. But I went right to the end of the hall, where I found a dimly lit panel with an image of my Mommy, and of me, too, as I was when I went to nursery school. She was sitting with her legs folded under her and was holding on to me with one hand as I was letting planes and rockets off into the sky, assembled from the blue mosaic. That was the artist's impression. In fact, Mommy had bought me a wind-up flying dove at Children's World. I let it fly in our room at home, and it flapped its wings and spun in the air until it hit a bare lightbulb, which burst and went out. And a long darkness came crashing down on us, along with the dove...

Paveletskaya Station

KOLTSEVAYA LINE

I t was not just the geography teacher who was experimenting. Our literature teacher, Yaroslav Yevstigneevich, decided that we would put on a show of Russian folk tales, based on his own interpretation and using his own script. For some reason, the action took place at Paveltskyaya Ring metro station, which was not too far from our school and where, incidentally, Yaroslav Yevstigneevich himself lived, by the entrance of Bakhruzhinsky Lane. The school's carpenter, Uncle Mitya (who at the time was being treated at Fyodorov's clinic), took me with him three times on expeditions to make sketches, on account of his poor eyesight and because of my grade-A drawing skills, and then we began to build the set in shop class. We decided to keep things to the bare minimum: two classical pillars (though with non-Greek ornaments), a passage between them, as though leading to the platform, and the parapet around the stairs that led to the stage below. And that was it.

And now to the tale of Yaroslav Yevstigneevich.

Once upon a time, a long time ago, there lived upon the earth a White God named Dazhdgod and his wife, the black-eyed Mara. And they lived very happily together. But it so happened that one day Mara met the Lord of the Underworld, the Black God Kosche Serpentovich, in a ravine, and fell in love with him. The Black God took her away with him into his underground realm, beyond the Black Currant River, beyond the Kalinov Bridge. Hearing the news of his wife's kidnapping,

233

the White God Dazhdgod set off after them in hot pursuit. But there at Kalinov Bridge he caught up with them, and a fight broke out, with Kosche and Dazhdgod beating each other down deep into Mother Earth, now to the knees, now to the waist, now to the throat until finally, with the help of Mara, the Black God conquered the White God and destroyed the sun chariot on which he had galloped to the border between the two worlds. The Black God crucified the White God on a huge tree by the Black Currant River, at Kalinov Bridge, and darkness fell over the whole world.

After the intermission, the action took an unexpected turn. The horses of the sun chariot, now left without a driver, galloped off in opposite directions, and if that weren't bad enough, Yaroslav Yevstigneevich joined the fray himself in the role of Veles the Almighty, who resurrected the White God, taking him down from the tree and healing his wounds. He proceeded to catch the sun stallions, who had roamed into dim, twilit corners (the gray stallion, played by Greygori Greyov, unfortunately got lost in the turmoil, leaving only the black stallion and the white one, representing night and day). Dazhdgod once again reigned over his station, Paveletskaya, which was once again filled with light and where the trains ran regularly. As for the Black God and Mara, condemned for eternity by Veles the Almighty, they descended along the interchange stairs to a world even further beneath the earth, and the earth glowed red before them...

You already guessed, of course, that Yaroslav Yevstigneevich gave me the role of the Black God, Kosche Serpentovich, although he did think about it for a long time, unsure whether it might be better for me to play the black stallion that drew Dazhdgod's sun chariot. But finally Galina Balueva, who played the black-eyed Mara (oh, if only Zulita was going to my school! After all, it was truly her role to play), persuaded him, arguing that not only was I always top of the class, but also I wouldn't need any makeup.

The biggest stir was caused by the scene with the fight on the Black Currant River, at Kalinov Bridge, when Slavka Malyetsev and I were meant to take turns hammering each other into the earth, now to the knees, now to the waist, now to the throat in our battle over Galina Balueva, who Slavka was truly in love with but for whom I had no feelings whatsoever apart from my solidarity with someone else who always got straight As. In the end we resolved it as follows: for each of us they sewed an earth-colored sheet with a hole in the middle, fitted with three hoops. As we struggled, we tried to make each other sit in those hoops, and then we grabbed them, pulling them up now to the knees, now to the waist, now to the neck. We became so perfect and proficient in this that Irina Rodionovna, who came to see the show as a parental surrogate, asked me later how we had managed to beat each other into the ground on the murky stage on the Black Currant River, at the Kalinov Bridge, while Yaroslav Yevstigneevich's sepulchral narrator's voice declared:

His good steed swam out
On the steep river banks;
His good steed ran o'er
To his pa and his ma
On the peak of a saddle
The edict was hung:
"The young man has drowned
In Moscow's deep waters,
The young man has drowned
In the Black Currant River!"

Everything was all well and good in that literary experiment except for good old Yevstigneevich's lengthy, tedious explanations about Prav, Yav, and Nav; about the battle between the

Black God and the White God, which took place in all our hearts; about the harmony flouted and then reinstated in the world by Veles the Almighty—but what did all this have to do with the harmony reestablished there in Paveletskaya, if now each time I was there I couldn't rid myself of the vision of Slavka Malyetsev crucified on one of the illuminated pillars or hanging from the ceiling like one of the tree-like lamps? And what's more, I felt guilty that I'd taken his little black-eyed Galina Balueva—and not my Zulita—away beyond the Black Currant River, beyond Kalinov Bridge, when I myself didn't love her at all.

Kurskaya Station
KOLTSEVAYA LINE

You have probably guessed that there was never a person lonelier than me. I could get through the day reading a book, or washing up, or watching TV, but once dusk fell—particularly when I found myself all alone in an empty room—my demons began to rule me. I would look at my body and not recognize it; it was like someone else's and didn't belong to me at all; it walked around in front of me, washed itself, cleaned its teeth, looked in the mirror, but it bore no relation to me. Then I would feel like phoning someone, going out onto the landing to throw the trash down the chute so I might accidentally bump into someone, or at least hear some stranger's voice—anything to get rid of the demons of loneliness in an empty room after a whole day. But that loneliness did not abandon me even when I was with people—in fact, when I was with people, among people, I hunted for it. I can tell you that there was never a person lonelier among people than me, and in the days of my loneliness, there was never a person more in need of people, albeit if only to find among them that same loneliness.

In my isolation I began to think that there had never been a Lita in my life, never a Zulya—I had made both of them up, just to intensify the gravity of my loss. As the heir of Russian literature, I knew that every gain eventually becomes a loss and this was what all Russian literature was about—starting from "The Overcoat" and ending with "Djan." And not only Russian literature. Even the things I had made up about Zulya—were they not just allusions to the Michelangelo Antonioni film *Blow-Up*, where the pantomime at the end recreates the very same game of tennis that I played with her?

Yet something didn't quite add up. After that memorable bruise that I received at tennis, Zulya turned up the next day bearing faint signs of a black eye, as if out of sympathy. "Dad beat me up, for getting involved with, with..." Zulya didn't finish her sentence, but I understood her halfway.

I looked with frustration at the little black-and-white beady eye now staring at me from its string around my own wrist. How come it didn't work? Was it my gain and her loss, or the other way around? Or maybe both...

Was it not for this strange, double-edged feeling, because of Zulya, that I would take any opportunity to go down into my underground realm for the price of five kopeks? I especially loved metro stations that led to railway stations, where throngs of unrelated people kept pouring upward and downward, but in the evening when all the elektrichkas had rumbled off in different directions and the long-distance trains had already pulled in, those stations would become just as orphaned, just as lonely and abandoned as I was, or so I thought: don't they know which kind of shameful business to busy themselves with?

One day Irina Rodionovna's relatives sent her a plucked goose and some sunflower oil on the train from Dnepropetrovsk to Kursk. She was tied up with a particularly complicated birth that day, and so it was me who went to Kursky railway station after school. As planned, the Dnepropetrovskis easily found me, the black one, at the information board: "Just look! Like the rind of over-baked bacon!" Mrs. Dnepropetrovski cooed maternally. She handed over the bag; I headed to Kurskskaya metro station, but instead of going straight home, I stopped under the hat of the Cyclopean central pillar in the entry hall, and my demons rushed in upon me, or rather, my little black imps...

I walked slowly around the mushroom-like pillar, led by my demons. The last passengers from the Dneipropetrovsk train were dragging their bags and suitcases here and there. A few Muscovite women (only a Muscovite could arrange to meet someone under that mushroom) were standing about with the bored expressions of those used to waiting for their husbands. I circled once more, and there was no one left in the station. I looked toward the stairs—not a soul. Toward the escalators—a murmuring silence. Blood began to pound in my temples; I anxiously asked myself what I should do in such desolation.

Pull out the goose and crucify it on the pillar as a fleshy coat of arms? Pour an even layer of sunflower oil over the red and gray granite floor? Piss, shit, or smear everything with blood? And suddenly in the midst of my convulsive loneliness and God-only-knows where from, a black person appeared—yes, yes, a Negro just like me, OK, a grown-up and dressed to the finest taste; I would even say he was wearing a top hat, but that detail is blurry. He walked by, heels clicking, while I, like clockwork, walked slowly round and round that poisonous toadstool of a pillar, out of inertia. I thought he winked, but he definitely smiled and disappeared behind the mushroom that blocked the stairs to the surface...

That snapped me out of my short circuit, and clicking my heels as he had done, I moved toward the escalator, where I was the only passenger in either direction. But somehow the isolation is easier on the escalator: as you go upward, you imagine you're a mountain climber; going down, you are jumping from a ski jump—just so long as no one distracts you or gets in your way...

Downstairs, right by the entrance, where on either side two niches gaped emptily, thinking of their absent lampposts, as though preprogrammed I stood on one of the empty pedestals along with my Dneipropetrovsk goose and my sunflower oil. I imagined that black guy opposite me in the other niche, on the corresponding empty pedestal, complementing, nobly, my raging demonic loneliness.

If I had my way, in each of those niches I would place a statue, two black humans catching sight of each other in the empty Moscow metro...

Komsomolskaya Station
KOLTSEVAYA LINE

But what is that living loneliness compared with my present loneliness, now that there is no one left for me, as I lie in the damp earth and wait for the brightness promised by the Book of the Dead? What bright thing can save my soul? What can haul it from this eternal counterclockwise circling? Where is that piercing light of thoughts, events, memories?

Bright, like my first love, my first betrayal, my first disappointment—Komsomolskaya Station, where time after time I search for my primordial innocence, my primeval happiness, my ancestral light...

Again and again, I come close to Shchusev's surface vestibule, built like a mausoleum to my searches, and like a heathen priest I descend slowly and surely to the underground hall.

As the first explorers of the Egyptian pyramids—or maybe the Pharaohs themselves—went down to their eternal rest, hidden from earthly eyes, so I walk in this late evening hour when the trains are few and far between, and the people are lonely and fearful; I walk, measuring every muffled step, observing every tiny detail of the perfectly measured pillars made of light Gazgan marble. I run my eyes over the flowing firmament of the ceiling with its smalti mosaics. There he is, mounted on a white stallion—Alexander Nevsky, from whom our Russian line of Rzhevsky descended—and there is Dmitry Donskoy, also one of us. I measure out steps so as to remember, each petal, each flower forever modeled in bas-relief.

Then comes the cartwheel of the next lamp, wheels like the ones with which my ancestors subdued Siberia, retracing the steps of Ghengis Khan from whom they inherited this passion for roads and conquests. The fires of history burn brightly in these wheels, and I go farther and farther, to Kozma Minin and Dmitry Pozharsky, to the delicate Alexander Suvorov, to one-eyed Mikhail Kutuzov. A small rivulet of the blood in my veins and arteries reaches my heart and chills it, and bursts, as though one quarter of my heart—one of the chambers into which that rivulet had flowed—had become cramped; it is too small for that quarter, which wants more, more, as though the whole of that hall where a Khakassian-looking Lenin endlessly, day and night, gives his mosaic speech, where for years and years my grandfather, Colonel Rzhevsky, guards his flag by the Reichstag...

But just as in the Russian music of Tchaikovsky, after the assembled orchestra has reached its inhuman crescendo and the music suddenly tumbles into a thin, absurd little voice, so I remember this station's incipient infidelity, its cruel betrayal.

On the day of the August coup, Gleb and I had arrived by train from the south where we'd been vacationing by the sea. As early as Ryazan we heard that Gorbachev was in Foros and that power had been transferred to the State Emergency Committee. Gleb flipped through his address book, putting little crosses next to the people who might have already been arrested. He handed me the book and began instructing me what to do in case of his arrest. For the first time in his absurd life he was preparing himself for real torture.

We left the train at Kazansky railway station and saw columns of soldiers. Despite the terrifying sight of all those soldiers in helmets, in their bewilderment they had (though I understood this only later) a certain air of comedy. Across the square, clueless soldiers, not as yet called upon to contain the crowds in the streets, whiled away their long hours waiting in line for soup from a field canteen, holding out their bowls; or they dangled their canisters in a line for some diesel fuel, as their tanks quietly rumbled nearby, puffing out exhaust fumes. These soldiers, meant to strike fear into our hearts with their very presence, looked more scared than we were, and the bulky tanks looked almost ornamental against the trashy old Zhigulis and Volgas whizzing past the square. There were armored vehicles around the station, although the station itself continued its normal, pointless life: transit passengers swarmed, loaders scurried around, and in those days each and every one of them was a Tartar, and the police were fining them with or without cause. The buffet waitresses filled the whole station hall with their clamor.

We stopped to watch, tucked in a corner by a machine that told you about all your previous lives. For a ten, Gleb found out that he had been a Nivkh, a poison-maker. "We won't check you. It has been revealed—you were Pushkin!" he said, and we went on our way, relieved.

But we still went down into the metro warily, and what happened there stayed with me, maybe the most important event of that time. Suddenly, the sound of the loudspeaker filled that crammed hall: "Citizen passengers! Komsomolskaya Ring Station is being urgently closed, all entrances and exits. Maintain order and discipline! I repeat: Komsomolskaya Ring Station is being closed urgently, all entrances and exits. Maintain order and discipline!" And that was repeated several more times...

Everyone became deathly still. Everyone looked up toward the smalt soldiers in iron armor, with spears three times the length of a man, from where the voice seemed to come. Fear spread through the crowd and caught us up in it. I knew many faces of my Moscow metro, but now I found myself in a crowd that was scared to death, and I suddenly realized I would never understand all of its possible faces. Could I have guessed, even in my wildest dreams, that the metro could become the very biggest prison, a prison for all nations...

Had the State Emergency Committee given the order to lock us all up behind the gates, designed with forethought in case of a nuclear attack, or had the civil defense decided to play out a war scene, or had the police simply decided to arrest us all and then sift us out one by one? Whatever was happening, the dread could not be dispelled by my glorious ancestor Alexander Nevsky, mounted on his white steed, or the bald and burring Lenin, forever waving his flag...

In the end, we were put on trains that took us away into the dark night, till the last man was gone and the station was empty...

That night, after a long chat with worried Gleb, we watched the repeat of that infamous TV press conference, which showed us the trembling hands of the ruling party. We couldn't fall asleep for a long time, each of us suffering from our own thoughts. But in the morning, for some reason, I woke up in a great mood, as if I had read the script of a vivid drama before watching it played out on stage.

Prospekt Mira Station

KOLTSEVAYA LINE

I spent the next day at the White House. Not to fight for democracy—who would let me do that?—but just to see what was going on. And do you know, ladies and gentlemen, it turns out that Pushkin with his keen desert nose was so right: the Russian spirit really smells! I did not participate in the October Revolution, but I suspect that its smell would be familiar to me, the smell that hovered over the square in front of the White House that day, too, where someone dragged a trashcan as a barricade and someone else shouted, "Come on, Lekha, rev the truck, let's smash the lamppost!" and someone else was getting the stage ready for the fervent Yeltsin. And faster than any orders, that spirit, with its scent of wastewater and urine, filled the square where more and more freedom-loving folk gathered and thronged.

I don't want to sound negative, but to my impartial eyes, it seemed like all the riffraff of the capital had gathered here, to delight in doing things they'd never get another chance to. They savored crushing the phone booth, extracting and dragging out all of its wires, storming up the steps, starting a fire in the middle of the square, using the top of an old street lamp as a kettle—come on, drink and be merry, everybody! When will we ever get another chance to live life this fully?

A little later, there on Kalinin Bridge, I bumped into Nazar, who in keeping with the new times had traded his gray cop's uniform for a long businesslike overcoat, almost to his heels: he was now engaged in property speculation on the Arbat, selling what had been so long destined for demolition. He was stepping into the square, not to defend Soviet power but—on the contrary—to protect his cooperative business. In the middle of that speech, Nazar glanced at his Rolex and said he had to rush off to Prospekt Mira Station for a business meeting. "Come with me!" he suggested. "You can learn some entrepreneurship!"

In the middle of the August Coup, we arrived at the station, and plunging through the archway of an ornate building, we found ourselves in a courtyard surrounded by simple apartment blocks. Here there was no hint of the coup or of a democratic revolution; here there was the smell of burning exhaust and the crisp courtyard trees. Nazar found the entrance he was looking for. We got into the unwieldy iron elevator and glided surprisingly smoothly up to the right floor, where we found ourselves outside an iron door with a peephole.

We rang the bell, and the door was opened by a pretty woman, probably of the Mediterranean Russian type, judging from her curly hair. "He's with me," Nazar had nodded in my direction, and she invited us in. She might have been more afraid of me than Nazar, although she didn't show it. The woman offered us a cup of tea. Nazar, like a true man of the world, tried to start a conversation about the coup; she apologized that she wasn't very up on politics and invited us through to the kitchen.

We sat and drank tea with strawberry compote, and I wasn't quite sure what the business of this meeting was about. Or maybe, I thought, that "meeting" was just a code and in fact we were sitting with the stallion Nazar's next conquest? But then again, why would he bring me along for that, and anyway, this lady—Innis—didn't seem like Nazar's type of prey...

So I sat, drinking tea in one of Moscow's Stalinist apartments, the type I particularly liked because they sometimes seemed like miniature metro stations—the same molded ceilings with huge chandeliers hanging from them, the same thick walls and elephantine columns, the same people!

Over a cup of tea, strange on such a historic day, Innis confided that she had borrowed ten thousand francs from some French people she knew and bought herself a second apartment nearby, which she was now renting out to foreigners and had already paid off. "And now that I've got permanent tenants who pay a year in advance, I want to buy up another one," she confided in us. "And you, Nazar, are going to help me..."

Maybe that was their business, I thought, delighted by the elegant simplicity of the female brain, creating a fortune for herself out of nothing, out of emptiness, and I kept drinking tea, cup after cup, in the kitchen of this stranger by the name of Innis.

Some kind of common sorcery of Innis's place—her tea, her coziness, her stories—wafted all cares and concerns out of your heart, your head, and when we left her place quite late in the evening and went to Prospekt of Peace Station, I put Nazar on a train on the circle line in the direction of his house on the Arbat, but I stayed on the ring line and walked around, admiring the huge Stalinist communal apartment that belonged to me, too: its high ceiling, sculpted marble bas-reliefs—a mother bending on her knee before her daughter, a vase of flowers between them; or a mother with her son plucking fruit from branches; or a mother with no children at all, but with scales, measuring out sins to some but to others virtuous deeds...

And so I walked through my communal Stalinist apartment in the night, waiting for someone to throw me out of it...

Krasnopresnenskaya and Presnya Stations

KOLTSEVAYA LINE

Ah, a black Sabbath is coming; I feel it, mark my words. It makes your head spin as if you were on a carousel, revealing only small bursts of light, epiphanies, fragments... I went through Red Press Station once, on my way back from the barracks on the River Moscow where Nazar was buying up cheap property. Right by the volunteer police memorial, just in front of the rotunda, I saw the old man, sitting on a shawl spread out on the ground. Maybe he was a Tajik or maybe an Uzbek, judging from his gown with its watermelon stripes, his white turban, and gray beard; in front of him were either dice or prayer beads.

I had seen this old man somewhere before, or Mommy had told me about him. Something awoke in me, cloudy, for a brief moment, and then went back to sleep...

I thought he was a beggar and—as my late Mommy had taught me—I reached into my pocket, which contained a few coins along with three tens that had been given to me by generous Nazar, who was now getting rich. I scraped out the change and tossed it onto the old man's shawl. I was through the station doors when the old man called me ominously by the name Mbobo, or maybe I misheard him, but either way it was clear he was singling me out from the crowd, and some sort of mysterious force pulled me back to the foot of the memorial. It was only then I noticed how disheveled the old man was, and he again seemed somehow very familiar, but I just couldn't fathom who he was...

"I'm no beggar," he said and pointed to the other side of the rotunda where a gypsy woman was sitting with her child. "Give it to her!" And he held my shameful change out to me. He whispered something else, too, and spat on his palm, and I was confused: should I give him a ten or go over to the gypsy woman and give her the change? But I couldn't just stand there either. Feeling my face grow red, I dived underground. Each torch on the escalator illumined me. Each lamp on the ceiling winked. Each blessed bas-relief grimaced and showed the scene of the fall. Was this old man the same witch doctor that Zulya's father and stepmother visited, who stuck the label of "evil spirit" on her and her elderly grandma?

I'll never know, but that day I was struck by an unprecedented fever; Irina Rodionovna called the ambulance, and for the first time ever, Ruslan was too scared to beat Akim. I dimly, dully remember the smell of vodka on the ambulance medic and vomiting repeatedly. They took me to the clinic and all night I had nightmares of wild Erlik...

It was only later, when I had recovered, that Irina Rodionovna told me Nazar had sold Gleb's old apartment that very day, leaving the poor drunk homeless, and that explained his generosity...

Kiyevskaya Station
Koltsevaya Line

Being well read, I knew of Hindu yogis, Tibetan monks, Siberian shamans, and Central Asian and Caucasian Sufis. I knew that all of them travel through stages of ascension, which are given different names—one of which, incidentally, is "station." I knew that their spiritual training includes the ascetic practice of going underground to purify the flesh, cleanse the spirit. "Die before your death!" That is their vow, which can last a day, a week, a month, forty days, years, a whole life... Now I remembered that Zulya had told me about it, as she was giving me the book about ants. And maybe, without knowing it myself, I was doing just that? And I don't need to look at the carvings and mosaics, the chandeliers and pillars. Maybe they are all for fun, to divert the uninitiated? So now I tell you: go to that station and look around you, but more than that—look deeper, into yourself! Can you see?

Before he passed away, Zulya's grandfather had been a bee-keeping enthusiast, and he loved telling his three-year-old granddaughter: "Remember my child, though bees are attracted to the aroma and beauty of the flowers, they but collect nectar."

Park Kultury Station

Spring had come to the underground world. It was late, but it had arrived nonetheless. First of all, the icicle-needles melted and the earth breathed damp and warm, then the roots swelled and suddenly began to grow, shifting our tendons and bones. A maggot accidentally brought a seed into my eye socket; its shoots crawled upward, and little roots began taking up strategic positions around it, checking my skull for cracks. Migrant ants began bustling nearby, setting off on foot, marching off for seasonal work and leaving their womenfolk and children in the dark ground for the time being. Such is the hustle of spring down here, but just imagine what is going on up there, on the surface!

But in that year, 1991, perpetual autumn reigned over Moscow. On one of those damp, miserable days when Irina Rodionovna's merciless rheumatism was flaring up and she couldn't stand still, despite the massages that Akim and I took turns giving her, Nazar called and asked me to go to Park Kultury Station, saying something about urgent business. Nazar, wearing a purple jacket and, again, a long coat that reached down to his feet—this is, after all, how the new Russians dressed—took me with him on all kinds of business, or so-called business lunches in those days. I think he was passing me off as his bodyguard in those new times, but as he now paid me thirty bucks for each performance, I had no reason to refuse.

A person quickly forgets about curses, doesn't he? Especially where there is real money to be had in such hungry times... so I left Irina Rodionovna in Akim's care, explaining why and where I was going because, after all, I brought my earnings into that house. I set off for Park Kultury, where Nazar gave me the low-down: "Gleb's waiting for us in the park with two slackers just like him. And those slackers, it seems, don't want to just sell their pri-vatization vouchers but their apartments, too..."

As we walked down along the station hall, Nazar was drilling into me that now is *the* time to make money, to take advantage of the cluelessness of drunks and little old ladies, that now is the time to ensure the survival of the fittest and that the "riffraff" are doomed to go extinct pretty quickly. "I have everything under my thumb—got my moles in the police and the government; so stick with me and you'll be alright. We'll make our millions, get some black butlers, and live happily ever after," he boasted, while I thought to myself, he already has a black pageboy, what more does he want?

"I've done my rounds of the old folks' homes and orphanages and bought up their coupons for pennies... then my moles helped out at the drunk tanks, so we rounded up a few hundred vouch-ers. Now I want to invest in a couple of vodka distilleries. We'll make vodka and groom future clients... like Gleb..." and he burst out into mad laughter. I suddenly felt scared for Gleb.

We went up and out to the surface and walked through the whistling winds of the Park Kultury till we found the hidden café where homeless Gleb was waiting for Nazar with two ar-ty-looking comrades (Rosencrantz and Guildenstern, I couldn't help thinking). But I was struck, not just by the fact that Gleb was dressed like a tramp and smelled like urine, but because he seemed not at all happy to see me; on the contrary, he appeared to be unpleasantly surprised—even, I would say, frightened. "Son, what are you doing here?" he stammered, confused, but then waved his hand and offered us a seat.

There was already a bottle and some kind of snack on the table, and it reminded me so intensely of the times when Mommy was alive that I was ready to forgive him and pity him for his unbearable stench and his homelessness... They began with a toast to Nazar. With nothing to do, I picked at the dry hula-hoop crackers scattered amid sausage, onion, and dark Borodinsky bread, and ground them with my teeth. It turned out that Gleb's friends were actors, and I thought vaguely I'd seen them somewhere once, a long time ago. They noisily toasted Gleb, who had introduced them to Nazar, "a person from a new barrel," then Nazar himself, and then me, who "would see a new Russia." One of them pathetically recited Pushkin for the occasion:

> Despair's true sister, faithful hope,
> Will bring you lively joy and cheer
> Even in gloom below the ground.
> The longed-for hour—you'll find—is near!
> Your heavy fetters will fall off;
> Your prisons crumble—bolt and ward.
> Freedom will greet you by the door
> And brothers give you back your sword.

Dramatically, he handed me a huge table knife, which had just been used to slice some sausage. I put the knife back on the table, placing several crackers on it.

With those toasts and the talk of vouchers and apartments, they talked away the two bottles that had been on the table. Nazar got quite sloshed, promising the artists he would invest their vouchers in a certain Dovgan bakery that would bring them endless profits as long as every mouth ate its daily bread. He chose not to mention his distilleries.

Gleb proposed a toast to our daily bread and pulled a bottle of moonshine out of what resembled his former briefcase and in which he now carried all his worldly wealth. "Give us this day, our daily bread," he said profanely, proposing a toast to Nazar, "with whom he had shared his very last and most favorite..." I sat there, and this drunkenness irritated me more and more, this drinking, this bragging, and this nonsense.

But as Nazar had knocked his glass back, he suddenly clutched at his throat and turned green, purple, and blue right before our eyes. At first I thought he was messing around, upstaging those artistic brothers on their own turf, but, holding his throat, he lunged backward, and his chair crashed to the floor...

The actors began to shake him. One of them cried out in a well-trained voice: "Ambulance! An ambulance!" just as he had probably once cried out in the theater: "Carriage! A carriage for him!" The café workers ran up; chaos broke out. But I remember as clearly as if it were this very moment: the three glasses stood untouched on the table while Gleb, that Gleb who used to chase my Mommy with a knife, Gleb, who was a preparer of poison in his previous life, sat there, holding the kitchen knife, and his jaw twitched as it had done in my near and distant childhood...

Oktybrskaya Station

And so it came full circle, and the circle closed. I found myself once again at this Oktybrskaya Station, which has forgotten its own name, and the wind blew as if God had cursed me for my arrogance and sent me to this underground temple to pray for my sins and those of others.

But in fact I was here as a witness. The dead Nazar was an officer of the MVD with connections in the police and the government, and so the MVD agents had taken the matter into their own hands. I was interrogated in front of the ailing Irina Rodionovna, who this whole terrible affair was simply killing. And one day they led us down some mysterious corridors and staircases in the deep cellars of the holding cell block, and in a stone room with a peephole in the door Irina Rodionovna and I were left alone and told not to worry. But how can you not worry when you are in the cellars of the MVD, where no human eyes can see you? I listened as hard as I could, and I can heard trains... It was a terrible feeling, then, to be on the other side of the metro, in a parallel world of fortresses and prisons, and I pressed myself against Irina Rodionovna's scrawny body as if she could protect me in some way.

Gleb was brought in, pale and stubbly. They had washed him and dressed him in prison clothes, and because he hadn't been drunk for a while, he was suddenly transformed back into my stepfather Uncle Gleb, teasing me or inviting me to the theater, to an execution.

They asked me for how long and in what capacity I had known Gleb; about how he had behaved on that ill-fated day during his last supper in that café; about whether he had been jealous of Nazar's relationship with Mommy, and a lot of other things that got all muddled in my head, but I remember how harshly the interrogator interrupted Gleb when he turned to me, tears in his eyes: "Son, you know me, don't you? Tell them..."

I tried with all my might to protect him. I remembered only the very lightest side of our life: the libraries and New Year trees, the Union of Writers and literary evenings, the ProfCom of Playwrights, and the House of Creativity. Gleb cried freely at my memories. I didn't say a word about his drinking bouts, his debauched nights, how he used to chase my Mommy with a knife, or about the night of her death...

But the case was soon brought to court, and they slapped the sentence "manslaughter by reckless indifference" on Gleb and deported him under guard as is customary in Russia—deep into the Siberian mines...

1992 Eternity

as if bumping into the morning in the twilights there,
a morning is wholly unable to bump into the morning...

Tverskaya Station

Everything turned topsy-turvy in the home of Irina Rodionovna Oblonskaya. Ruslan, just blossoming into manhood, was suddenly stricken by peritonitis and died on the operating table. Akim was again an orphaned creature, needed by nobody, so he ran away to one of his Caucasian uncles. As if her unbearable rheumatism were not enough, Irina Rodionovna was the victim of an armed robbery in her apartment by three masked bandits who came in search of Nazar's money, who also waited for me to come home from school. Luckily, or unluckily, I was held up that day by a politics class on the collapse of the Soviet Union and, by the time I got back to her apartment, the whole place was bathed in blood. The neighbors had already called the ambulance to take the half-dead Irina Rodionovna to her own Pirogov Hospital.

For the rest of the day, I scrubbed bloodstains from the walls. When night fell, I armed myself with a little axe and hammer and waited for the return of the bandits. But they didn't come back that night, or the next day, or after.

Everything around us was topsy-turvy too: the empire was crumbling; the old money was changed; the streets, regions, and towns were given new names. People changed overnight. Kirsa was now ruling one of the bands in Long Ponds; Vanka Korenovsky held some position in the youth wing of People's National-Patriotic Orthodox Christian movement; Gleb's actor friends were opening a Moscow stock exchange with Borov...

But worst of all, they began to rename the stations of my metro! In those days, I would look in the mirror and not recognize myself. Others didn't recognize me, either. Now the old ladies who used to stroke my curly head, lamenting, "Ah, our poor little orphan boy" would scorn me as they stood in line for milk powder: "Just look! Now all kinds of niggers have turned up!" At school I slid from straight As to straight Cs. In art class, sketches I'd abandoned were picked up by pure-Russian Borka Kluchnikov and turned in for As. The drawings I'd really sweat over would be handed back with a big, red C.

My Siberian grandmother suddenly descended on our place on Bolshoi Tatar Street, to look after poor Irina Rodionovna—or so I thought. Actually, she had come to wrangle in court for Nazar's pension, on the grounds of her "loss of sole breadwinner." She spent a month making the rounds of all the echelons of the MVD and the social security departments, but not once did she set foot in Pirogov Hospital where poor Irina Rodionovna was healing her broken bones. Finally she won the case and disappeared just as abruptly as she had appeared, with no warning, and without so much as leaving a note.

Yes, everything had gone topsy-turvy in the Oblonskaya household.

It reminded me of a literary joke, which Gleb, whom I now remembered fondly, liked to tell after his trip to Europe in 1988. While in Graz he'd visited the home of Ivan Bunin (now a museum) and was even shown the certificate of the Nobel Prize, which, as you know, Ivan Alekseyevich was awarded. But imagine Gleb's surprise when he saw a drawing under the certificate that depicted a man lighting the way for others with the torch of his heart; yes, yes, a drawing of Danko, that very same Danko who can be seen in the bas-reliefs of Gorkovskaya Station, now renamed Tverskaya Station.

"Imagine," Gleb would say, tipsy. "They gave it to Bunin, but they were thinking of Gorky, I'll bet. Gorky, who Bunin couldn't stand! And then he had to live with the stigma the rest of his life!"

But in my naked loneliness, my confused thoughts ran counter: "So they should have called the metro station Bunin, then, or what?"

Teatralnaya Station

Call me "pot" if you want, but at least don't bake me in the oven! Not only did they bake me in the oven, but they also burned me until I was black! Oh, that "teacher of humanity" from Red Press Station cursed us all, he cursed our arrogance!

But I'll tell you everything, in order, without losing my head. In a studio across the hall lived a bachelor of sixty who liked the company of our lonely Irina Rodionovna. And it was this man, of some half-Eastern blood (a fact borne out by his name, which was either Marat or Murat), who would visit Irina Rodionovna in Prigorov Hospital every other day, bringing her a bag of sweet apples or a hot homemade pastry. I remember another feature of his brotherly relationship with Irina Rodionovna: Marat or Murat (Irina Rodionovna used to pronounce it somewhere in between, "Mrat") looked uncannily like Gorbachev, though he didn't remind you of Gorbachev obviously, directly, but more insidiously, subconsciously. You would meet him and ask yourself, Where did I just seen that person? Where did I hear that voice? Where was it I just saw those gestures? Ah, of course, it's our Gorby!

He was always very kind to me, too. He might have been the only non-relative in my life who simply didn't notice the color of my skin. Unable to find another explanation, I suspected he must be color-blind. During the days when my Siberian grandmother was besieging Moscow, I would simply drop in on Mrat, helping him to bake pastries in his gas oven or cook some thick beetroot soup the way our Irina Rodionovna liked it.

Despite having worked all his life as a bookkeeper in some publishing house, Mrat was an excellent storyteller, and not only a storyteller, but a stylist, to boot. He told me he was editing Tolstoy's "Strider" for some reason, and how he had found a mistake even Tolstoy himself had missed in his description of a harness. When I would daydream aloud, telling him how one day I would shoot a film about Anna Karenina in the metro, he would smile and say: "You, my friend, are like a cow from the plains cocking your leg at a mountain bull," and we would both laugh at the image of that bow-legged cow...

It's no wonder that Mrat loved Nabokov, but for some reason *Lolita* was his favorite. One day when we were coming home from visiting Irina Rodionovna, after we had stopped into the Central Department Store where he had bought some little presents, when we got to Theatre Station, Mrat sat me down on the bench next to him and began to describe all the passersby as though through the eyes of Nabokov's Humbert. "Look at how coarse those women are, even that one who thinks she's so beautiful. If you squeeze her, she'll leak, like an overripe melon... And that one, a peach, with a dewdrop of morning sherbet. She isn't playing vulgarly at being a woman yet, and that sits inside her like pure nature, like a bud..."

That night I dreamed of Nabokov in my future, and for the first time in my life I wrote down a dream.

* * *

After he had handed out his books to a few Khakassians and they had wandered off to the sea, he bent over another pile and dug out a really luxurious book, Selected Works, *which had just been published in Russia. The book had been printed to the highest standards—on glossy paper, the edges of the pages were deckled, as if they had been scorched. I leafed through the book but said I already had those novels. He turned to another stack, choosing something else to give me, as I was thinking to myself how I might present myself in the best possible light. As I flipped through the Selected Works I noted that one of my books had, incidentally, been published in the same style. "Oh, by the way, did I give you a copy?"*

"I don't remember."

I started to tell him the plot. He remarked, gently, "So you've become a well-known poet?" I mumbled something in reply, along the lines of, yes, they've written about me, saying I'm the new Pushkin, and, well, I write novels, too...

"You know, you and I have something in common. You see, in many ways, my situation is an echo of yours. You wrote in English, and I, too, was a Russian-speaking writer who lived in Moscow for a long time."

He agreed, adding: "I'm turning back to Russian more and more."

"Well, recently I've been writing in Amharic more and more. Which reminds me, my latest Ethiopian novel is about to be published in Paris any day now. C'est bizarre, mais c'est vrai."

He holds another of his sad books out to me: "Take this one, then. It's my latest." He gives me the book and leaves the room for a moment, and all sorts of delicacies are suddenly served. "Taste our strawberries..." Without too much regard for table manners, Mommy and I start tasting those strawberries, surrounded by all those open books. After a minute or two, Vladimir Vladimirovich sits down at the head of the table, and, in a way that reminds me uncannily of Vsevolod Vasilevich Timokhin (incidentally, I wonder if he is all right), takes a glass of ruby-red wine, not champagne, from the ice bucket, and begins his lunch. How this wine—provided by some society of fans for his daily luncheon—suits him!

Novokuznetskaya Station

ZAMOSKVORETSKAYA LINE

As we were taking the metro from Theatre Station to Novokuznetskaya Station, Mrat continued to whisper in my ear his evaluations of the women sitting across from us in the half-empty car. With some sixth sense, they caught our glances and, realizing we were talking about them, turned crimson with indignation; all except for a fourteen- or fifteen-year-old little nymphet who made eyes at us while rearranging her bangs or tugging at her dress. "You can tell by the way that blonde is sitting how unsure she is of herself. And to hide that insecurity, she's preemptively aggressive..." Mrat whispered into my ticklish ear. "Look how fitfully she tugs at her collar, how she turns her head—she already knows she's pre-packaged goods."

Any minute now, I thought, he'll fling himself at that young girl and start... But luckily the train pulled into our station, so I took advantage and got up quickly.

But in the station, under one of the Deineka's mosaics, Mrat decided to tie his untied sneakers. The lamp lit up the mosaic nymphet, hoisted high into the sky by a muscled sportsman, and Mrat asked: "Do you want me to share a terrible secret with you?"

I agreed at once, as though he were about to hand over the last secret of the Soviet Union to me. Mrat pointed at the Deineka maiden and whispered faintly: "I have an underage girlfriend..."

I thought I had studied Mrat well enough, because of his misleading likeness to Gorbachev; after all, what secrets could Gorby have that I didn't know about?! But no! Mrat had turned

264

out to be a box with a false bottom. At first I was cautious—was he trying to corrupt me? But he wasn't even looking in my direction, and then I sensed that the man just needed to let it out, much as Gleb had said things to me over the years, and Nazar too. He had met the girl by chance; she had asked him for a cigarette. He had offered her a cigarette in the twilight, not noticing her age, but as he held it out to her he began to tease her, saying playfully: "Is it all right to smoke at such a tender age?" The girl retorted cheekily that she could do a lot more than just smoke. "What else then?" Mrat had asked with a pounding heart. "Give me some money and I'll tell you!" the girl had replied, lighting up. "Well you see, I haven't any money on me just now, but... if you come up to my place... I can offer you a coffee, too... and give you some money, of course..." It turned out that Mrat had later been to a psychoanalyst and had talked over every detail of that conversation, explaining his behavior and his motives for that behavior and the girl's reactions. His voice suddenly trembled as he said the last words, as he added the phrase "my girl."

She'd nodded by way of consent and jauntily waved the smoke away with her hand.

"I've got a dog at home, you see, so I'll go and tie it up, and you come upstairs to flat thirty-two in a little bit, my girl..." Mrat lied, trying to control the heavy breathing that was giving him away. Of course, there was no dog at his place, but he was afraid of the neighbors' prying eyes, and so he hurried up to his flat, glancing around: had anyone seen him with that underage girl?

She went up after him. Before she could even ring the doorbell he flung the door open and gave her a sign to come in quickly. No sooner had she crossed the threshold than he bolted the door and locked it from inside and invited her into the kitchen.

"No," Mrat said, looking at me at last, "there was nothing like that. We drank coffee, sat a bit, smoked, and talked, and I sent her off with a present. But since then she's been coming to visit me..." He ended his tale and pointed to the present he'd bought in the department store that day. "It's for her..."

I didn't know how to react to that story: what of it? Nabokov's Lolita. Or look at Goethe, who in his old age had fallen in love with the young Bettina von Arnim. And what of it? There was no lustful saliva drooling from Mrat as there had been from the old Karamazov. There he was, dragging himself along with his empty string bag and little present, past Deineka's heroic bas-reliefs, going up to the surface in his sneakers, unbecoming at his age. But in that case shouldn't we demand he marry old Irina Rodionovna?! But then the law of the Soviet underground goes like this: everyone forges his own happiness. And what's the big deal if Mrat-Gorbachev is one of the New Smiths?!

Paveletskaya Station
Zamoskvoretskaya Line

Two weeks later we said goodbye to Irina Rodionovna, still decrepit after her spell in the hospital, from Paveletskaya Station to Kuban. It turned out that, as early as the previous year, she had traded her apartment in Moscow for what in those days was an enormous additional payment. She only admitted it to me at Paveletskaya, which was—to use a phrase of one of Gleb's friends—"Mozarty." Under the light, elegantly linked pillars, which resembled Mozart's leaping trills, Irina Rodionovna asked me to forgive her for leaving, saying she had a sister and niece down south, that she didn't feel safe in Moscow anymore.

I felt guilty in a way for all that had happened; after all, her place had been attacked because of my paltry inheritance, left to us by Nazar. Although she didn't say so, it was me who had brought this calamity down that she was now fleeing. I remembered Mommy's tale of the cliff that swallowed up dear ones. "Rock, crack open! Crack open!" I wanted to cry out in Mommy's words. "Let me see Mommy again!" Alas, the decrepit Irina Rodionovna went to Kuban forever, another loss to enter on my long list...

Mrat told me what had really happened with that apartment swap. Irina Rodionovna, torn between her nobility and her citizen's weakness had asked advice of Mrat, a man with a bookkeeper's mind, about a possible exchange. And although it was a fantastic exchange at the beginning of 1990—a two-roomed apartment in Moscow for a four-roomed one in an ObKom block in the center of Krasnodar, plus 120,000 rubles in cash—Mrat had talked her out of it. He sensed some inevitable calamity. After all, wasn't he Gorbachev's anonymous double!

Maybe it was Ruslan's death, maybe it was the flight of loyal Akim, maybe it was the attack, or maybe it was something else, but all this took its toll, and Irina Rodionovna changed her mind and decided to go. No, those people from the Party in Krasnodar didn't rip the poor lady off; she got her four-roomed, furnished ObKom apartment and that very summer she got her 120,000 rubles—an enormous sum for Soviet times. But what were they worth now, lying in her savings account, after the Pavlov reforms? "A bundle of toilet paper," as the bookkeeper with Gorbachev's face and mannerisms put it, and added cruelly, "to wipe her decrepit backside..."

Taganskaya Station

KOLTSEVAYA LINE

After Irina Rodionovna Oblonskaya's sudden departure, I was left with nowhere to live. True, Mrat let me live at his place for a month, but I think the kind Irina Rodionovna had paid him for it. Should I go looking for Akim's Caucasian uncle, or Gleb's Russian-Jewish friends and drinking companions, or Nazar's Asian kin, or my mother's Siberian branch—where was I supposed to go, which gypsy band should I join? I remembered again how Zulya and I had once planned to run away from home. At the time, I didn't rack my brains about exactly where or how we were going to live in my metro; it was all the same to me.

But now, in that huge city I was like a little ant whose anthill had been scattered. And here in Taganskaya Station the inhabitants were completely alien: auburn predator-ants had eaten my whole family. I sat down and looked through Mommy's address book. Everyone I knew had either died or moved away, and their names had been crossed out. As for those not already crossed out, I didn't know them, and their names looked out at me frostily from the address book, like the nameless bas-reliefs of that station. And it's true, it is hard for a person when he has nowhere to go, I thought, with Dostoyevsky in mind.

In those years, the *Foreign Literary Journal* ran a story by someone or other about people living in the metro. With a touch of mysticism, the story portrayed them as quasi-aliens, recognizing one another by their pale skin, which never saw the light of day. But in my case, there was no mysticism; life had simply turned out such that maybe there was nothing for me to do but move into that scattered anthill, the metro?

I had somewhere read an African tale about an ant left alone, homeless, and with nothing to do. He crawled and crawled in his pointlessness until he had crawled right up to the end of the earth, and from there he carried on crawling, right up to the God Nyar himself.

The God Nyar saw the little ant and asked him: "Little ant, why have you crawled up here?" And the little ant complained about his homelessness and pointlessness. Nyar took pity on him and gave him a job keeping watch over an underground well of the waters of life in the desert. By day, the little ant kept watch over the well, but at night, moved by old habits, he would drag drops of water to his old anthill to bring life back to it.

The animals would come to the well and ask to drink, but the little ant would answer them sternly: "No, Nyar ordered me to guard the water!" He wouldn't give them so much as a drop. But each night the little ant would once again go back to his old business: drop by drop he carried the water off to his anthill.

The animals were angry and went to complain to Nyar, saying that they were dying of thirst. Hearing this, the God Nyar flew into a rage over the little ant and went to the well—but there was no well and no ant...

Maybe that was what I had done, I thought. I had dragged all the life-giving moisture of my memories into this underground realm, into my Moscow anthill, and now there was no more life for me up there, on the surface, where the thirsty beasts and the raging gods were ready to trample me down!

Kurskaya Station
KOLTSEVAYA LINE

There is, alas, more darkness in the cosmos than light. And you can see that much with the naked eye, and with the naked soul. And there is more darkness in the metro, too, than there is beauty in the stations. Why then am I—black of skin, black of face, and black of soul—so alone in this darkness? The dead in the neighboring chambers creak and rasp; fresh ones, new arrivals, grind their teeth; the smell of their decay is carried along by the maggots, but my soul sees not another soul... Oh, if you only knew how I longed for my Mommy... Just as during my last days on the surface I longed for that girl whom I had called Lita, no longer searching for her, merely holding on to her memory.

The light of snuffed-out stars, the pain of an amputated arm, the echo of a stifled sound...

Strange to say, Irina Rodionovna had left, but a parcel with a Dneipropetrovsk goose and sunflower oil arrived once again at Kursky railway station. Irina Rodionovna's replacements, the Krasnodarskis from the ObKom flat, promoted to Moscovites, told us about it. So as before, I went to Kursky to meet the Dneipropetrovsk train.

You know the feeling of déjà vu, don't you, when present events already seem familiar to you, like you've already lived through them? I stood under the information board just as before, the station announcer's muffled voice proclaimed the arrival and departure of trains, then when the passengers poured out from the Dneipropetrovsk train, a woman waved her hands

271

about and exclaimed: "Look, there he is, the black guy, as black as the rind of over-baked bacon!" She handed over the same canvas bag with the same heavy goose and the same sloshing sunflower oil. Everything was just as it had been.

But this time, I had somehow lost control of my thoughts: they flared and flamed out, ran together. Had I answered aloud or only thought my reply in advance? I didn't grasp anything anymore. Now I went to the foyer and saw that mushroom in the middle of the hall—for some reason, I was thinking in the past tense, but in reality I was only opening the glass doors leading to the hall. Nothing like this had ever happened to me before; it was as though my weary brain had retched, and whatever was left in my skull was all scrambled up, knowing neither future nor past.

I remember that mushroom—I was forcing myself to put things in order—and I do remember that dolled-up girl, about my age, wandering around the mushroom, around that gigantic toadstool. Who was she waiting for? Shouldn't I be the one wandering around? Where? In what reality? Concentrate! Concentrate on her face! Putting out her cigarette, as though waving away invisible smoke, there was nothing more in her hands, no bag, no violin case... and everything was spinning, spinning...

I should go off to the side, stand still, force my brain to be still. I'll lean against the cold marble wall; I'll merge with the black pillar. The girl goes around and around, and there's no stopping her. Her bare baby-bird knees pitter-patter like a tongue, like a clapper in the tiny bell of her little skirt, and just keep ringing and ringing in my ears; lipstick on the cigarette, lipstick smeared over half her face; I had never seen such a large moth flitting around a lamp, but where were her wings?! Like the she-ant of a scattered anthill looking for new semen, she fretfully quickens her circle, and then turns back again in the opposite direction...

My thoughts are cluttered. No, this isn't even déjà vu, it is something more uncanny, something black should now appear in that hall, I can feel the goose struggling in my canvas bag, the oil spills onto the shining floor, something black is threatening, but where from? From which chapters in my mind? From what sign in my memory? And the young girl is still circling and circling around the gigantic phallic lamppost, and my trousers are starting to swell, and I fear that moment, pressing myself all the harder against that black pillar.

And now huge snow-white sneakers descend from that nightmare down into the underground. I can see how they pitter-patter on the steps, extremely long legs growing out of them, first to the knees, then to the waist, in jeans, a kind of slow-motion movie, or the sticky sludge in my brain, in my trousers, swollen at the loins, one step and a T-shirt; one step and the sign "fucker"; one more "mother," and there it is, the toothless face of the black sportsman, hooking this underage girl and leading her deep into the fathomless vaginal depths of the earth...

I need to keep quiet so my head won't burst; keep quiet, so my brains won't spurt out onto the floor; keep quiet, until I choke on myself as I ride the escalator and think my next thoughts, about how he will climb onto the empty pedestal where a lamp was and imagine in front of him on such an empty pedestal that little stone girl, that little stone prostitute...

Ploshchad Revolyutsii Station

If I had only known then that this was just the foyer! Over these fifteen years of black death (I have died more than I lived), my brains gradually dried up, squeezing the memories out as they went. In the end, what remained in my skull was at best the size of a nut or maybe even a dried-out black peppercorn, rolling from side to side as the trains pass. Or has it turned into the beady eye of the protective charm that Zulya gave me to carefully observe my forlorn life? Whichever way...

And so I took control, and there was no need to swill slush on the floor, no need to spill thoughts over the marble...

And so it was that I bore a stranger's goose and a stranger's sunflower oil unto Mrat, and Mrat was pleased at the unexpected gift, so he made up his mind to set out a feast. In riddles did he speak unto me: "Then shall we eat this goose in a threesome? I shall call my beloved, I shall call my young girl!" How could I object, how could I refuse? I lived at his place like a little church mouse, so I held my tongue and said not a word. And so he called that young girl, he called his dear sweetheart and invited her to the feast. And that is how the tale of the roast goose and the anointed guest goes, but that is not how the rest of our story unfolds...

Ah, that last little black peppercorn—or maybe even less, the last sprinkle of hash—which rolled around in my empty skull, unable to disappear, now burning me with bitterness, now maddening me with its drunken smoke the whole of the next day, as, picking and plucking the goose, stuffing it with the apples left over from Irina Rodionovna's hospital ration, I prepared myself for the meeting with my peeress, the young girl, Mrat's underage lover, and again my soul went through the same lurches as it had yesterday at Kursky Station, not so much déjà vu as *nous reverrons* (not "already seen" but "we'll meet again"), thought shoved against thought, like the apples in the innards of the goose, and I roasted in my suppositions like that fat goose roasted in the oven. It's not Christmas, after all, I thought, then came another flare: What if yesterday's dolled-up girlie shows up? But the thought was overtaken by another: And with her the white-toothed black sportsman in a T-shirt with the evil promise "motherfucker?" How would the old lecher Mrat behave, and how should I act?

All day long my pants swelled, so from time to time I would run to the bathroom to extinguish my flesh with cold water, but something I couldn't fathom nagged at my heart.

Mrat had a quick wash in the tight gap between cooking and setting the celebratory table—though just what we were celebrating remained a mystery. Then he began combing his thin Gorbachevian hair, tied his old-fashioned bowtie into a fat knot (in the "Windsor style" he called it), and set about glancing periodically out of the window into the yard. He was riled up, jealous in advance of my age, my presence, my goose... "Just don't start talking to her about that rock music!" he warned me.

That's what my long-gone friend Zulya had once said to me after a tennis lesson, "Just don't start talking with me about rock music; I don't know anything about it." This thought brought with it a pang that evaporated as suddenly as it had appeared. Mrat repeated himself: "Just don't go talking to her about rock music..." I couldn't answer him; my voice no longer fit in my throat after a whole day of silence, so I just shook my head.

By six o'clock the goose was done. I skewered it for the last time with a fork, hands trembling, and turned off the gas. The oven gave an unhappy twitter. Or was it the goose's spirit, saying a last farewell to its body? Or maybe it was a ring at the door? Mrat leapt up to look through the peephole. He flung open the door, an empty-handed shadow scampered into the hall and I, bent over with a huge kitchen knife in my hand, even without straightening up, realized: it was her...

It was her, my girl, Lita... How overjoyed I was for a split second, how I cried out, how I—probably—leapt up as high as the ceiling, stabbing it with the knife. And all at once Mrat, old, lewd Mrat, exclaimed, "Moscow, all mine, Moscow is my guest!" and reached out to her like a spider's web, and she flung herself at his neck, like a butterfly, like a little ant, like a fly. They twirled around, under the lamp and only her bare, bent knees, sticking out from below her short little bell of a skirt, like a tongue, like a clapper, rang and rang in my head, in my heart, ensnared in a net...

And everything exploded inside me. I don't remember how I threw myself, hacking with my knife at this cobweb, I don't remember the screams that floated into oblivion. I don't remember how I got to the metro, at Ploshchad Revolyutsii Station; I don't remember by what power I was carried there, the bloody knife in my hands; how I found myself at that heathen altar at my Mommy's feet... I cried unseen tears, like that ant, punished by the God Nyar for wasting the well of life. The well dried up my tears. I tried to make Mommy move with the knife, but its sharp point only scraped over the slippery stone and finally plunged into my thigh, and the fresh blood mingled with the dried blood and a thin little trail spread toward the silent altar...

As I looked at the knife, I discovered to my horror that the charm was missing from my wrist, that small eye, keeping me alive. Oh, where is my Zulya, who could bind my wounds now?

The wound ached with a dull, drawn-out pain, my soul ached with a drawn-out, dull pain... What was that river called? Black, was it? The one where I fell down into the abyss, someone screaming my name after me. Yes, that's it. There's surely more darkness in the world than light... The blood on my inflated pants dried the color of black currants... But what was that river called, the one where only a bridge remained, a smith's bridge? Why shouldn't it be New Smith's? The river had dried up, her two banks had disappeared: the bank of heaviness and the bank of tenderness, and all that remained was the bridge over them, linking them together like a primeval clamp. They repaired that bridge after all, put it back together again. A bridge over what? Did I fight with Mrat—who had shouted that terrifying "Moscow, all mine, Moscow!"—at that dried up river, pounding him into the ground? What had happened? Where is my mother, and where is my girl? Lita, Zulya. To the heart it seems that, as with any loss, all you need to do is give it a little shake and you will find what you lost; it is just lying forgotten in some wrong place, and you are already on your way back, where the thing you lost peeks out from every elephantine arch, as though it had just been standing there, or further on, under the next arch? No, maybe one passage further on... and these thoughts rumbled on to the very end of Kuznetskiy Most, and what is lost is not there, not there. There is neither the river, nor time, nor truth—only Hades' underground realm. And the piercing metal nails...

Trains race back and forth, but Anna Karenina is not on them, nor is my Mommy Moscow, by the name of Mara, Marusia... Neither Zulya, nor Lita is there...

Emptiness, complete emptiness... and the bridge over it, the scanty ant bridge between my present, otherworldly reality of death and the former unreality of what I called life...

Pushkinskaya Station

I know what black Pushkin felt before his black death. A great sense of betrayal. As though the old countess had dealt out the wrong cards... and a great sense of impotence in the face of it all... deceived and betrayed in every way: by my father, who left me even before I was born; my mother, who so strongly bound me to her and then left me an orphan; my stepfathers, who threw me into the abyss between them. Deceived by Zulya, in whom I found a kindred soul and a close friend and maybe something more, who disappeared into the ether; Lita, the airy Lita, who preferred the angel of death and lust over me; by Mrat; by the ever flowing and ebbing underground; by the no longer recognizable city; and by my crumbling country... No matter what you do, it all comes to the same thing. Deception, deception, deception... or maybe I have deceived myself—with this made-up world, these invented relationships, this dreamed-up warmth of human hearts, which doesn't really exist...

A sense of the never-ending, mind-boggling circle, to break out of it with integrity is to be like a child thrown from a carousel. Look, these lines spurt in all directions from the print of the Moscow metro map.

Drop by drop I dragged the living water from the God Nyar to cleanse myself and my anthill from the aina-devil's spit, but I lost my way between two worlds: my brains, sliding back to the first dot, the primordial point, no longer remember where they are—had they decided to run the metro through the cemetery?—the train comes ever closer... Was it that I had resuscitated the world of the dead at the cost of death to the living, or the other way around? The wheels are already screeching on the rails...

Believe me, I know what Pushkin felt after his encounter at Black Currant River, but did he know how I would feel? Faithful and betrayed, the only one left to close the doors honorably, which he had left open a crack, so that a thin ray of light still swirls in the dusky, pungent darkness, but enough... The sound of the train over my head... or under my feet... Is it Mommy's voice that I hear ahead out of the thundering darkness or is it the cry of the young prostitute, of Lita-Moscow, coming from behind. Who is it calling my name: "Kirill, Kiriiill? It is time!"

The wheels are rumbling overhead... The black little ant closes the black well. The black rooster mounts the black tree once again and calls out in a black, inhuman voice: "Watch the closing doors..."

And as I fall from the platform under the train's wheels, I catch a glimpse of Zulya, who has at last tracked me down in the labyrinths of the underground, screaming out my still-living name and her two eyes, like the beads of two protective charms trying to save me... "Kiriiiill!..."

And yet...

About the Author and Translator

Born in an ancient city in what is now Kyrgyzstan, Hamid Ismailov is an Uzbek novelist and poet who was forced to leave his home in Tashkent when his writing brought him to the attention of government officials. Under threat of arrest, he moved to London and joined the BBC World Service, where he is now Head of the Central Asian Service. In addition to being a journalist, Ismailov is a prolific writer of poetry and prose, and his books have been published in Uzbek, Russian, French, German, Turkish, English and other languages. His work is still banned in Uzbekistan. He is the author of many novels, including *A Poet and Bin-Laden* and *The Dead Lake*. He has translated Russian and Western classics into Uzbek, and Uzbek and Persian classics into Russian and several Western languages. You can visit him at www.hamidismailov.com

* * *

Carol Ermakova studied German and Russian language and literature and holds an MA in translation from Bath University. She first visited Russia in 1991. More recently, Ermakova spent two years in Moscow working as a teacher and translator. Carol lives in the North Pennines and works as a freelance translator.

Restless Books is an independent publisher for readers and writers in search of new destinations, experiences, and perspectives. From Asia to the Americas, from Tehran to Tel Aviv, we deliver stories of discovery, adventure, dislocation, and transformation.

Our readers are passionate about other cultures and other languages. Restless is committed to bringing out the best of international literature—fiction, journalism, memoirs, poetry, travel writing, illustrated books, and more—that reflects the restlessness of our multiform lives.

Visit us at www.restlessbooks.com.